FEELING
LOVE
BEYOND
DEATH

AVA WIXX

First Edition: September 2023
Published in the United States of America by
Wicked Wixx Press.
The Wicked Wixx Press Logo is a trademark of
Wicked Wixx Press.
Originally published under the title
Feeling Death: May 2013

Cover Art, Ava Wixx Logo, Wicked Wixx Logo, & Interior Book
Graphics by Lindsay Tiry of LT Arts
Edited by Melissa Ringsted of There For You Editing

Print ISBN: 978-1-955950-21-3
Kindle ISBN: 978-1-955950-22-0
EPUB ISBN: 978-1-955950-23-7

For more information visit: avawixx.com

Content Warning

Dear Readers,

The characters in this trilogy are extremely flawed, which translates to a ton of questionable behavior. In other words, if you're not a fan of morally grey MCs who fuck up a lot, then you might not want to read this series.

And on that note, if swear words bother you, then this series might not be for you. (Personally, I don't think there are a lot of F-bombs or anything like that, but I cuss so much that I don't notice anymore. Although I do keep the language cleaner when I'm writing ... it's easier to spot on page. *shrugs*)

Also, I need to mention that there is a rape scene committed by a murderer on page, and a decent amount of graphic violence on page as well. (Hello ... serial killer.) And let's not forget the spicy sex scenes ... there are a few.

Basically, this is not a light and fluffy story, but rather

a dark romance. Although in comparison to what's out there nowadays it's more dark-ish than anything.

I will say that the series gets darker as it goes along though. *Feeling Love Beyond Death* is setting you up for all the dark, delicious fun to come in the next two books. So if you do read this book and it's straddling the line of what you can handle, I'd recommend not continuing the series.

Now that we have all of that out of the way, if you've decided to proceed ... Happy reading!

~Ava

*For those of you that take things to the darker side when wondering **what if** ...*

DEATH IS THE
ULTIMATE ADDICTION...

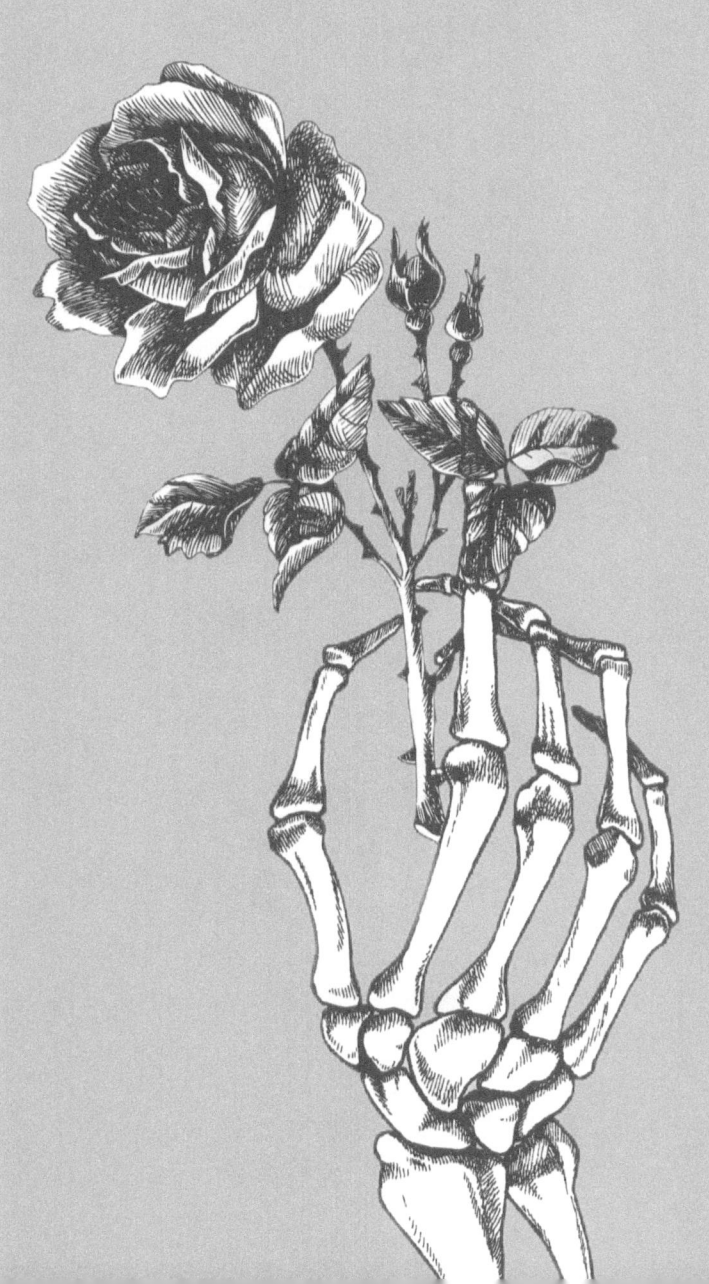

Chapter 1

"I'm having an affair."

Dr. Gray shifted forward, her worn leather chair creaking, and her auburn curls bouncing around her face.

"Well, not in reality, just in my mind." Completely unbidden, the all-consuming azure gaze of my dream man skidded across my brain, elevating my heart rate. "And it's the best sex I've ever had." I nibbled on my bottom lip, a flash of his hand around my throat as he licked—

I shook my head, dislodging the image.

"Mmm hmm." Dr. Gray nodded as she relaxed back into the cradle of her chair. Her brown eyes darted towards her notepad, and her freckled cheeks hollowed out as she pursed her lips. After another few moments of silence, she said, "You told me you were getting better at blocking out unwanted emotions. You specifically—"

"I am," I snapped.

I should have known she'd react this way. Of course she would think it was my old problem rearing its ugly head. It was a constant uphill battle being an empath, trying to keep any unwanted emotions out and separate from my own. There was a time when I'd almost lost myself—quite literally.

"This is different." I met her gaze steadily, silently challenging her to disagree with me.

"Oh?" Dr. Gray raised her perfectly groomed eyebrows. "Do explain then."

I knew she was patronizing me. I could *feel* it. The urge to shake her nearly overwhelmed me. I wanted to remind her that she couldn't hide her emotions from me. Or maybe she wasn't trying to? Perhaps she wanted me to know.

Digging my nails into my jean-clad thighs, I forced myself to remain seated. "Yeah, well, I've changed my mind and don't want to talk about it anymore." I flicked my gaze to the window, the outside world a blur behind my haze of annoyance.

"I'm sorry, Samantha." Dr. Gray's voice washed over me in a soothing tone. "I didn't mean to offend you, but you have to be aware of how it sounds to me."

"I guess." Sagging, I crossed my arms over my chest. "It just feels different, okay? I'm not really sure what it is— what's causing these dreams and waking fantasies—but I know they're mine."

He's mine.

I shuddered at my mind's declaration of ownership

because it felt right. Whoever he was—real or fictional— he was all mine, and every fiber of my being knew it.

"Are you having problems in your marriage? Perhaps that is the root of the problem. Or it could be ..."

Closing her notepad, she exhaled. "I'm sorry, Samantha. What I'm trying to say is that I have patients who aren't gifted like you are, and they've suffered from an imagined affair similar to what you're describing due to issues in their relationship. Their fantasy lover, for lack of a better term, fulfilled things for them that they weren't getting at home. Is it possible that the problem lies with you and Nixon?"

"Or maybe the problem just lies with me," I mumbled.

Because Nixon was perfect. Since day one with him, we'd shared a special kind of connection. If not for him, who knew where I'd be now? Certainly not working for the government as part of a special ops team that handled cases no one else could. Nixon had already been part of the team when he found me. He was the one who brought me to the agency that helped me learn how to focus my abilities. He was the one who picked up the pieces of my shattered life and built a new one with me. He was my rock—my everything—and I was currently cheating on him. It didn't matter if it was just in my mind, the guilt was still very real.

"I thought you'd moved past your feelings of being inadequate when it came to Nixon. Things were going so well for you—"

"And things have changed!" I hissed, jerking upright.

3

"Or maybe I was just lying to myself before, pretending that anything in my life could ever be normal. Maybe I'm just not meant to have a happily-ever-after. Maybe this whole imaginary affair is me sabotaging my relationship with Nixon any way I can."

"A-ha!" Dr. Gray exclaimed. "And there we have it. I think that's exactly what you're doing."

Beeps erupted from a timer sitting on her desk, signaling the end of our session. She reached over and silenced the alarm. "I think that's a good place to stop for now. Next time, I want to continue talking about why you might want to sabotage your relationship with Nixon. Think about what may have triggered your old feelings of inadequacy, and by all means do not discuss this with Nixon ... just yet anyhow. You'll only hurt him."

"Aren't doctors like you supposed to encourage open and honest communication in relationships?"

I knew some of the things Dr. Gray advised me to do weren't normal, but I was a special case with special needs. She was brought in as one of the experts in her field to help me when I had been at rock bottom. Admittedly, Dr. Gray helped me a lot in the past, and just like with Nixon, I didn't want to know where I would be without her. But just like with everything lately, things felt different.

Dr. Gray's peach-glossed mouth twisted down into a frown. "I'll see you next week, Samantha." *Apparently, she doesn't want to dispute her methods with me ... again.*

"Yep, next week. Same Bat Time, same Bat Channel," I replied, gathering up my things, and heading for the door.

———

SUBMERGING myself up to my neck in the bathtub, I sighed loudly, the warm water and soft bubbles sliding blissfully over my aching skin. I leaned my head back against the small bath pillow, closing my eyes. Encased in silence, except for the occasional drip of the faucet and the almost inaudible popping of bubbles, I breathed in and out deeply, the faint scent of lavender and vanilla curling around me. I attempted to relax my mind, to think of nothing so all my stress would melt away into the void. But somewhere in that void lurked the image of the very man who was causing my volatile emotions.

And I don't even know his name.

My hands ran lightly over my slick skin as I tried not to think of his vivid blue eyes fringed by long, inky lashes. I tried not to think of his strong, chiseled features that were framed by slightly wavy, nearly black hair. Or his lips ...

Mmm ... yes. His lips would be soft, full, and supple, with just the right amount of give to—

Suddenly, I found myself locked in a full-blown fantasy with my fictional lover.

He slid into the bathtub to join me, his lithely muscled chest glistening in the dim candle lighting. My gaze ravenously devoured each dip and swell of his body, everything about him *utter perfection.*

But how can that be? No one is perfect, not really. Then again, he was a fantasy ...

Leaning forward, he captured my lips with his, stealing my breath as his tongue pushed in to dominate my mouth. He pulled scant inches away to lock gazes with me, his eyes glittering with the knowledge of how much I wanted him.

After abruptly yanking me from the tub, he turned me against the wall, where I braced myself with both hands. He pressed himself firmly against me, his breath cool on the side of my neck after the warm water.

"You like it when I take control, don't you, my good Sammy girl?"

I couldn't respond with anything more than a moan.

Positioning himself at my entrance, he nudged ever so gently, causing goose bumps to erupt across my flesh and my body to quiver with need. I'd never been able to let go sexually with anyone like I could with him. Whatever he wanted, I would willingly give him with a smile.

Too bad none of it's real.

"That's what I thought," he said gruffly.

Barely a heartbeat later, he plunged into me, pinning me fully against the wall. He moved in and out of me slowly at first, his large, callused hands sliding up to grip my wrists tightly.

"I love you, Austin," I rasped as his pace became

harsher, brutal, skating the line between pleasure and pain.

He chuckled close to my ear. "You're supposed to wait until after I make you come to say that."

A soft knock was the only warning I got before the bathroom door swung open. Flustered, I whipped my hand from between my thighs and tried to appear nonchalant as my husband stepped into the small—suddenly much too small—room. When I met his deep brown, amused eyes, a wave of guilt crashed over me, and I sucked in a few ragged breaths.

"What's with the face?" he asked.

"What face?" My heart quadrupled in time. *Shit. Shit. Shit. He knows just by looking at me.*

Nixon laughed. "Oh, come on, babe, I know what you were doing. Why the sudden shyness?"

Because I was just touching myself while having a very, very real fantasy about another man. A man I have now named. A man I told that I loved while he took me roughly from behind.

"You startled me is all," I croaked, my cheeks heating. It was almost as if Nixon had actually walked in on me with another man. And yet a small part of me wanted to ask him to leave so that my fantasy lover and I could be alone to finish up.

How screwed up am I?

"Want some company?" Nixon didn't wait for my response to begin stripping off his clothes. Of course he'd take it as a given that I'd welcome him when I was feeling frisky. I never would have turned him away in the past.

But that was before Austin. *God, I can't believe I've named him.*

Nixon reached for me as he sank into the tub. "Hey, babe, come here."

"I need a minute … to um …" *Stop thinking about Austin.* But, of course, I couldn't say that. "You just startled me, like I said, and I need to take a minute."

His lower lip jutted out in a faux pout. "I'm sorry. I didn't mean to startle you. Here." He snagged my foot and began to masterfully massage it. "This should help you relax."

Groaning in pleasure, I let my head fall back against the bath pillow, my eyes sliding shut. My thoughts swirled around my interrupted fantasy, and as I replayed it briefly in my mind, I got worked up again. Obviously reading my body language, Nixon rose to his knees and lifted me so he could slide between my thighs.

My eyes fluttered open as I gripped the sides of the tub. Disappointment rocked my system when I took in dark brown hair instead of nearly black, brown eyes instead of blue, bronzed skin instead of pale flesh. Squeezing my eyes shut, I pictured Austin in my husband's place as Nixon began to make love to me.

What is wrong with me?

The worst part was that I knew my fantasies weren't brought on by my empath abilities. No, because if that was the case, then all of it would have stopped the instant I was with Nixon since he was a void. Normally, I enjoyed knowing I was grounded and safe since what I felt with my husband was always completely me. And all of that changed in an instant. Now I knew my feelings for some unknown or fictional man were completely mine.

Attempting to clear my mind, I focused on the sensation of Nixon moving in and out of me languidly, his pelvis swiveling expertly against my clit with each downward stroke.

No! I don't want this! I don't want languid lovemaking! I want all consuming and rough! I want Austin!

No, stop! What am I thinking? Nixon is the man I love, not some fantasy guy named Austin. I need to stop sabotaging myself.

"Fuck me," I whispered, my eyes still squeezed shut. "Please, Nixon, fuck me hard." *Let me lose myself in you so I can forget about him.*

Not needing any other encouragement, Nixon shifted to find a better angle and began to pound into me. Gripping the edges of the tub tighter, water sloshed over the sides, and my moans mixed with Nixon's grunts echoed off the walls of the bathroom.

Teetering on the edge, my muscles coiled tight, I rushed eagerly towards release, but wasn't quite able to get there. Nixon was close, his muscles bunched with the extra effort of holding himself off until I came—*if* I could come.

Finally, in equal parts desperation and frustration, I did exactly what I'd been trying to avoid. I pictured Austin buried deep inside of me instead of Nixon. And for my treachery, I was rewarded with a mind-blowing orgasm.

Shit. What did I do?

I'd pictured someone other than my husband to get off. And not just for help like a normal fantasy, no. It was as if I were wishing Nixon would actually become Austin. I'd wanted it so desperately that it was as if I almost willed it into reality.

I need to move up my appointment with Dr. Gray because my marriage is in more trouble than I originally thought.

Chapter 2

"Is something bothering you, Sam?" Nixon's gaze met mine, a deep furrow marring his brow.

My eyebrows lifted. "You mean besides the dead body lying in front of us?" I pushed away the lingering guilt from our sex session the previous night. We were on a job, and I had no time for personal issues while I was working a case.

Completely unsatisfied with my answer, Nixon studied my face intently. "We'll talk later?"

"Yes," I snapped. "Now get out of here so I can do my thing. I can't sense anything with you and your void powers standing so close to me."

He nodded, reluctantly making his way across the field. I knew the instant his void powers were rendered useless by distance. I gasped as the emotions of the murder scene slammed into me, the intensity familiar and yet unique like each death imprint I stepped into.

I hated it. All of it. But I had the power to do what no one else could. I felt the victim's last emotions before they died. My skills were obviously invaluable.

"Surprised ... she was surprised," I whispered.

I knew Trixie was standing close by, recording everything I said. I tended to forget when asked to recall scenes when not on sight. "She never thought he'd find out. His anger is too much. She loves him. She hates that he still loves that bitch even though he thinks the bitch is dead. That bitch never deserved his love. He's too good for her. Why can't he see, that unlike the bitch, she would worship the ground he walked on, do anything for him? Hell, she did. And yet he's killing her. He doesn't mean it. She knows that. She still loves him anyways. He can't control his gift. He's so angry she stole the bitch from him. So angry. Can't see anymore. Hate. She feels such hate for ..."

An image of myself flashed before me, but my hair was shorter, and I was different somehow. I turned and smiled up into the face of the man who'd been starring in all of my fantasies lately.

"Austin," I heard myself say before I could prevent it.

I'm going crazy. That's what this is.

Despite the jarring image, I didn't lose my grip on the victim's emotions. *I need to finish my job.* "She wishes the bitch really was dead. She hates her so much ... his Sammy girl." Gasping, I pulled myself out of her emotions, my mind reeling.

The shock of that term of endearment—the one that

Austin used in my fantasy just last night—was too much for me to handle. *Something's wrong, all wrong.* I stared at the lifeless woman lying at my feet. She was beautiful, even in death. Her long, fiery red hair fanned out around her like a pool of blood cradling her pale face. And yet there was no actual blood to be seen. She looked like she was sleeping, no obvious signs of trauma.

What killed her?

I turned to Trixie, who was eyeing me speculatively from a few steps away. I felt the worry in her for me, the lines of it etched into her otherwise smooth, brown skin. "How'd she die?" I croaked.

Trixie's dark bob swung back and forth as she continued to try and get a read on me. "No idea yet. We're going to need an autopsy. But—"

"But you think it's going to match the MO of the others?"

She scowled. "Don't. You know I hate when you pull on my emotions like that."

"Sorry," I muttered, not feeling sorry at all. "But there was never this much left behind for me before." Which was strange. This murder scene, on the other hand, was a whole different story.

"You okay, babe?" Nixon asked. "What'd you get?"

I couldn't meet his eyes. "Trixie recorded it."

With Nixon's presence, I could relax and stop concentrating to keep everyone's emotions out; his gift of being a void did the blocking work for me. *Maybe I rely on him too much. Perhaps he's becoming a crutch.*

He gently swiveled me around to look at him. "Tell me what's wrong. I don't have to be an empath to read your emotions. They're written all over your face, Sam."

For some reason, I had the instinctive urge to hide from him what I found at the crime scene. Was it more sabotage at work? Well, that was the problem with such things, you usually didn't see it when it was you doing the self-sabotaging. "I don't think she gave us anything useful." The art of lying without lying—I had perfected it years ago.

I slipped out of his grip, intent on seeking refuge in the car. "Let's head back, let the rest of the team do their job now. We can talk about this when everyone's there." Of course, I was just angling to get more time to think about what I was going to say to him.

"Sam, no," Nixon growled. "We need to talk about this now. Something's wrong."

I fought the urge to laugh. He had no idea how true his statement was. Something was *very* wrong. The problem for me was figuring out if it was all in my head, or something more sinister. "Not now, Nixon," I ground out between clenched teeth. "Let's focus on finding the killer, and not anything else, at least for now."

Nixon's hand clamped down on my shoulder, spinning me back around to face him. His features were twisted in a combination of confusion and frustration. "What else is wrong, Sam? You need to stop shutting me out."

"I'm not shutting you out!" I shouted. "Don't do this, not here!"

His cheeks flushed with anger. "Why do you always try to make it seem like I'm the bad guy? I'm trying to help you. I need to know if you're having problems with things again."

Blinking rapidly, I sputtered for a moment before I found my words. "Fuck you, Nixon. Right now, I don't have to make you out to be anything, especially the bad guy, because you are him—the bad guy!" I spun on my heels, stalking towards our car. How dare he say those things in front of our co-workers! How dare he embarrass me like that! They all knew what he was referring to when he implied I was having *problems* again.

"No, Sam—wait!" Nixon called as he jogged after me.

When he caught up, I refused to look at him, keeping my head down as I sprinted for the car.

"I didn't mean to say it like that … I just … damnit, Sam!"

He grabbed my hand but didn't force me to stop. I halted and turned, just to humor him. "Talk to me. Please." He ran his hand through his thick, brown hair, gazing down at me with exasperation. "I love you."

I bit the insides of my cheeks so hard I tasted the metallic tang of blood. I wanted to tell him that I loved him, too, but in that moment, it felt like a lie. So, I decided to go with an emotion I knew to be true. "I'm sorry." And I was. Nixon didn't deserve the treatment I was giving him. He deserved better—so much better.

"Come here." He pulled me into his warm embrace.

I exhaled deeply, attempting to let his arms comfort

me, but instead my muscles tensed. I found myself thinking about the image I'd pulled from the victim's mind, the one of Austin and me. *What does it mean?* And why did everything suddenly feel so different between Nixon and me? Off. Wrong.

Sliding away from Nixon, I gave in to the urge to put some physical distance between us. "Can we just go back to HQ? We'll talk later. I promise." And hopefully by that time, I'd have something better to say than the truth.

He sighed. "Yeah, okay. But we *are* going to talk about all of this."

"Yeah, yeah," I mumbled as I strode around to the passenger side of our car.

We rode the entire way back to HQ in silence. Nixon didn't even bother to turn on the radio. He apparently enjoyed long, awkward silences all of a sudden. I just couldn't manage to peel my mind away from images of Austin, both the ones I'd created in my mind, and the ones I'd picked up from the victim.

There's more going on than my abilities running amuck. I know it.

Of course, I'd heard that the insane rarely knew that they were … well, actually insane. Maybe—finally—after all these years I was in the middle of a full-blown psychotic breakdown. If that was the case, I was lucky it'd taken me this long.

"We're here," Nixon said gruffly. He unfolded his large body from the driver's seat, slamming the door shut behind him, not waiting for me.

Instead of scrambling after him, I decided to give myself a few minutes to try to collect myself. Leaning back in the smooth leather seat, I allowed my eyes to slide shut. *In two, out two, in two, out two ... clear your mind. Focus on me, Samantha Bevans. Feel only Samantha Bevans' emotions ...*

"I love you, my Sammy girl, like I never thought I'd be able to love anyone." Austin's low voice rumbled next to my left ear, and a flash of his intense blue eyes staring down at me played inside my mind. *"Let me go after him alone. I can't bear the thought of losing you."*

Springing up, I almost banged my head against the roof of the car. I gasped for air as I tried to process what just happened. It felt like a memory, but that was impossible. Someone else's maybe, but not mine.

I scrambled out of the car, panic pushing me to sprint for the elevator. After a few too many seconds of waiting, I ran all six flights of stairs in another burst of panic. Arriving at the debriefing room sweaty and out of breath, I paused, leaning against the wall next to the door.

"I need her off this case," Nixon demanded. "It's too much. I don't think—"

"It's not your call," David, the head of our department, spat.

"It should be," Nixon growled. "You need to trust my judgment on this. Something could go wrong—"

"What good is she to the team if she's so easily broken? We need to know now if that's the case. We should push her and not coddle her like you've been doing. We need—"

"God damnit, David. Please. Just give me some more time to work with her, and then you can push her if that's what you really want."

David clicked his tongue. "Is it for her sake or yours? Are you that desperate to keep him from winning?"

"It's for her, me, and the entire team," Nixon grated.

"No. I think it's time we test her. And I had just the opportunity to do so present itself to me this morning. I've already—"

I couldn't listen anymore without the risk of getting caught eavesdropping. I crept softly away from the door and down the hallway to the ladies' room. Only when I was locked safely inside a stall did I let out the breath I'd been holding. I wondered what kind of test our illustrious leader was planning for me. I shuddered with apprehension.

"I'M GOING TO BE A STRIPPER?" *This is some kind of mistake.* David said he wanted to test me, not punish me.

"You're going undercover. You won't be a stripper in actuality," David said, his fingers tapping rapidly against his oak desk.

I opened and closed my mouth several times, regarding my boss with uncertainty. He was still the same suit-wearing, strait-laced, moderately-in-shape, middle-aged white man that he'd been five minutes ago. But somehow, he'd morphed into an unpredictable liability as far as I was concerned.

"Will I be taking my clothes off in front of strangers?" I asked as I stared at what was to be my new identity. *Raven? Really?* I didn't think I could pull off the name Raven—not without black hair or some serious ink. Probably both.

"Yes," David responded flatly.

"I don't like the idea of my wife taking her clothes off in front of complete strangers," Nixon growled from the chair beside me. "Especially at the club she used to bartend at when she—" He clenched his jaw, not wanting to finish the sentence.

"Go ahead and say it, Nixon," I hissed, not meeting his gaze. "Where you found me … at my lowest." I couldn't even bring myself to say the rest. When Nixon brought me in, I'd been strung out on cocaine that I was using in an attempt to numb myself, shut out other people's emotions. The reasons for my past drug use didn't matter—I was still an addict.

"But I've been clean since the day I met you. I'm not that girl anymore." Wasn't I? I still had all of the emotional issues that had driven me to use drugs. Maybe I was able to suppress them when I was with Nixon, but what would I do without him? David was right. It was time for me to find out just how broken I really was.

I lifted my gaze to meet Nixon's. "I need to do this. Without you. I need to know if I even can." His countenance clouded over. "It's sink-or-swim time," I added. He still didn't respond. Anger built within me. "I'm doing it."

Standing, I loomed over David's desk. "Who's going to be on my team?"

Nixon's chair toppled to the floor as he stood abruptly, stalking from the office in a thunderstorm of dark emotions. I didn't even need my empath abilities to feel them. I didn't try to stop him, or even acknowledge him either. Maybe some time away from him was exactly what I needed, on all levels, to figure things out.

David chose to ignore Nixon's dramatic exit as well. "It's not finalized yet, but I've already started working on putting together your team. In the meantime, we'll build the rest of your fake identity."

"I'm ready," I said, not sure if I was trying to convince him or myself.

"Good, because you're going in as the lead on this one, Sam. We've been trying to keep this case out of the press as much as possible, but it broke yesterday." David slid a folder across the table to me. "It looks like there's a serial killer loose in Pittsburgh targeting dancers at the club where you used to work. There is no one better suited for this job. You know the people, and you know the area."

"Yeah, and they know me. How are we going to make that part work?" Strange how that hadn't even occurred to me before that moment.

"Everyone thinks you're dead. We went through a lot of trouble to make people believe that. With a little help from a very talented colleague to change your appearance, no one will know it's you."

"You think?" I quirked a skeptical eyebrow at him. And what very talented colleague was he referring to? My curiosity was officially piqued.

"I don't think, I know." A small smile played across his aging face, his hazel eyes twinkling.

"All right, you're the boss. But it'll be on your head if I'm recognized the instant I step through the front door."

Why do I have such a bad feeling about all of this? Maybe it's the whole taking-my-clothes-off-in-front-of-strangers thing? Nah ... couldn't be.

Chapter 3

I rolled into the parking garage across the street from Club Elite on Raven's brand-new, custom Harley-Davidson Cruiser. I'd always wanted a bike of my own and was quite satisfied that Raven was turning out to be a badass biker chick. Maybe Sam would discover she was a badass biker chick, too.

After I found a space on the second level and parked my shiny new toy, I removed my helmet and shook out my altered tresses. I ended up getting black extensions to lengthen and add volume, along with a matching dye job for my natural hair underneath. I wasn't a fan of the choice—the dark color made my already pale skin appear ghostly white in contrast—but I also knew I wouldn't be able to pull off a name like Raven without going dark as the name implied. After all, it was all about image in any service industry job. Plus, it wasn't a bad look exactly, if you liked the curvy, inked-up, Snow White vibe. It simply

AVA WIXX

wasn't me, which I supposed was precisely what I was going for in this situation.

Rifling through my bag, I double-checked that I had everything I needed for the night, pushing down my anxiety. *I can do this. It's just acting.* And although Sam would be entirely too self-conscious to dance almost completely naked in front of a bunch of strangers, Raven would suck it up and do what she needed to do in order to catch the bad guy. *I wonder if this is how multiple personalities start? Hmm ... something to ponder later.*

I took off my leather jacket and slung it over my bag as I crossed the street. It was going to be odd, to say the least, seeing people who were once my friends, but hopefully would no longer recognize me since they all thought I was dead. David had assured me that a specially skilled associate managed to alter everyone's minds, replacing my image with a girl who was actually dead. *How convenient.* I mean, making them all think I was dead and then me waltzing in the front door, pretending to be someone else, wouldn't exactly fly without that little trick. I supposed that's why David was so confident about no one knowing me.

Although, the whole situation raised a new set of questions. For instance, why wasn't I previously made aware that David had someone working for him with that particular skill set? And how many other people with nifty little talents like that one were kept hidden away from us? *Or maybe it's just me?* An icy chill ran up my spine as an eerie sense of trepidation settled over me. Choosing to

26

ignore it, I forced myself to focus solely on the task at hand.

Hesitating outside the club, I swiped at the sweat collecting along my forehead, before pushing open the side doors to head back to where I knew the office was. Bert, the owner, had all but officially hired me from my fake reputation alone. He just wanted to meet with me first before I started my shift. Basically, unless he thought there was something horribly wrong with me, I'd be naked and on stage in about an hour. I swallowed around the sudden lump in my throat.

Bert was casually standing outside his office door, obviously waiting for me, chatting with my once favorite barback and friend, Joey. Seeing the two of them there— Bert in his black tailored suit, and Joey in jeans and a T-shirt—talking about business like any other day, made a small part of me wish I could go back in time to before I met Nixon ... to before my life had spun off into a strange, new land. I missed my friends even if I didn't regret my choices.

My Harley boots clomped on the dingy floors, drawing Bert's attention. "You must be Raven," he said, smiling as his dark eyes roved over me from head to toe with satisfaction. The thing about Bert giving a woman the once over, at least in his club, was that it was all about business. There was never anything sexual behind it.

"Yep. That's me." I notched my chin up, internally cringing, almost positive he would recognize me despite his memories being tinkered with.

Joey gave me a hand gesture somewhere between a wave and salute, winking as he not-so-casually attempted to flex his bicep. "And I'm Joey."

Completely thrown, I blinked at him. *You've got to be kidding me.* I'd witnessed Joey put the moves on girls so many times I'd lost count, but never once had he ever shown any interest in me. We'd been friends, nothing more and nothing less. But then again, I was now Raven.

"Hey, Joey." My gaze darted over him briefly, noting that his dirty blond hair had grown past his chin and that his normally pale skin was a tad sunburnt.

Bert cleared his throat, drawing my attention back to him. It was then I noticed that his hair was greyer than it used to be, and his tanned face carried a few more lines. The sands of time continued to fall after I left Club Elite, my old friends changing and moving on without me, and something about that made my heart fist.

"So, I read your press kit and am quite impressed. What I really want to know is why here? Pittsburgh, I mean. Because, of course, my club is the only clear choice while in our city, but why leave Vegas to come here? You're not going to make the same kind of money in Pittsburgh."

Raven. I am Raven. I needed to stop thinking like Sam pretending to be Raven and just be her. *I can do this. Just remember my backstory and become Raven.* "The usual pathetic tale. I came here for a guy, he screwed me over, and now I need to earn some money to get back to my old life."

"So you won't be here long then?" Bert nodded in acknowledgment, letting me know he thought he'd figured Raven out already.

No. Not Raven. You. He thinks he's figured you out. You are her and she is you. "No. Only as long as it takes to make enough money to blow this pop stand." *Pop stand? Really?* I'd been watching too many old movies lately.

"As long as you let me know beforehand and don't just disappear, I'm fine with that. Pretty much what I expected anyhow after reading your kit."

I smirked. "No mysteries here."

"I'm sure that's not true," Joey interjected with a half-smile.

I shot Joey a withering glare. "You'll never know." I knew he didn't recognize me, but I never realized how much of a pig he could be until his snout started sniffing around me. But then again, I wasn't Sam to him anymore. I was Raven, and Raven was just Joey's type.

Bert eyed my bag. "I assume you brought all your stuff with you to go on tonight?"

"Never assume, my man, it makes an ass out of you and me. But yes, I brought my stuff. Anything else I need to know?"

The smile on Joey's face wilted, and he quickly turned away. I was surprised when his amorous mood suddenly dipped into darker territory. Then it hit me—that line was something I used all the time as Sam, and although not original, it obviously reminded Joey of her. I mean me. I mean, the old me that he thought was dead. *Shit, I think I'm getting a headache.* Despite that, I couldn't suppress my grin. After all, who doesn't love to be missed?

Bert's own smile turned brittle as he tried to remain casual, but he obviously was thinking about the same thing. "House fee is ten percent. No drugs on the premises, no exceptions, or you're out of here permanently, no questions asked. You can drink but don't get shit-faced or you're done for the night. I think everything else is pretty standard. Any questions or problems, just ask me, Joey, or one of the bartenders."

"No problem. Where do I get ready?" I asked even though I already knew the answer.

"Joey will take you up and point you in the direction of where our dancers get ready." He glanced at his watch. "Can you be ready to go on in forty-five?"

Physically it wasn't a problem, I just wasn't sure if I'd be mentally ready. "Yep, probably sooner."

"Good. I'll put you in the rotation. Just let our DJ know your song choices before you go on, otherwise his call, and no complaints from you." Bert hooked his thumb at Joey and then in the direction we needed to go. "Nice meeting you, Raven. I hope you enjoy working for us while you're here." He then slipped into his office, shutting the door behind him.

"This way." Joey jerked his head to the right, trudging along with his hands in his pockets.

I fell into step beside him, wishing I could talk to him like old times. His gaze danced along my exposed skin as I pretended to take in the already familiar surroundings.

"Nice ink. Did you get it because of your name, or did you pick your name because of it?"

I glanced at my left wrist where my expertly done, yet very fake raven tattoo stared back at me. Since I have small wrists and forearms, the head of the raven took up the entire top surface of my arm just above my wrist, with its wings wrapping up and around to reappear farther up on my arm. Its head was turned so only one eye was visible, and its feet curved gracefully down onto my hand. The feathers were expertly shaded black, fading to a rich, dark purple.

A small part of me was saddened by the fact that it would eventually come off, and I idly wondered if I should get it inked on for real to add to the half dozen other tattoos I already had. Although, if I was truthful with myself, I didn't like having one that I couldn't cover up if I chose to. The rest of my ink was hidden unless I wanted people to see them. Tonight they'd all be hanging out, though. My gut churned around the knot already formed in my stomach.

"I picked my name because of it," I said, rubbing my fingers absently over the raven.

Leering, Joey asked, "Any more?"

I mentally shook myself and fell back into character. "Guess you'll find out soon enough. If you catch me on stage, that is."

Clearing his throat, he peeled his eyes off of my body. "Well, here we are. The changing area along with showers, a place to get ready, and lockers are all through there." He gestured at the old red door with flaking paint that I'd already been through countless times. "Come see me if you need anything else." His lips twisted up into a flirtatious smirk, letting me know exactly what he hoped I'd come to him for later.

Annoyance flared. "Not going to happen, Joey, so you might as well save your energy."

Joey was good-looking enough, but he was no Nixon or Austin, and even though Joey didn't remember me, I still remembered him. Plus, his behavior was weirding me out and adding an unnecessary complication to my already anxiety-inducing situation.

"Oh, well …"

I'd obviously flustered him with my directness. I knew he was used to all the girls at Club Elite at least flirting with him, except for Sam. He needed to realize that Raven wasn't going to either.

Pivoting on my heels, I strode into the changing room without another word. I didn't have time to worry about Joey and his possible hurt feelings. As the door clicked shut behind me, I let out an audible sigh of relief. *Okay. I've made it this far, maybe it won't be so bad. Yeah, right.*

I chose a locker at the end of the row, relieved to discover I was the only one in the dressing room, at least temporarily. Most of the girls who worked night shift usually got to the club early to take their time getting ready. Then once everything was laced up, fastened, and taped, they went to scope out potential marks, and hopefully get a head start on their evening's drinking. Bert never cared if the girls drank so long as they behaved and didn't get completely hammered. After all, it made him more money, and therefore everyone was happy.

Not wanting to lounge around in pasties, a G-string, and my flimsy cover-up gown, I decided to do my makeup first. I wasn't completely cool with doing casual nudity. Being naked while having sex? Yes. Being naked just because? Not so much.

Once finished with my makeup, I reluctantly pulled black, sparkly pasties out of my bag along with a black G-string, a long, flimsy black gown, a pair of mile-high, black-topped, clear-heeled stripper shoes, and of course, a black garter to keep any money I made in. *Shit. I'm really doing this.* Holding my stripper gear in my hands made it suddenly all too real.

Time crawled by as I finished getting ready in a daze, and about twenty minutes later, I stood in front of the full-length mirror completely decked out as Raven. I was nearly unrecognizable even to myself. I, at least, looked the part of a seasoned stripper, and I prayed I could pull off the rest as well. *You can do this. You can do this.*

The trip from the changing area to backstage was a complete blur, adrenaline and nerves carrying me through the motions my mind wasn't on board with. I'd seen both Joey and Bert again, I was sure, and I knew they had approved of my look, otherwise I wouldn't be standing backstage getting ready to go on.

Somewhere along the line, I'd picked up a bottle of beer and was holding it in my shaking hand. *You can do this.* I didn't even remember the two song choices I'd made. *I guess they'll be just as much a surprise to me as everyone else.* I brought the beer to my lips, tipped it back, and chugged nearly the entire thing.

That's when I heard: "Next up on the main stage, all the way from Las Vegas—a veteran to the stage, but a virgin on ours—the ravishing Raaaven."

Oh. My. God. I'm being announced. This is it. I was about to dance in front of a bunch of strangers in nothing but a G-string and pasties. My stomach gurgled in rebellion from the combination of beer and nerves. *Shit. Please don't puke.* How could I expect to be taken seriously at my job if I ralphed on stage? And I wasn't talking about my fake job as a stripper.

But wait ... I'm an empath. Why not use it to my advantage for once? I was constantly feeling everyone's emotions unless I concentrated on blocking them out. So why not focus on one person specifically, and pull on their emotions to get through this situation? It was worth a shot, anyways.

As I stepped out onto the stage, the first song in my two-song set began. I froze in the low lights, the music indiscernible to my anxiety-addled brain, my focus turning to who was dancing on the rear stage. *Please let it be someone I can use.*

Squinting, I spotted long, platinum hair, so blonde it appeared white, glinting under the dim stage lights. *Skyler. Yes! It's Skyler!* If I could manage to channel her, it would be perfect. She was one of the rare dancers who got off on the attention she got while performing. No sad backstory for her. She was just an everyday, run-of-the-mill exhibitionist. *Hooray?*

Never having pulled on one person's emotions on purpose, at least not a living person, I wasn't quite sure how to go about it. *Think, think, think.* Sweat gathered around my hairline and on my upper lip. I was just standing there ... not dancing. *Think ... What would Skyler do? What would she do? How would she feel?*

Foreign emotions crept to the forefront of my mind, overwhelming the rest. *She likes this, wants it, all these adoring men. She gets off on the power it makes her feel.* It wasn't enough though. I didn't just need to feel her emotions, I needed to channel them. I had to think like her, feel like her—to be her. I had to open myself up completely to her and her alone.

I briefly slid my eyes closed, concentrating. A moment later there was a sort of mental click. *I'm in!* I still had control, but it was like I was wearing Skyler over me, letting her emotions run the show.

The rhythm of the music pulsed through my body, forcing me to move. It wasn't a choice, but rather a compulsion. Adrenaline coursed through my system as my gaze traveled over the sea of adoring men's faces, giving me a kind of high I'd never experienced. If they wanted a show, I would give it to them.

My mind blanked, going fuzzy around the edges as I performed, exhilaration weaving its way through every pore. I reveled in the power I held over my adoring fans as

I writhed on the floor and gyrated to the music. My heady laugh filled the air as money was thrown at me.

And then it was over.

My second song came to an end, and dazedly I pulled up my gown to the sound of boos that I was leaving the stage. Afraid my nerves would come back, I held on to my Skyler guise. What would I do if someone asked me for a private dance? I couldn't exactly say no without blowing my cover, but the mere thought of touching a stranger made my skin crawl, despite holding onto Skyler's emotions. *Maybe she hates that part, too?*

I sat down at the back VIP bar and ordered another beer, not sure what I asked for. I brought the bottle up to my bright red-painted lips for a sip, letting the amber liquid roll around in my mouth for a moment before actually swallowing.

"How about a dance?" a familiar voice asked, causing me to nearly choke on my beer.

I lifted my gaze to meet the hazel eyes of one of my teammates, Simon. *What the hell is he doing?* Maybe he was trying to save me from having to give someone else a dance? Although giving one of my co-workers a lap dance would probably be more awkward than giving a stranger one.

"Umm ..." I was having a hard time holding onto Skyler's emotions and reaching out to probe Simon's mind at the same time.

"How much for a private room?" he asked.

Did he want to talk to me in private? Was that what

this was really about? Perhaps he had something pertinent to the case to share. "Twenty per song, but you have to rent the room. Fifty for a half-hour, a hundred for an hour."

I tried not to view Simon through emotions tinted by Skyler's motivation, but I found my mind sizing him up like a real dancer would—Skyler, to be specific. He was young, good-looking in a professional business-type way, had an expensive-looking watch on, nice shoes—he would probably be a decent tipper, and I could work him over for a lot of money, being that he might believe I was attracted to him.

"Talk to Dewayne." I pointed at the massive bouncer standing back by the row of private rooms. "You can book a room through him, if that's what you want."

Simon stared at me with a glazed expression. "Yes, I want to book a private room for us."

"Okay, then," I said with false cheer. "Follow me." After sliding off the bar stool, beer in hand, I lead Simon over to Dewayne. "Hey," I said to him. "He wants to book a private room."

Dewayne's pale, bald head glinted under the lights as he turned to address Simon. "How long you want it for?"

"I want to buy her off stage for the night," Simon said, his tone devoid of emotion.

What? This isn't part of the plan. How am I supposed to scope out the club for the serial killer if I'm not working the crowd? "I don't think—"

"Do you take credit cards?" Simon asked Dewayne as he pulled his wallet out of his pocket.

Dewayne scowled. "Of course, what kind of place do you think this is? I'll take you over to the bar where they'll run it for you."

Dumbstruck, I leaned against the wall as I watched Dewayne and Simon make their way to the bar. I wondered again what was going on. But instead of worrying about it, I decided to center myself and let go of Skyler's emotions. I certainly didn't want them riding me when I went into the private room with Simon.

Before I met Nixon, I hadn't possessed the knowledge of how to fend off the lustful emotions of others, specifically my past boyfriends. When I was with one of them, I usually ended up taking things further than I wanted physically. Afterwards, no longer caught up in their emotions, I would feel dirty and used. It didn't matter that my exes had no idea what was going on, I was still left feeling emotionally raped, and physically violated in ways I couldn't explain to a normal person.

"You're good to go," Dewayne's deep voice broke into my thoughts of self-pity. "Room five."

My body suddenly numb, I stiffly made my way to room number five with Simon close at my heels. Since I was no longer letting Skyler's emotions guide me, I was self-conscious in my state of partial nudity. My heart thrummed in my ears and sweat dribbled down my spine. *Stop it. No one's staring at you. At least not more than any of the other girls. You're in a strip club. Suck it up and do your damn job.*

Stepping into the small room, I allowed Simon to move past me before I yanked the velvet curtain shut behind him. "What are you—" I gasped as someone grabbed me from behind, sliding a hand over my mouth. My nostrils flared as I sucked in the familiar scent of—

"Shhh … I don't want anyone to know I'm here." Nixon's warm breath tickled my bare shoulder.

I focused on Simon as he sat down on the corner of a couch, slumped back into it, and closed his eyes. Nixon removed his hand, and I whirled around to face him.

"What the hell is going on?" I hissed.

Nixon's eyes sparked with anger. "I was worried. I—"

"Didn't trust me."

Nixon's jaw ticked with tension, his gaze flicking away from mine. "It's not that I don't trust you. It's just with everything that's been going on with you lately, I was worried you wouldn't be able to handle this assignment … at least not without doing something you'd regret."

My stomach twisted, my emotions warring between anger and guilt. Hadn't I just been thinking that if I didn't let go of Skyler's emotions, things might go badly for me? "I know it's a test, Nixon. You can't take it for me. I'm sure David isn't going to approve of this."

"That's why he isn't going to know I was here." His lips tipped up into a sly smile. "How about a dance?" He pulled me to him, running his lips along the side of my neck.

Giggling, I slapped at him playfully. "What about Simon?"

"What about him? He's not going anywhere anytime soon."

I eyed Simon speculatively. He was still slumped into the couch, completely unaware, as if he was sleeping. Apprehension tightened my chest. "What did you do to him, drug him?"

"Something like that." Nixon's hands roamed my body with intent, caressing and squeezing in all the right ways, but I was still consumed with anxiety and couldn't concentrate.

"What about the rest of the team? I can't let this affect our jobs."

Nixon heaved a huge sigh, breaking contact with me, and flopped back onto the smaller couch that was closer to us. "Stop worrying, I've got it covered." He grinned, his eyes alight with mischief. "Now, I paid for you and this room. I want you to dance for me."

"Fine," I grated. "You win. For now."

Why is he doing this? Maybe he was worried about me, but it felt like more than that. I resented him just a little for not letting me discover if I could control my ability—control myself—without his help. But perhaps it was about control for him as well. Quite possibly, up until now, I ignored Nixon's need for it because I was okay with him having it. *But not now, not anymore.* If he wanted me to play a role for him, then I would. *Be careful what you ask for, baby.*

As the next song began, I stepped in front of him, dropping my gown. Knowing he would be pissed if I pretended to actually be a stripper and not his wife, I decided to stick to my role as Raven. Sure, I'd play his game, but he wasn't going to win.

Smiling saccharine sweet, I spit out the cliché stripper line I'd heard more times than I could count when I used to bartend at Club Elite. "Keep your hands to yourself, big boy. I can touch you, but you can't touch me." Dropping to my knees in front of him, just like I'd seen so many dancers do with customers, I slid up to press my breasts into him.

"Don't do that," Nixon growled.

Smiling innocently, I batted my eyelashes. "Do what? You said you wanted me to dance for you, so I am."

"You know what I mean," he snapped. "Don't do it like you don't know me."

"You mean, don't dance for you like I'm Raven? Do I sense a little resentment? Did someone forget that I'm supposed to be undercover? You should consider yourself lucky that you're getting a dance at all with me being on a case."

Focusing on Skyler, I attempted to open myself up to her emotions again, but it was pointless with Nixon being so close. His void abilities were completely blocking my empath gifts. Instead, I went with plan B, otherwise known as the dumbest choice possible.

Austin. I conjured an image of him in my mind's eye. Wrapping myself in his essence, I shivered with delight.

Nixon no longer lounged on the couch in front of me. Instead, Austin's azure gaze glittered with lust as it met mine. *Yes. You, I want to dance for.*

The music pulsed through me, my heart rate dancing steadily along with the beat as I undulated my body and swiveled my hips. *Mmm ... yes.* My temperature seemed to spike, the power I was holding over Austin heady. I slid up his body, pressing tightly against him, inhaling his spicy scent. *So good.* I wanted to lick every inch of him, map the ridges and planes of his body with my tongue. I wanted— needed to taste Austin.

Straddling him, I leaned over to whisper in his ear, "You like that, baby?" I ground my hot center against the hard erection pushing against his pants, letting out a moan.

His hands slid up to cup my ass, grinding me into him with force.

Grabbing his wrists, I flung his hands away. "Huh-uh. I told you the rules. I can touch you, but you can't touch me." I placed his hands on the back of the couch, rewarding him with a swivel of my hips.

Austin's eyes sparked with a dark lust. "Sam ..."

I stilled, shooting him a glare. "That's not my name anymore. If you want me to play, then I'm Raven to you here and nothing else."

Indecision rolled through his eyes before lust finally won out. "Yeah. Okay. Raven."

"That's better." I punctuated my words with a slow grind against his crotch. I let the music pull me under again, carrying me away to a place dominated by my desires. Sliding back down to my knees, I ran my hands up his inner thighs to cup him. I wanted to hear Austin's moans of pleasure as I took him into my mouth. I wanted to taste his vulnerability while he touched the back of my throat. And most of all, I wanted to swallow him down when he finally came, all while he couldn't touch me. I wanted—*needed* complete control over him, and I would have it.

The sound of me undoing his zipper caused him to jolt upright. "What are you—"

I slid his entire length into my mouth in one go, stealing his words as I choked on him. He fisted my hair, but I reached up and flung him away from me. *This is my show, baby.*

I licked and sucked him while using my hands to stroke and cup. I swirled my tongue, loving the taste of him, lost in the act of giving him pleasure. Too soon, he spilled into my mouth, and I moaned as I lapped up every last drop of what he gave me. After it was over, I was reluctant to let him go, but I did.

Shakily making it to my feet, I gazed down at Austin who was slumped back on the couch. His hands gripped the cushion above his head, and his pants were undone, his cock glistening from my saliva, red lipstick ringing the base. I loved seeing him like that, knowing I'd been the one to unravel him so completely. His heavy-lidded gaze followed me as I reached for my beer. Taking a sip, I let some of it dribble down my chin before wiping it off with the back of my hand. I set the bottle down so I could pull up my gown. "I'm leaving now."

My words set him into motion. He stood abruptly, struggling to get his pants zipped. "Wait, Sa— Raven. I bought you off stage."

"I'd say that was well worth what you paid for." I strode out of the room with him hot at my heels.

"Raven, I said to wait," he grated, reaching for my arm.

"You don't get to tell me what to do." I glared at his offending hand, shaking it free. "And you never touch me without my permission."

"We need to talk." His eyes flashed dangerously.

"No. I'm done talking, or didn't you notice? I gave you what you wanted. That should make you happy. But you don't get to fuck this assignment up any more than it already is."

"What do you want from me? Tell me, Sa— Raven."

I stared up into Austin's baby blues, blinking in confusion as they faded to a deep chocolate brown. No longer was my fantasy lover standing in front of me. *Not Austin. Nixon.*

A wave of dizziness washed over me, and I staggered on my ridiculously high shoes. "I'm not doing this right now, Nixon." I had to say his name to remind myself who he was. "I'm on a case, and you shouldn't be here. Go home, don't try to follow me."

I strode away from him quickly, making sure to swing my hips provocatively, wanting him to regret how he was behaving.

"Excuse me," a man said, trying to get my attention as I walked by.

"Not now. I'm done for the night," I snapped, not registering what the man looked like.

"What? Too good for me? I heard what was going on in that room with that other guy. You're nothing more than a pretty whore, and you think you're too good for me?"

I wanted to deny what he was saying, tell him that he was mistaken—that he heard me with my husband, not a stranger—but why waste my time? I simply kept walking, not even bothering to respond. People like him would think what they wanted to think, regardless of how wrong they were. Although in this case, I could see his point. He didn't know who Nixon was to me. He thought I gave some stranger a blowjob for money, and under those circumstances, I would be a whore—literally. *Whatever.*

Ignoring everyone and everything, I marched through the club, intent on my destination of the changing room. I had quite an interesting first night as Raven. In the short amount of time since I became her, I'd managed to screw things up royally. Drama had found me like it seemed to find any real stripper. *Maybe it's part of the job, which means I'm playing the part better than expected.*

I stalked to the locker I'd stored my stuff in, slamming it open. How could I have let that happen with Nixon while I was on a case? Sure I'd wanted it at the time, but to top it all off, I'd been imagining he was Austin. Didn't that make it worse somehow?

Ugh. Stop. Let it go. Either way, it happened, and I couldn't change that fact. I'd given Nixon a blowjob, in a not-so-private private room, while I pretended he was someone else. If I was honest with myself, in that moment I wanted him to be someone else. I wanted him to be Austin. How were we going to get past this in our marriage? Or maybe the real question was: how was I going to get past it? Hopefully, Nixon didn't have a clue, because I couldn't bear the thought of losing him. *What a piece of work I am. I don't want to lose the man I was just wishing was a completely different man.*

"Rough night?"

I glanced over to see none other than Skyler sitting in a chair on the other side of the room. "We all have them once in a while. You just can't let them get to you, you know?" She gave me a genuine smile that warmed her dark eyes. "You must be new here. I'm Skyler, but my real name is Destiny." She laughed. "Yep, I know my real name sounds like a stripper name, too. We used to have a Destiny here, but she left a few months ago."

I returned her smile, hoping mine passed for genuine. "Yeah, the night hasn't gone as smoothly as I would have liked, but I guess it never does." Although without siphoning her emotions the night could have, and probably would have, been a hell of a lot worse. "My stage name's Raven, but my real name is Samantha, Sam for short." *Whoops ...* I probably should have used a fake name, but the thought hadn't occurred to me until the words had already spilled from my mouth. *Yep, I'm doing a real bang-up job of this undercover stuff.*

"Nice to meet you, Sam. So what happened? I mean besides the fact that men are at the center of your woes. They always are."

Funny how I'd never liked Skyler all that much before, but now that I had insight into who she really was, I found she was growing on me.

"Of course men are the center of my problems. You know what they say ... can't live with them. But I'm not attracted to women, unfortunately." I chuckled.

Skyler snorted. "Ain't that the truth?" She paused to take a drag of her cigarette. "So did it have anything to do with tall, dark, and broody? I saw him grab you coming out of one of the private rooms."

I supposed there was no harm in telling her a little bit as long as I didn't go into too much detail. Besides, when this assignment was over we'd all be long gone, and she'd think Raven had just gone back to Vegas. I grimaced. "How could you tell?"

"Oh, honey, I'd have to be blind not to see the tension between you two. You knew him before tonight. And don't try to deny it. That kind of heat takes time to develop, but don't fret, I won't tell any of the other girls if you're worried it'll spoil your rep. So who was he? Boyfriend? Ex-boyfriend?"

I sighed. "No. Neither."

"But you want him to be?" She gave me a knowing smile. "So he's what, married or something, but he wants to have you on the side?"

"All right. I'll tell you, but only because I need to tell someone. If you repeat this, I swear I'll kick your ass."

"You know, I think you would, but I'm not worried because I can keep a secret. I like knowing the tea more when nobody else does. So ..." She sat forward in her seat ready for me to spill.

I swallowed, my eyes burning from the smoke swirling in my face. "Okay. The guy you saw me with, he's my husband. Things are strained between us right now. We had a fight before, but I'm working, and he won't let it go. I just wanted him to give me some space. He shouldn't have come here at all tonight." I exhaled, releasing some of the tension from my chest. It felt good to say it out loud. "But he thinks he's protecting me."

Skyler frowned. "Protecting you? From what?"

Shit. I shouldn't have said that part. "I don't have enough time to explain the entire backstory. Let's just say he's worried I won't be able to handle myself here." Oh yes, I was still the queen of lying without lying.

"I don't think it's as complicated as you're making it out to be." Skyler took another drag of her cigarette, exhaling a long stream of smoke. "Right now he's controlling the situation. Take the control from him and make him crawl to you on his hands and knees." She nibbled on her bright red lips, the edges curling up to complete her pleased expression.

She fiddled with her cigarette before snuffing it out in the ashtray sitting next to her and then winked at me. "Well, I've got to go. No one bought me off stage for the night … yet. All the girls were talking about the new girl getting bought off after only two songs. But don't worry. Like I said, I won't ruin your rep by telling them he's your husband. Well, as long as you don't go around telling people I'm nice." And with that, she clicked quickly out of the dressing room.

Huh. Who would have thought? Apparently, just because one is an empath doesn't mean you have everyone all figured out. Her advice wasn't half bad either. It was time I stopped letting Nixon run our relationship, even if he claimed to do it because he loved me.

After changing back into my street clothes, I grabbed my cell phone from my bag. *This is going to end tonight.* Nixon and I had a lot to work through, but I believed we could manage. Every marriage has its rough patches. As long as both partners were willing to work on the relationship, everything would be fine. Nixon and I loved each other, and my fixation on Austin—a fantasy guy— was exactly what Dr. Gray said it was: me sabotaging our relationship. But admitting the problem was half the battle.

Everything will be fine. Nixon and I will work everything out.

Chapter 4

My heels clacked rapidly on the pavement as I moved across the street to the parking garage. It was still pretty early, and I was hoping to get home before Owen went to bed. The novelty of having someone to go home to was still relatively new, but I was starting to like it. Things were different with him. Easy. He accepted every part of me, and I was developing real feelings for him. Okay, maybe more than just developing them. I was even willing to consider quitting dancing for him if he asked, but only if he asked, not demanded. And I'd never considered giving it all up for any man before. Maybe I am in love.

As I hurried to my car, I hit the button on the automatic opener just as I heard footsteps behind me. My hand fumbled on the door handle, my heart pounding in my ears. I should have had Joey walk me to my car, but he had to bring some beer up first, and I was in a rush. Almost—

I screamed as a hand slid over my mouth, muffling it before

I could get any real volume. Hot breath fanned the side of my face. "You think you're too good for me, don't you? But you're wrong. You're nothing but a pretty whore." He laughed, the sound sending chills up my spine.

I wrenched to the side, struggling to break free.

"But not when I'm done with you. When I'm done with you, you won't be so pretty anymore. You'll be nothing but a whore. Or maybe not even that since you'll have to pay guys to give it to you."

Not strong enough to fight off the man who was attacking me, I was pushed up against the side of my car. I whimpered as he managed to keep me in his grasp with only one hand while smashing my face into the hood. With the other hand, he shoved up my skirt and tore off my flimsy thong. My heart exploded in my chest as realization settled in. This man was going to rape me, and there was nothing I could do about it.

Pain ripped through my core as he rammed himself into me, my thoughts scattering into a billion pieces, my mind hiding in nonsensical places, keeping me isolated and numb.

It only lasted a few minutes, or an eternity, I wasn't sure, but when I heard his pants zip back up, I decided to remain as still as possible to not draw any more of his attention. He'd done what he came to do and now he would leave if I didn't cause any trouble.

He lifted me from the hood of my car by my hair and threw me to the ground. Curling into myself, I kept my eyes averted as I prayed for him to finally leave. But instead of hearing him walking away, the sharp snick of a knife clicking open echoed in my ears.

Adrenaline surged, giving me the strength to pull myself to my feet. I stumbled over the pavement as I tried to run, but he was faster than me, and I only managed a few steps before I was on the ground, this time on my back. Recognition hit me when I saw the man's face. "You," I croaked.

He grinned, the sight utterly terrifying. "Yeah. Me. The guy you didn't have the time for earlier. But you'll have all the time in the world for me and guys just like me when I take away that pretty face of yours."

He lunged, knocking my head into the pavement—hard. My world tilted, dark spots dancing in front of my eyes, and I idly wondered why no one had walked past us yet.

Fire ripped across one cheek and then the other, then my forehead. The agony of the wounds was slow to form, and belatedly I cried out in agony. Why didn't I wait for Joey to walk me to my car?

I screamed again and again, each one intermingling with my prayers for it to stop—said in my mind or out loud, I didn't know anymore. I just wanted it to stop, needed it to. And it would soon ... it would have to stop soon. And then he would leave me, and then someone would find my bloodied body before it was too late. I just had to make it to the other side—to survive this and everything would be fine in the end. Yes, it would be okay. All of it would be okay. It was just my face, there were plenty of amazing plastic surgeons in Pittsburgh, I just had to survive. For Owen. I wanted more than anything to be in Owen's arms again.

That's when I felt it—cold hard steel slicing across my throat. I struggled to breathe, choking on what I knew was my own blood. The pain ebbed as darkness pushed heavily down on my chest. I was so cold.

Am I dying? Yes. *With calm certainty, I knew I was. But why? Why did he pick me now, just when I was finally in a good place?* At least there's no more pain. *Regret filled me that I wouldn't get to see Owen one last time, to tell him how I felt ... If only I could see him one last time ...*

Screaming, I sat up and ran my hands over my face and neck with relief. It was a nightmare, just a nightmare. I blinked in confusion as I took in my unfamiliar surroundings. *That's right, I'm working a case.* I fell asleep in my hotel room while waiting for Nixon. I'd texted him to come meet me so we could talk.

I reached for my phone, which was lying beside me on the bed. I had a handful of missed calls and text messages, all from Nixon. Just as I was about to call him back, my phone rang in my hands, startling me. The screen lit up with Thomas' name, another member of my team.

"Hello," I croaked.

"There's been another murder," he said with no preamble.

My stomach dropped into my feet. It hadn't been just a nightmare after all. I'd picked up on the latest victim as the murder was taking place. It wasn't unheard of with an empath, but it wasn't a regular occurrence either. Although with me having just spent my night in the club, it made sense. "Who was it?"

"Don't know yet. Her face was pretty screwed up—"

I stopped listening to what he was saying. I already

knew the rest. Hell, I'd been in the victim's head as she was brutally raped and murdered. My gut twisted. I had a sinking feeling I knew exactly who the victim was.

"I'll be right there." I hung up on Thomas.

I'd explain later how I knew without asking where I was headed.

I DROVE Raven's prized Harley past the garage where the murder scene was. I couldn't just drive up and risk blowing my cover. I needed to be as incognito as possible, so I donned baggy clothes and a baseball cap pulled low over my ponytailed hair. Raven's black hair extensions and black hair at the base of my neck were still visible, but lots of girls dye their hair black. The less common shade of strawberry blonde that was my natural color was completely hidden.

After finding a spot to leave my bike a few blocks down, I walked briskly to the parking garage. Unable to shake the feeling of being watched, I keep my gaze down and my body hunched, making sure my face remained hidden.

As I went to slip under the crime scene tape like I normally would, a local Pittsburgh cop grabbed my arm to stop me. "No civilians allowed. This is a crime scene, ma'am."

I frowned, realizing for the first time that I hadn't thought to bring my badge with me. *Shit.*

"Sam, is that you?" Simon strode forward with an unsure look on his face. Peering up at him from under the brim of my hat, I met his gaze as recognition washed over his features. "Let her through. She's with us."

The cop begrudgingly released me, his feelings of annoyance wafting over me.

I scurried towards Simon, wondering if he remembered anything from earlier, or if whatever drug Nixon slipped him prevented it. Our employers were always coming up with nifty new drugs and technology to do all kinds of things that would probably make the public run screaming with paranoia. Rightly so if Simon's complete lack of embarrassment or guilt was any indication. *Shit, he doesn't remember anything at all.* I wasn't sure if I should be relieved or worried.

"I didn't want to blow my cover."

"Right," he responded. "We've been waiting for you. Thomas was starting to get nervous that you wouldn't show. He wasn't happy with how you disappeared earlier from the club, and then he said you hung up on him before he could tell you where to go."

I'd never been a big fan of Thomas, mostly because he had never particularly liked me. Guess that hadn't changed. "I didn't need to ask because I already knew. I had a dream about the murder right before he called. I also think I know who the victim is."

"Oh," Simon said. His anxiety pushing at my senses was his only other response.

Some of the people I worked with got a little weirded

out by my empath ability. They usually felt better when Nixon was nearby to dampen my power. I didn't completely understand why, although I supposed people didn't like to think that someone could dig inside their head, even if I just picked up on emotions ... mostly. There were times when I got thoughts, or thought fragments, if they were attached to strong emotions. That was probably why I was pulled inside the mind of the victim earlier. Obviously, she had some strong emotional shit going down; rape and murder will do that to someone.

As I followed Simon to the victim's body, a weird sense of déjà vu washed over me, but I shook it off with ease, needing to focus on the task at hand. I rolled the information I'd garnered from my dream over in my head, considering some of the contradictions. Why did the killer go on about wanting to disfigure the victim so she wouldn't be pretty anymore, but he went ahead and slit her throat anyways? If I had to guess, I would say it spoke of a lack of control as if he couldn't help himself—but I wasn't a profiler, just an empath.

"Nice of you to show up," Thomas said, not even bothering to make eye contact with me.

Anger surged at his tone. "Last time I checked, I'm the one in charge of this case. Not you." I stalked closer to him. "You called me twenty minutes ago."

I knew why Thomas didn't like me. He was older and more experienced than me, and yet he kept finding himself below me in rank on cases. He was convinced it was because I was married to Nixon, who was David's favorite. I couldn't deny his logic, but the fact was that I did make sense to head up this case, all things considered. The rest of the cases … yeah, maybe it was because of Nixon. Not that I would admit that to even myself.

Ignoring Thomas' attitude, I jumped right in. "I was already in the victim's head. I saw the killer through her eyes. Finding him won't be difficult anymore. He'll be back—at the club—to find more victims."

What I didn't share was that I was one of his next possible targets. The killer was the same guy that insulted me on the way out of the club earlier. Even though I hadn't seen his face with my own eyes, I recognized his rant when he repeated nearly the same thing he said to me earlier to his latest victim.

And what I refused to even think about was that if Nixon hadn't been where he wasn't supposed to be earlier, and his void abilities wouldn't have canceled me out, quite possibly we'd already have the killer in custody and the victim would still be alive. *She would be with Owen.* My heart fisted painfully. *No. I can't think about any of that.*

Thomas' annoyance was immediately replaced with excitement. "You saw his face?"

"Yes. And I think I know who the victim is—was. Skyler." My gut clenched as I let myself acknowledge my suspicions out loud.

"We just confirmed her identity as one Destiny Miles, aka Skyler, yes."

"Okay, so you don't need me here. We'll go back in

tomorrow night and get the bastard. Now that I know what he looks like, this should be a walk in the park. I need to get some sleep."

Thomas glared at me, his too-tan face contorted with the effort to contain his displeasure that I was right. "Yeah, all right, go get some sleep. We'll go back in tomorrow night, or tonight, technically." He tugged at his dark greying hair in frustration.

I smirked, hoping my attitude would give him another clump of grey hairs. "Mmm hmmm ... yep, see you tonight then." I waved a hand dismissively at him. *Yeah, that's right, you don't matter because I'm the one in charge of this case.* I stared him down a few seconds before pivoting on my heels and stalking off.

Stupid, misogynistic asshole. This is supposed to be about catching the killer, not about turning this whole thing into a power struggle. Does he even care about the victim at all?

As I approached where I left my bike, apprehension slid up my spine. Someone was leaning against the brick wall right next to it. Even though he was lurking in the shadows, I could still tell he was one large individual.

Stopping where I was, I watched as he moved out into the streetlight. Doing a quick assessment, I guessed he was about 6'4" or 6'5". His long, dark hair was pulled into a low ponytail at the nape of his neck. He was stacked with muscles, but also had sharp features and striking bone structure refined with a tawny skin tone. Belatedly, I also noted that he was quite attractive, yet nonetheless intimidating, especially considering the circumstances of our encounter.

The man's amber-colored eyes traveled over me from head to toe and then back up again before locking gazes with mine. He swallowed once as if in shock. "Sam?" His voice was a deep baritone, very pleasant, and not threatening at all.

I blinked in confusion. *Wait. Do I know him? He seems to know me. But how could I forget knowing someone like him?* "Do I know you?"

His emotions pushed at me—ones of sadness, pain, and regret—before he spoke again. "I guess not. Sorry, I thought you were someone else."

"With the same name as me?" He was lying. I just wasn't sure about what.

"Yeah, sorry," he mumbled as he turned to jog off into the night.

Weird. No, more than weird. Freaky. But I had more important things to worry about at the moment. I got on my bike and roared back towards my temporary home.

Chapter 5

"**D**o you trust me?" Austin's penetrating gaze roamed my features like a physical caress, waiting for an answer.

"Always," I breathed, my heart hammering against my ribcage.

A wicked grin twisted his full lips as he secured my wrists to the bed with a piece of nylon cord. "You're so beautiful," he murmured.

I couldn't believe I was letting him do this, but I knew what it meant to him—to us—for me to trust him like this. To trust him in a way I'd never trusted anyone before.

"Austin," I chastised as he ripped my bra and underwear from my body. The man destroyed more undergarments than anyone I'd ever known.

"Shhh ... I'll buy you more."

I smiled because that's what he always said, my naughty husband.

He stood at the foot of the bed, studying his handiwork while he stroked the dark stubble on his chin like he was debating some complex problem.

"Austin," I hissed. "What are you doing?" I didn't like him just standing there staring at me while I was tied to the bed completely naked.

He met my gaze, his baby blues glinting with mischief. "It's missing something."

I gulped, unable to read his emotions since he'd closed them down to me, on purpose no doubt.

"Don't play with me, Austin! What are you planning?" I kicked my legs on the bed restlessly.

"I'm planning to do just that—to play with you. To play with my wife's beautiful body until she screams."

My nipples pebbled, and my skin tingled, my entire body zinging with anticipation when he pulled a long, black scarf from the top drawer of our dresser. "Austin, we never talked about a blindfold."

"Ah ..." He approached me slowly as if not to spook me. "But what would be the fun in that?"

I remained mute as he slid the scarf over my eyes, tying the knot firmly behind my head. He checked to see if it was secure, and once satisfied, I heard him back up, his clothes rustling as they fluttered the floor.

"No fair," I whined. "I want to see you. Now only you get to see me. I don't like it."

"Guess you're just going to have to rely on your memory." I could hear the smile in his voice. "No more complaining. You're mine to do whatever I want with."

"When am I not?" I asked, my voice sounding huskier already.

Ignoring my question, his tongue invaded my mouth, taking control, as his fingers pinched my nipples. Pleasure and pain spiked through me simultaneously, and I moaned around his tongue, rising up to push more firmly into his hands. He broke apart our fused mouths, blazing a path down my neck, licking and sucking. He caught my left nipple between his teeth, nipping, before continuing his journey down my body. I writhed in anticipation, lifting my hips off the bed in open invitation.

"Impatient tonight, aren't we?"

Austin's tongue glided against my pulsing center, causing me to arch sharply off the bed. He kept his pace, slow, agonizingly so, teasing me to the brink before backing off, over and over. Pleasure and frustration intermingled within me. I bit my cheeks to keep from cursing him out, afraid he would stop if I did.

I screamed his name when he sucked on my clit, the elusive orgasm rolling over me, a kaleidoscope of colors exploding behind my eyes. It was almost too much, my flesh too sensitive from Austin's ministrations. I lifted my legs to push him away, needing a break, but my actions only made him redouble his efforts. My entire body convulsed as another orgasm slammed into me, mindless screams tearing from my chest. Austin owned me, controlled me as he wrenched orgasm after orgasm from my body with only his tongue.

"Please ..." I heard myself whimper as if someone else was working my mouth. "Please, I need you now."

"You already have me."

"That's not what I mean," I panted. I wanted him inside me. Now.

"My good little Sammy girl, so fucking needy."

Instead of denying me like I thought he would, he slid his body up so his hard cock rested at my entrance. "But then again, so am I tonight."

He plunged into me in one fluid motion, causing my breath to catch in my throat. He began a brutal pace that was part pain, but mostly pleasure due to the size of him. I wrapped my legs around his back, wishing I could hold him with my arms too, but grateful I wasn't completely bound. Inside the forced darkness of the blindfold, colors danced behind my eyelids, and Austin's spicy scent surrounded me, cocooning me completely. My muscles coiled tight as I hung on the edge, everything in me stilling for an instant.

I erupted, screaming Austin's name again and again. A moment later, he groaned, long and loud, pulsating within me.

"Damn," he rumbled, collapsing on top of me. "I wanted to play with you for longer than that." He slipped the silk scarf over my head, and I squinted against the blinding lights in the bedroom.

A scowl tugged my lips downward. "You mean like all the girls you were with before me?" Despite everything, sometimes my insecurities still came to the forefront of my psyche when it came to Austin. He had quite the reputation as a player before I came along. And we'd only been together a short time when he somehow talked me into marriage. What if he got bored with me one day? I couldn't bear the thought.

"My poor insecure, Sammy girl." He brushed his lush lips

over mine briefly. "You still don't get it, do you? I've never loved anyone but you. And I love you more than I can begin to explain. We're perfect for each other, perfectly flawed." He opened his mind to me, his emotions washing in to cocoon me in warmth, happiness, and intense satisfaction.

Yes. He belongs to me. He's mine. We're flawed perfectly to fit each other.

"So much love, so much trust. It's a shame really." A deep voice skittered through my brain, menace trailing in its wake. "Have you forgotten me, like you've forgotten him? Because I remember you, Samantha. I remember you."

"No!" I shouted, jolting up with a start. I rubbed my bleary eyes. It was just a dream. *Holy shit—I'm never sleeping again.* Every time I went to sleep lately, I either had super-realistic dreams that involved Austin, sex, and me, or I dreamt about murders. But the creepy voice at the end of my last dream was new, and definitely not welcome. Maybe I needed to take some cues from the *A Nightmare on Elm Street* kids and try to stay awake indefinitely.

"Sam? You okay?" Nixon's voice caused me to flinch, and I whipped my head around just as he exited the bathroom. He wore nothing but a white towel slung low on his hips, obviously just out of the shower.

"What are you doing here?" Confusion nettled. Why did the dream with Austin feel so real? And what did that voice mean about forgetting him? How could I forget someone I never knew?

"You left me a key at the front desk, remember? You

said you wanted to talk." His forehead furrowed with concern. "When I came in you were sound asleep, so I figured I'd take a shower first before waking you."

"Oh, right." I ran my hand through my hair absentmindedly. *I remember now.* Meeting my husband's gaze—my real husband, not my imaginary one—I gave him a wan smile.

He remained where he was, studying me while I studied him. Nixon really was an attractive man. His body was all strong, chiseled lines under smooth, bronzed skin. Dark brown, wavy hair framed a handsome angular face, which held soulful chocolate eyes. Anyone attracted to men would consider themselves lucky to have someone like him, and here I was panting after a fantasy instead. Much to my horror, I felt my face crumple up, and hot tears erupted from my eyes, burning their way down my cheeks.

Nixon came to me immediately, and I let him take me in his arms. "Sam, baby, tell me what's wrong?"

"I don't know," I sobbed. "I just don't know." That was the truth. I had no idea why I was obsessed with Austin, an imaginary man, or why everything else in my life felt so wrong lately, as if I were living one big lie.

"Maybe you should let Thomas take over the case. Come home with me, Sam. We'll fix this, I promise."

Standing, I stumbled away from him, sudden anger consuming me. "I'm not leaving this case, Nixon. I saw his face—the killer's. No one else can identify him. And maybe I need to figure these things out for myself. Maybe with you always trying to save me I've become too dependent on you."

"You're my wife. What else would you have me do?" he responded through gritted teeth.

"Not smother me!" My voice crept up a few octaves. "I may be your wife, but I need to be my own person, too!"

"You think I smother you?" Hurt rolled across Nixon's features, pinching them.

"Yes … no." I didn't want to hurt him like I was already doing, just make him understand. "I love you, Nixon. It's just—"

"You're pulling away from me lately. I can feel it," Nixon whispered.

"I don't—I don't mean to." And that was the truth, too. I didn't want to imagine Austin in his place, I just did. It was a compulsion. Undeniable even if I regretted it with everything in my being.

"What's more important? This case or our marriage?"

Fresh tears burned the corners of my eyes, rolling down my cheeks a moment later. "Don't make me choose. That's not fair and you know it."

He turned away. "You're right. I'm sorry. I just don't want to lose you."

I watched his muscular shoulders rise and fall for a few heartbeats before I went to him. I hated not being able to read Nixon's emotions when we fought. Wrapping my arms around him, I pressed my face into his back, inhaling his freshly showered scent. "You're not going to lose me if you don't want to. Just let me finish this case, and I'll do whatever you want me to do. I can't let this psycho get away."

He placed his hands over mine, squeezing once. "I know." He then pulled me around the front of him and dipped his head to kiss me.

"I've never loved anyone but you. And I love you more than I can begin to explain. We're perfect for each other, perfectly flawed." Austin's impassioned voice echoed in my mind, forcing me to slip away from Nixon.

"I can't," I whispered. "Not now." *But why?* Why did it suddenly feel like being with Nixon was cheating on Austin, a man I'd invented in my mind? Just the thought of letting Nixon touch me right now twisted my insides.

"Sam ..." Desperation was laced into Nixon's tone.

"I'm sorry," I murmured, unable to meet his eyes. "We'll fix everything after this case is wrapped up. I promise."

"Yeah, all right, fine. Do what you need to do and then come back to me. Please just come back to me."

Silence engulfed us as Nixon waited for a response, and I searched my mind for an acceptable one. "Thank you." Those two words hung in the air meaning so much more than the simplicity of them.

I slumped on the bed as Nixon moved around the room, getting dressed and gathering what little stuff he brought with him. When he was finished, he stood before me, tipping my chin up with his index finger. "I love you. I'll always be here for you. You know that, right?"

Tears trailed down my face again, and I bit back a sob. "I know."

And then he was gone, the door ominously clicking shut behind him. Wrapping my arms around my middle, I curled into a ball in the center of the bed.

What the hell did I just do?

Chapter 6

I'd fallen asleep with my phone right next to my face, its cheery alarm tone my not-so-pleasant wake-up call. Somehow, I'd managed to get a few hours of sleep even though the noises in the hotel during the day kept me awake until I was too exhausted to resist the pull of dreamland any longer. Of course, I'd been rewarded with more dreams of Austin. Thankfully, no more murder nightmares. After what happened with Nixon, I wasn't sure which was worse anymore though.

I had just enough time to shower and eat before needing to be back at Club Elite for the evening shift. My thoughts were scrambled, floating back and forth between memories of my fight with Nixon and my super-steamy dreams of Austin. What I really needed was to focus on the case, the rest I could deal with later.

Once out of the shower, I quickly dressed in street clothes and went to gather Raven's things. But when I opened my bag, I was greeted with empty space. My blood heated, and a colorful array of swear words directed at my husband spilled from my mouth. Obviously, despite Nixon's claim that he understood my desire to finish the case, he didn't mean it. His petty actions spoke louder than his words, his very clearly stating that he wanted me off the case and at home with him.

Nope, not happening. If he thought something as small as taking Raven's work gear was going to stop me then he was in for a rude awakening. I still had the most important things: the fake tattoo on my arm, and my hair extensions. Everything else I could work around.

I glanced at the wall clock. Yep, I was going to be a little late, but all things considered, I was willing to bet Bert would be thrilled I showed up at all after what had happened with Skyler.

You will not control me, Nixon, whether it's out of love or not.

I ARRIVED at Club Elite in a cab, a cold fury simmering in my veins. Nixon had taken it a step further by snagging the keys to Raven's Harley. *I will be getting those back, asshat.*

Bert scowled when I entered the club in a huff, even though I felt his relief at my appearance. "You're late."

"I'm here now." I cocked my hip and tilted my head. "I had some issues with my stuff walking away on its own.

You should be glad I showed up at all though with the less-than-stellar record you have of protecting your dancers around here."

Bert's gaze dipped to the floor. "There is that," he mumbled, turning to go into his office without another word.

I made quick work of getting ready, and before I knew it I was standing behind the main stage, preparing myself to dance mostly naked for a crowd of strangers—again. *Talk about job dedication.* My nerves weren't as debilitating as my debut, and when my name was called, I sashayed onto the stage with confidence. Completely from memory, I let Skyler-like emotions settle over me, the music doing the rest.

A twinge of guilt nibbled at my attention. *She's dead. Skyler's dead and you're still using her for inspiration. Damnit.* If I'd used my empath abilities to scan the club yesterday instead of being so wrapped up in what was going on between Nixon and me, then maybe Skyler would still be alive. The killer tried to stop me, he even insulted me, and I didn't bother to check him out with my gift. It was the reason Nixon wasn't supposed to be there. With his void abilities …

No. Stop. You've gone over this. You can't let yourself think about it. What's done is done. All you can do is save the next girl.

When I finished up my two-song set on the main stage, I pulled on my borrowed gown, aiming for the VIP bar, and a view of what was going on around the club.

"What took you so long?"

I spun around, coming face to face with Nixon.

"What are you doing here?" I hissed. I fought the urge to hit him, knowing it would most likely blow my cover. *What the fuck is his problem?*

"I talked to David. I got him to understand what's at stake, and he let me join the team on this case."

"What does that even mean?" I plastered a fake smile on my face. "You think I can't handle this by myself, and I'll screw the case up?" Nixon's marked silence was all the answer I needed. "Fuck you, Nixon. I thought you believed in me."

"Sam, wait!"

I strode away from him as if he was nothing to me. But underneath my mask of neutrality humiliation threatened to suffocate me, my entire body trembling with it. *How will it look to the rest of the team now that they know my own damn husband doesn't think I can handle one case without him?*

"Excuse me. I would like to book a private room with you."

My head snapped around at the sound of the man's voice—the killer. *Is it really going to be this easy?* A shiver of apprehension ran up my spine. There was something not quite right about all of this.

"I ... w-well—" My face heated as I stammered. Should I get him to the private room and then call in the rest of the team? Or should I call them in now and risk making a scene? Would it even matter as long as we got him? My mind went blank, overwhelmed by the decision.

Apparently, I didn't need to worry about it though. With Nixon leading the way, my team swarmed the guy. One minute he was asking me for a dance, and the next he was being led out of the club in handcuffs.

And I just stood there blinking, confusion warring with relief. *How did they know it was him? I didn't signal them in any way. Something is very wrong with this entire situation. But what?*

"Come on, Sam, let's go." Nixon's rough voice broke into my inner musings, and I numbly trailed after him. It all seemed so anticlimactic. Or maybe I just needed to stop watching overdramatized TV crime-solving shows.

My attention moved idly over the crowd in the club as we passed through to the exit, my gaze snagging on a familiar face—the tall guy who had been lurking by my bike this morning. His amber eyes met mine for one intense moment before he turned to spear the back of Nixon's head with a death glare.

I staggered, a sudden and sharp pain spiking through my head. "Nixon?" Darkness pushed around the edges of my vision.

"I got you, Sam," Nixon said, scooping me up in his arms.

"That guy back there—" My vision tunneled, bright spots flashing before my eyes.

"Shhh … I've got you. Just relax."

Abruptly, my tension morphed into calm. Everything would be fine because Nixon would take care of me, just like he always did. My eyes fluttered shut, drowsiness overwhelming me. It was a relief in contrast to the forced sensation of losing consciousness I'd been fighting a moment ago.

Just before everything completely slipped away into oblivion, a familiar voice slithered through my mind, winding anticipation and fear together in my heart.

"Sam ... my Sammy girl ... I'm coming for you."

I KNEW I was dreaming with one hundred percent certainty. But even though I knew it was a dream, it was extremely realistic, as if I'd stepped back in time to when I'd bartended at Club Elite. To before I met Nixon ...

Yes, it was like reliving that moment, and yet, I had a separate train of thought as the dreamer, which altered things a bit. I was observing from an outside perspective while remaining the main character simultaneously.

Obviously, my subconscious needed to show me something, so I decided to let it without a fight.

"What kind of beer do you have?" the probably-fake-ID-toting, baby-faced kid called to me over the booming music of the club.

But what did I care? He made it past the not-so-discerning eye of our bouncer, so it wasn't like I'd be the one to lose my job if Baby Face got busted.

I glanced over my shoulder to see my partner in crime for the evening, Jenn, mixing up a row of flaming shots. It was Friday night, we were stacked at least five deep all the way around the bar, and this stupid kid wanted me to tell him what kind of beer we had. I shot him an impatient look as I began rattling off our limited options. "Iron, IC Light, Bud, Bud Light, MGD, Miller High Life, Coors, Coors Light, Miller Lite, and Yuengling."

He tilted his head, puzzled. "Don't you have any imports like Stella or Heineken?"

I quirked my eyebrow, resisting the urge to skip right over him to take the order of the guy wearing a very expensive suit who would probably be a much better tipper. "If we did, I would have listed them!" I yelled over the music.

"Umm ..." Baby Face stammered.

"Aw, come on, kid. Just order something so I can wait on some other people. You're not the only thirsty one here." Seriously, what kind of selection did he expect to find in a strip club? Another minute rolled by, which was the equivalent of twenty in bartender time.

Eh. Time's up. *I mentally dismissed Baby Face and pointed to Expensive Suit Guy, signaling to him that I wanted to take his order instead. He pushed in closer to the bar, giving me a hundred-watt smile meant to dazzle.*

"Kid, huh? You can't be much older than him. How old are you, darlin'?"

I wasn't dazzled quite that easily. "Hasn't anyone ever told you never to ask a woman her real age? What can I get you to drink?"

"Aw, darlin', you look much too young to be worried about your age already. What are you, twenty-one?"

Ugh. He wasn't going to just order without small talk.

Couldn't he see I was trying to work, and having him try to flirt was not going to endear him to me? "Fine. I'm twenty-five. Happy now? You cracked the code. So what can I get you to drink?" Please just order and leave me alone, for fuck's sake.

Suit Guy's smile widened ever so slightly with a look of triumph. "How about a name to go along with your pretty face?"

"Look, mister, I'm just the bartender here. I make your drinks, you pay me, hopefully tip me if you feel I did a good job —which I always do, by the way—and then you go give your A-game to the ladies who actually have the time and inclination to receive it." I motioned to the main stage with a flourish. I mean, why was he bothering me anyways when he had a bevy of almost naked dancers waiting to vie for his attention?

The smile on his face slipped, and he fumbled for a response. "I ... uh ..."

I rolled my eyes. Apparently, he wasn't used to that kind of rejection. He was probably one of those types who tried to pick up the bartenders in places like these because he thought we'd be so flattered he wanted to talk to us instead of the dancers. He had the wrong bartender if that was the case. Jenn would totally fall for that trick.

A hundred-dollar bill sliding onto the bar caught my attention, especially because the guy wasn't waving it. I hated when guys waved money in the air to get my attention. But something about the subtle way this guy asked for my attention made me want to give it to him. I took a step to my right, leaving Baby Face and Suit Guy both drinkless and confused. I quickly sized up Hundred-Dollar Guy.

That's right. This was the night I met Nixon for the first time.

"No, that's not right," a voice whispered in the back of my mind. "This was the night you met Austin."

My attention swung back to the scene as I watched Nixon's image flicker and morph into Austin's. My dream/memory then continued as if it had been paused in my mind for a moment before I hit play again.

He was tall—about 6'2" or 6'3"—muscular, but not bulky by what I could see of him in his jeans and T-shirt. He sported cropped, dark hair, his shockingly blue eyes stealing the show. In fact, I had to pry my gaze away from his eyes to take in the rest of him. His features were striking, almost feminine, yet the proportions were much too large to be anything but masculine. He was extremely attractive, the allure of him going beyond his appearance into undefinable territory. It was like he had his own gravitation pull, and suddenly I found myself trapped in it.

"What can I get you to drink?" I asked in a neutral tone. Despite thinking that Hundred-Dollar Guy was hot, I wasn't about to allow myself to act on it in any way.

A slight smile quirked his full lips. "A Yuengling."

I nodded with approval. Finally, someone who knew what they wanted. I whirled around, dipping my hand into the cooler to retrieve a bottle of Yuengling just before Jenn slammed the cooler shut. I flipped the top off with my flat bar, setting it down in front of Hundred-Dollar Guy. "That'll be $5.75."

He slid the hundred at me. "Keep it."

Now, that brought a smile to my face. "Thanks." One of the reasons I worked at a place like this: awesome tips. It offset the rest of the bullshit I had to put up with.

"Totally worth it," Hundred-Dollar Guy said before he turned, disappearing into the crowd. For some reason, that intrigued me. What was worth it exactly? My mind swirled with possible answers I didn't have time to contemplate while I was working.

The rest of my evening passed in much the same way until everything blurred together like every Friday night at Club Elite did for me. Soon I found myself sitting at the almost empty bar, having a beer while counting tip money, chatting it up with Jenn and a few of the dancers.

"You should come with us to after-hours tonight," Jenn said before taking a long draw from her cherry vodka and Dr. Pepper, her favorite.

"Nah. I have to be back here at noon tomorrow. It's bad enough having to come back at all, let alone with no sleep." I paused to take a swig of my beer. "I just don't see the point."

"The point is," Nikki interjected, while applying a fresh coat of ruby red lipstick without using a mirror, "that you need to unwind and have some fun with your friends."

"I can unwind tomorrow night when I don't have to work the next day."

"Nope. You're coming with us tonight. I'm leaving for Florida tomorrow and won't be back for a couple weeks. You need to hang out with me before I go," Tristin stated with force. She knew she couldn't bully me. And as long as she didn't try to guilt me, I'd be able to resist her brand of persuasion. "Please,

Chloe. For me." As if reading my mind, she went straight for my Achilles heel.

I frowned. "It's not like you're going for good, and you won't even be gone that long."

"How do you know that? I'm an exotic dancer. What if I love it so much down there I decide to stay? I'm sure I could find work there pretty easily."

"Then I'll come visit you," I retorted.

"Puhleeeeeease, Chloe? I really want you to hang out with me tonight." Tristin stuck out her lower lip in a mock pout.

Confusion washed over me—why would Tristin call me Chloe? The first time I thought I'd heard wrong, but not the second.

"Because that was your name," the same deep voice rasped in the back of my mind.

"No! This was the night I met Nixon, and my name is Samantha."

"But it was Chloe," the masculine voice calmly insisted.

"Who are you? Why are you trying to screw with my mind, my memories?" His voice was familiar and yet hidden from me—masked. The more I concentrated on it, the further away its identity seemed to slip.

"I'm not the one who distorted your memories. I'm simply the one trying to help you put them back the way they should be. Just keep watching." And with that, I received a mental push, one I couldn't resist, and my focus went back to the dream/memory.

I laughed. "I'm sure that works on some of your regulars, but not on me. And besides, even if I did want to go, I'm not going wearing this." I motioned to my black pants and crisp white shirt. Club Elite was the only strip club I'd ever heard of that made their bartenders dress so frumpy. No way was I going to after-hours wearing my uniform.

Tristin pulled out some clothes from her bag, waving them in the air. "Way ahead of you. I brought you a change of clothes. And before you protest anymore, I brought your favorite pair of go-out jeans, your favorite tank, and your comfy slides. Personally, I would have picked something much cuter, but I didn't want you to have any more excuses."

That's it. I'm taking my spare key back from her.

"Shit. You really are pushy sometimes." I shook my head in dismay. I knew it was a losing battle at that point. "Fine. I'll go. But I'm not closing the place down. I'm just going to stay for a little bit, have a few beers, then I'm going home to pass out for a few hours before I have to be back here."

Tristin, Nikki, and Jenn all whooped it up, only making my desire not to go even stronger. Who was I kidding? I knew I'd be there until the sun came up. The crowd that made up after-hours largely consisted of bar industry people: bartenders, waitresses, bouncers, dancers, and so on. The energy of everyone being out of work, unwinding on a Friday night, most of them having money to burn, could be intoxicating to someone like me. There were too many people to shut out completely in a scenario such as that. I would get swept away in the tide of emotions that weren't mine.

Although I had to admit that it would be better than the loneliness and depression that had been threatening to suffocate me for the past nine hours. Most people found on the inside of a *strip club, be they customer or employee, were nothing like the outward appearance they presented to the world. The loneliness and depression was far louder than any kind of lust. I didn't understand why people bothered.*

I sighed loudly. *"All right, just let me and Jenn finish splitting our tips, and then I'll go change."*

My gut twisted with the knowledge that I was going to regret my decision. But then again, who was I to say? I didn't get premonitions of the future. I was just your run-of-the-mill, everyday empath.

"Okay, I kept watching. So now what? What was the point of that? I was there, I remember my thoughts and feelings, and I remember what happened next. I go to the after-hours club, and I see Nixon again. We—"

"No," the voice growled. "I'm trying to give it back to you—the real memory of that night. Just keep watching. You may think it's pointless, but every little bit matters to make the memory complete."

I didn't want to listen to the voice inside my head, but I didn't seem to have a choice.

I ended up driving my car to the after-hours club. It was only a few blocks from Club Elite, located in an innocuous building in downtown Pittsburgh. I could take a cab home to my North Side apartment for under ten bucks and not have to worry about my car until morning. The parking meters usually weren't checked until late afternoon on a Saturday, so I could just take a cab back to my car in the morning, move it to the garage across from work, and I'd be golden. Tristin, Nikki, and Jenn were on their own, not that I worried about them finding a ride home. The three of them always managed somehow, just like I did.

As the four of us spilled out of my two-door Honda Civic and made our way across the street, I already felt myself getting pumped up from the energy leaking out of the club, and we hadn't even made it to the door yet. Yep, it's going to be a long day at work tomorrow.

I plastered a smile on my face, still attempting to mentally shield myself from emotions I knew weren't mine. I didn't know why I bothered. I usually just gave up in the end and figured if I was going to hell, I might as well enjoy the ride.

"Ladies. Good to see you," Jimmy, the big, burly bouncer, rumbled as we made our way to the front of the line. "And, Chloe, I can't believe they got you to come out tonight. I feel like the only time I ever see you is behind the bar." He bent down and delivered a much-too-tight bear hug that left me gasping for air. "First drink is on me tonight, Chloe. Tell Rocco to put it on my tab."

After I caught my breath, I smiled. "Thanks, Jimmy."

I went out so seldomly that I usually ended up not spending any of my own money when I did. Everyone wanted to be in my good graces for when it was their turn to get hooked up. Bar industry people knew how to pay it forward with their peers. As Jimmy held the door open for us, a slew of complaints were thrown at us from the people left outside in line. Like I said, there were advantages when I did make it out.

Tristin grabbed my hand, propelling me up the stairs and into the club. "First drink is on me! I can't believe I actually got you out! Someone better check the thermostat in hell!"

As Tristin pushed her way to the front of the bar, dragging me with her, I glanced over my shoulder, noticing that both Nikki and Jenn had already disappeared into the crowd. That was a record even for them. It hadn't even been five minutes and they'd spotted marks. It looked like neither of them would be spending any of their own money tonight either.

"Here's to foolish men and parting them from their money!" Tristin saluted me as she handed me a bottle of beer.

"Hear! Hear!" I clinked her bottle with mine and smiled, letting the electric emotions of the people around me seep in and fill me to the brim. In another few minutes, I wouldn't know that the emotions I was feeling weren't mine. It was easier to just let go and stop thinking, at least when the emotions were positive. It was the type of high that no drug could duplicate. But just like with any high, I would suffer doubly tomorrow. I would be left feeling empty and void, worn out. Better make the cake worth the bake.

"Let's dance! They're playing my song!" I said, taking a swig from my beer. Truthfully, I had no idea what song was currently playing, but I already was feeling good, and about to feel better.

"See, I love when you get like this, Chloe! You're so much fun! So carefree!"

Tristin led the way to the center of the dance floor. Funny how we always seemed to own the place when we were here. We both started moving to the music. Our styles were very different, her a much better dancer than me, but I didn't care, I was having fun. As we gyrated, we laughed at nothing and everything. I reveled in the feelings of excitement, hope, and *lust. I could almost taste all of it, sweet and decadent, like a treat I rarely had the pleasure of enjoying. Life was good, at least for the moment.*

After a few songs, I was draining the bottom of my beer and in desperate need of a refill. I left Tristin grinding on some guy she'd probably end up going home with despite the fact she'd just met him. But I wasn't judging. Her body, her decision. Still swaying to the music, I fought my way to the sidebar where I waved at Rocco. He nodded, letting me know he'd get me next.

"Let me buy you a drink," a masculine voice rumbled much too close to my right ear, hot breath tickling my cheek. I turned, finding myself face to face with Hundred-Dollar Guy.

But it was Austin and not Nixon. "Hey!" I shouted in my head. "This isn't right!" No answer came, and I was again forced to turn my attention back to the dream/memory.

Was he following me? Wait, why would I think that? If he wanted to keep the party going after Club Elite, it would make sense that he'd end up somewhere nearby. Even still, something wasn't right. But I wasn't getting a creepy vibe, just a few niggling-doubts accompanied by suspicion.

Reaching into the waist of my jeans, I slid my fingers down my hip to retrieve a twenty, waving it at him. "In a way, you already have."

His azure gaze glinted in the low light as his lips turned up slightly. "That's not what I meant, and you know it."

"Sorry, I don't accept drinks from strangers."

He tilted his head slightly and donned a smirk. "But you'll accept a tip of ninety-four dollars and twenty-five cents from a stranger without any problem?"

"Yep. I was working—that was me getting paid. Totally different." I winked and turned away to wait for Rocco, who was taking too long if you asked me.

"Mmm ... I see. I'm Austin, by the way."

Good for him. I grinned at Rocco as he slid my new beer across the bar. About time. *"Jimmy said to put it on his tab,"* I called out, and Rocco gave me a thumbs-up.

"Jimmy can buy you a drink, but I can't?" Austin asked as he followed me towards the dance floor.

I glanced over my shoulder at Austin. He was looking pretty good to me right about now. But I couldn't tell if my reaction to him was mine or if it was the overwhelming lust permeating the club. Feeling good, happy, carefree, and even lustful enough to maybe dance with a stranger was as far as I ever pushed it. *"Jimmy's not a stranger. You are."*

"I just introduced myself. All that's left is for you to tell me your name, and voilà, we're not strangers anymore."

He grabbed my wrist and spun me towards him as if it were a dance step. My head swam, and I gasped. Every single one of his emotions surged through me as all of mine filled him up, and at the same time he was getting his own emotions filtered back to him through me as I got mine through him ... it was a tangled, bizarre, jumbled loop.

"What the fuck?" he muttered, his eyes wide and transfixed on mine.

"How—what—Don't touch me!" I yelled, stumbling away from him.

I maneuvered in and around people, going deeper into the crowd in an effort to lose him. What the hell just happened? Was my weird ability going wonky? Or did it have something to do with him? I wasn't going to stick around to find out, that was for sure.

I made a beeline for the back door, slipping out before Austin or any of my friends spotted me. I paused to breathe in the cool night air once outside, before hastily making my way from the back alley towards my car. I only had one beer, so I'd be fine to drive because if I wasn't, I'd probably run all the way home instead of waiting for a cab. I was shaking uncontrollably, even though I wasn't cold, the weird incident with Austin rattling me to my core.

Once inside my car with all the doors locked, I heaved a sigh of relief. I'd made it, and in mere minutes, I'd be in the safety of my apartment. As I pulled out of the parking lot and onto the main road, I had the sudden urge to look in my rear-view mirror, and sure enough, jogging across the street from the club was Austin. His head swiveled in the direction of my car just at that moment, and I knew he saw me—felt me. I just knew. Shit. *I slammed my foot down on the accelerator, leaving him in my dust.*

I parked my car in a back alley by my apartment, something I didn't generally like to do, but I didn't want Austin to get any bright ideas if he happened to spot my car. After all, I was only a five-minute ride from where I'd left him. It wouldn't be implausible for him to figure out which direction I'd gone and keep an eye out for my car. I had this odd feeling in my gut that he would know I was somewhere close by—call me paranoid.

I scurried into my apartment, making sure to fasten the handle lock and the deadbolt. Flipping all my lights on, I made my way to my bedroom, locking that door as well. Only then did I feel a tad bit more secure.

All my windows had bars on them since my unit was on the first floor, and if someone wanted in, they'd have to first go through the main building door, then the front door of my apartment, then my bedroom door. By that time, I'd be well alert, and armed and ready, locked behind my bathroom door as well by that point. At times like these, I really loved the set-up of my apartment—a lot—although I wasn't sure why I was freaking out so badly.

I hadn't felt threatened by Austin, just ... ripped wide open. It was as if he would have been able to see into every dark and dusty cranny of my mind without any effort if I'd given him the chance. And I'd sensed him more clearly than anyone ever before.

Even in the safety of my apartment, isolated and alone, I was aware of him out there, his presence humming within me. He was intrigued by me, his thoughts laser-focused on finding me again, and he knew I felt him just as much as he felt me. Somehow, that one touch, that one moment when his fingers closed around my wrist, it had forged a connection between us. And the biggest problem was that I didn't know how to turn it off ... to break it. I didn't understand any of what was happening. Was it possible that he had some kind of ability similar to mine? Yet he'd seemed just as surprised as I was. Could he—

Suddenly I was standing in an empty, white room with no windows or doors.

"Isn't it funny how you can't remember your 'coke problem,' yet you accept it as a part of your past as well?"

I swung my gaze around in an attempt to locate the owner of the voice, but I was still alone in the room.

"That's because I was always too fucked up on the drugs to remember things clearly," I retorted.

"But the memory I just showed you, aside from the dispute of your name and who you met that night, the rest is accurate?"

"Yes," I said, crossing my arms over my chest.

"So you went to an after-hours club that night, where coke is handed out like candy on Halloween, and the thought to do some didn't even cross your mind?"

Why did I have the feeling that the owner of the voice was wearing a smug smile at the moment? "I ... well—" Okay, fine, it did seem a bit odd.

"I know you don't want to believe your memories are all lies, that Nixon is lying to you, but you need to start asking questions. You need to discover the truth for yourself. You need to come back to me."

I was hurled into darkness.

Chapter 7

My pulse beat out a staccato rhythm inside my skull, my thoughts sluggish and fuzzy around the edges. *I didn't drink last night, did I?* Rubbing my temples, I tried to remember.

"I know you don't want to believe your memories are all lies, that Nixon is lying to you, but you need to start asking questions. You need to discover the truth for yourself. You need to come back to me." My eyes fluttered open as the words from my dream ricocheted around in my head, adding another layer to my confusion. Groaning, I attempted to pull myself out of bed.

"Hey, baby, don't. Let me help you." Nixon carefully propped me up on a pillow. "Here." He handed me a glass of water. "You're probably dehydrated."

As I gulped down the cool water, I met Nixon's eyes over the rim of the glass. His worry was splashed across his solemn expression. "What happened? I mean, after I passed out?"

The seeds of mistrust planted by my dream sprung to life inside of me, pushing tendrils of doubt through my mind. *Is his concern genuine? Could the man I'm married to be lying to me about my past? But why? What good would that do?*

Nixon hesitated a moment before sitting on the bed beside me. "Isn't it obvious? I brought you back to our home in Virginia. I was worried when you didn't wake up right away, but Tina looked you over and assured me you were fine."

"Right ... Tina," I mumbled.

"How are you feeling, besides the headache?"

My heart twisted and dropped into my stomach. "How do you know I have a headache?"

For the first time since meeting Nixon, it struck me how odd it was that he always seemed to just *know* things. *What if being a void isn't his only gift? No. Don't be ridiculous. Why would Nixon hide any abilities from me? He loves me. I'm his wife, end of story. Stop being paranoid.*

"I mean, I guess Tina told you ..." I mused out loud. Of course, that was the answer. Not some paranoid delusion invented by yet another weird dream. Tina was a healer. She also had a gift for diagnosing illnesses, which went hand in hand with being a healer. She must have told Nixon what to expect when I woke up.

Nixon's phone chimed, and he reached over to pick it up off his nightstand. "Hello? ... Yes. I understand. I'll talk to her." He ended the conversation without so much as a good-bye. Staring at the phone in his hand, his jaw muscles flexed.

It's times like these I wish I could read him with my gift. "Well? What's going on?"

"There's been another murder."

"Okay?" I raised my eyebrows. "And?" We dealt with murders all the time. It's what we did.

He slumped down onto the bed next to me without making eye contact. "It's more than one murder." Nixon turned his phone over in his hands slowly. "One matches the MO from the bodies we've been finding here in Virginia, and the other matches the murders from ..." He heaved a sigh and pursed his lips. "From Pittsburgh."

"What? I don't understand." My mind reeled. How was that possible? The two cases weren't linked, and we'd just caught the serial killer from Pittsburgh. "I don't understand," I repeated, hoping to prompt him into an explanation.

"They're connected somehow," he muttered. He just sat there, his face impassive, before he stood abruptly. "Come on, we have work to do." His nostrils flared as he eyed me warily. "That is, if you're feeling up to it."

I pulled myself from bed, staggering slightly. "Of course I'm up for it. A little headache isn't going to stop me."

"I'M READY."

Nixon roughly pressed his lips to my forehead before he turned to walk away.

"Wait," I snapped, grabbing his forearm.

Swallowing compulsively, I tried to combat the dryness in my throat. Nixon just stood beside me quietly as I stared at the macabre scene in front of us. Two women, both beautiful, one with blonde hair, one with dark brown hair, lay on the ground. The brunette's face was cut up in the same manner as Skyler's had been, and her throat was slit, too. The blonde appeared to merely be sleeping. There was a message there, and I was certain I would discover it when I tapped into their dying emotions.

But this case, these murders, something about all of it had shaken me to my core and stolen what little confidence I'd managed to scrape together for myself. For the first time since joining the team, I had to fight the urge to tuck tail and run.

I took in a deep, quivering breath, forcing myself to release my tight grip on Nixon. "Okay. Now I'm ready."

Nixon silently moved away from me, taking his void ability with him. I didn't lift my eyes from the gruesome scene filling my vision.

But no death emotions slammed into me like I'd been expecting. Instead, a vaguely familiar voice, one I couldn't quite place, spoke, filling my head with its raspy tone. "Testing, testing, one, two, three. This is a prerecorded message that I left for you, Sam. I was hoping you would get to it first. But don't be alarmed—this is a gift. I want you to remember who I am. I want you to remember the good times we had together before you forgot who you really are."

A dark chuckle swam through my mind. "Remember how I used to leave you such beautiful gifts so you could join me in the ecstasy of their deaths? Remember how I tried to teach you about the rush of being in someone's head when they died—and living to walk away? There is no bigger or better high, and yet I still want to share it with you. Yes, I've missed our games. But not to worry ... a new one is afoot, and I think this one is going to be the best one we've ever played."

A sharp pain ripped through my skull, dropping me to my hands and knees. My vision blurred, and bile burned its way up my esophagus. Swiping at the sweat gathering on my upper lip, I accidentally wiped the Vicks from under my nose. The foul odor of decay stung my nostrils and rolled down the back of my throat, gagging me.

Strong arms encircled my waist, lifting me into a firm chest. I turned my face away, inhaling Nixon's scent. I clawed at his shirt, shaking my head as I processed what I'd just picked up from the crime scene. It was essentially a prerecorded emotional message. I didn't even know that was possible. Plus, whoever left the message had also erased the death emotions, leaving behind only what he'd wanted me to find. At least we now had the answer to how some of the other scenes I'd worked on had been devoid of emotions. They'd been erased, too.

"He knows me," I mumbled, my lips partially numb. "He left that message for me." Goose bumps erupted across my skin, and I shuddered. "He said it was a gift for me, and that he wants to share the experience with me."

I lifted my head to gauge Nixon's reaction. His gaze was shuttered, and his expression blank.

"He said this game is going to be better than any we've played before."

My stomach flipped and twisted, tying itself in a knot. "I-I don't understand."

None of it made sense. I had no recollection of anything pertaining to what the insane, and yet mentally gifted, serial killer was alluding to. But then again, he was clearly insane, so maybe it was best if I didn't pay attention to anything he said. Maybe I'd simply become a part of his delusions.

"Come on, let's get you home. We'll figure this all out later, I promise. We can't sort through this here when you're in this condition."

I didn't protest when he carried me to the car, not caring that everyone on our team would probably see me as weak, broken. None of it mattered, not anymore. There was a mentally gifted serial killer on the loose.

"Chloe?" Nixon rumbled softly.

Icy fingers danced along my spine. "Wh-What did you just call me?"

His forehead furrowed as he regarded me with

confusion. "What do you mean? I just called you by your name. Sam."

"No, you called me—" A sudden roar swept through my ears, blocking out his response. I saw Nixon's mouth moving, but I couldn't hear what he was saying. Instead, I listened as voices replaced the roaring in my head.

"Why Samantha Bevans?" Austin's deep voice murmured as if he was right next to me. "Why choose that name for your new identity? After all this time I never thought to ask you until now."

"I don't know ..." I heard myself say. "I picked the name when I was still trying to convince myself that I hated you. I didn't realize until later, but my subconscious was trying to call me on my bullshit, obviously." I laughed. "When I was a little girl, my mom used to watch Days of Our Lives. *There was a character on the show who was obsessed with this guy named Austin. I don't remember the rest. I was just a kid, and it was a soap opera, so it was kind of confusing to me, but somehow I guess my subconscious just thought, I don't know, her name was Samantha, but they called her Sammy for short. You think it's stupid, don't you?"*

"Marry me."

"What? You can't be—"

"Shhh ... Sammy, my good little Sammy girl. I'm just as obsessed with you, if that's what you're trying to tell me, and I have been from the beginning. I want to spend the rest of my life with you. Marry me."

"I-I don't—yes. I'll marry you. But I thought that kind of thing didn't matter to you. The marriage thing."

"I never thought it would, but I want everyone to know you're mine. I need you to be mine officially."

"That means you'll be mine officially, too."

"Sam? Can you hear me?" Nixon's voice broke through, as Austin's faded away. "Tina, tell me what's wrong with her, now!"

"Nothing, as far as I can tell," Tina's spritely voice chimed in.

Blinking my surrounding into focus, I realized that I was on the ground with Nixon and Tina hunched over me. "I'm fine. Really, I'm okay." My face damp, I reached up to wipe away tears I hadn't realized I was shedding. *What the hell?*

Nixon grabbed me by my shoulders. "You're not fine. You—"

"Don't touch me!" I shrank away from him, my skin crawling. "I mean—I-I'm so confused." *Confused, yeah, try completely falling apart.*

"It's okay, baby, I'm here for you." There was fear in Nixon's voice—real fear. "Can you give her something to calm her down, make her sleep?" he asked Tina.

"Yeah, sure. I can inject her with something to knock her out if you think that's what's best for her."

"Yes, she just needs some rest, and then we can sort all of this out."

I didn't argue with Nixon, because truth be told, I wanted an escape. I couldn't handle reality at the moment, or what it meant that I couldn't.

Tina tugged at my arm gently. The sting from the

needle only lasted a second, and moments later my eyes fluttered shut.

"That's right, baby, sleep. I'll take care of you. I'll always take care of you."

I mumbled the only thing that came to mind before everything slipped away. "Austin."

Chapter 8

Darkness shattered, giving way to a cacophony of sights, sounds, and emotions. *Memories? These feel like memories. But whose? Mine? That can't be right.*

My thoughts were muddled, confusion the primary motivator to keep me focused on the scene unfolding before me, framed in the eyes of a body that seemed eerily like mine ... and yet not.

"Please, let me help. You can't expect me to just sit back here and wait, doing nothing while you guys go after him."

"You won't be 'doing nothing,'" Natalie stated patiently. *"You'll be training, getting better, so when the next person like Malcolm comes along, you'll be ready."*

"You're right. I won't be doing nothing ... I'll be worrying," I mumbled. *"I'm just not the stay-home-and-wait kind of girl. Even before I started training, I would have wanted to be*

involved." I turned my best puppy-dog eyes in Austin's direction. "Please. Let me go with you."

"No, Sam. I'm not putting you in that kind of danger."

I hit the desk with my fist and cringed at the stab of pain. "What about you? You're going to be in that kind of danger. I can't sit back here and worry."

Austin's fierce gaze softened. "We have more training and experience. Besides, Malcolm isn't targeting us."

"Yes, he is! It may be through me, but he's still targeting you. If he gets the chance to go directly to the source and just take you out, who's to say he won't jump at the opportunity?" I wouldn't be able to go on without him, no matter what I'd promised him.

Austin cupped my face in his large, callused hands, forcing me to look up at him. His eyes shone with a determination I'd never seen in them before. "He won't take me out. He doesn't want me dead. That would be too easy. He wants me to suffer the same way he did when he lost Maggie. That's why he's going after you. He knows the worst thing he can do to me is hurt you."

I pulled away from him, letting out a frustrated growl. "I can't just wait here for you!"

The scene changed, and I stood in a small room with a table and chairs … and Austin.

"But you still want me, don't you?" His gaze bore into mine with challenge.

Before I could respond, or even process his words, he was on me, and his tongue swept in to take control of my mouth. A shockwave of pleasure rocked my system, and I was carried *away, our connection electrifying.*

No! What are you doing? Stop!

Jerking away, I slapped him across the face with all the strength I could muster. "You asshole. You fucking asshole! You don't get to kiss me after you fucked her. Especially not when you're probably going to fuck her again."

I raised my hand to slap him, but he caught my arm that time, eyes brimming with fury. I withdrew my attack, spinning on my heel to leave. "Nixon's your friend. Your best friend. And I'm with him now. If you don't care about Jessica's feelings or mine, then maybe you'll care about his."

"You forget, I know the real reason why you're with him now. Why you accepted his advances so suddenly."

Trembling violently, I demanded, "Why do you even care? Why, Austin? Why do you care?"

His lips—the same lips that had just been pressed passionately against mine—pulled into a sneer. "I don't. Not really. I guess I had at least hoped I would get to have you first."

His words landed like a punch to my gut, and I fought not to double over as if they were an actual physical blow. I was sure—so sure, about our connection, and about the things I felt from him. How was I so wrong? How could I, as a friggin' empath, not get it right? Could he fake feelings? I had no idea about his abilities, or anything else apparently. Because I was a fool—a complete fool when it came to Austin.

And again, the scene morphed, taking me somewhere new.

"I need you, Chloe." Austin's heated breath skated over my flesh as he kissed his way down my neck.

"Yes," I moaned, throwing my head back to allow him better access. "I need you, too."

"We need to go somewhere." He'd somehow managed to get my shirt up, capturing my nipple between his teeth. "Can't do this here."

"Your room," I rasped.

"No ... Jessica," he said around my other nipple.

Irrational anger caused my gut to clench. Then I remembered Nixon. He was waiting for me in my room. Guilt replaced every other emotion.

I pushed at Austin's chest. "No, Austin—we can't. What about Nixon? He's your best friend."

Austin's voice was low and gruff with unspoken promises of pleasure. "I need you."

He offered me no other explanation, no argument, no rationalizations, just that he needed to be with me, plain and simple. And I wanted it—oh how I wanted it. I wanted him in any and every way he would let me have him.

What little will I had to resist melted away as he stumbled, with me wrapped around his waist, into a nearby room. He yanked my shirt off and deposited me on a desk. Leaning back, I clutched the edge of the scarred wood as Austin tugged my pants and underwear off. The cool air skated over my overheated flesh, causing goose bumps to erupt.

Austin paused, his gaze running over me from head to toe, as if he was planning what to do with me next. I swallowed, my throat suddenly as dry as the Sahara.

"You're so beautiful," he said, echoing Nixon's words the first time we'd been together.

I forced my mind away from the guilt that knowledge brought with it.

He shucked his clothes quickly, coming to stand between my quivering thighs. It was my turn to give his naked body the once over. He was exactly how I'd imagined him—perfect. I knew it was ridiculous to even think, but to me he was. Austin was absolutely perfect in that moment. His long, lean muscles gleamed with a fine sheen of sweat, his toned abs flexing under my scrutiny as I drew my gaze down the line of his body ... lower, lower, and lower until it snagged on his massive erection.

I gulped. I knew he was large, I'd felt him before, but seeing him standing there in front of me, completely naked and ready to go ... it was both intimidating and awe-inspiring.

I abruptly hooked my legs around his back, causing him to pitch forward. Grabbing his hair, I pulled him down until he was mere inches from my face, our breath intermingling. My lips curled up at the corners as I said, "Fuck me, Austin. Fuck me now."

His eyes flashed as a pained sound erupted from the back of his throat, his nostrils flaring. I threw my head back when he plunged into me. His fingers bit into my hips as he pulled out and slammed back in, falling into a brutal, demanding rhythm. The desk inched its way across the floor, the metal legs scraping loudly, blending with our moans and grunts. Oh, yes. Yes, this is what I want—need. *I'd never had rough sex before, but then again, I'd never been running on my own emotions during sex before either.*

Austin gripped the sides of my face, forcing my head down.

"Look at me, Chloe," he growled. "I want you to look at me when you come."

As if his words gave me the permission I needed, my body exploded in pleasure, and I screamed. Austin held me steady even as I tried to thrash my head, his gaze capturing mine for the entirety of my unraveling, followed shortly after by his. His eyes held a single-minded intensity that spoke of possession, passion, and in that moment, we completely belonged to each other—and each other alone.

A silence fell over us, even as our hearts thrummed in our chests like hummingbirds. I kept my breathing shallow, afraid if I moved, I'd break the trance, this one perfect moment when nothing else mattered but us.

Austin moved first, gliding his thumb over my bottom lip. I nipped at him playfully, which caused him to dip his head to deliver me a long, sensual kiss, much different from the ones he just gave me minutes earlier.

Threading my fingers into his hair, I pulled, eliciting a grunt of approval from him. As our kiss deepened, I felt him grow hard inside of me again. I rocked my hips in encouragement. The slow, steady rhythm he built was the opposite of what we'd just finished, but I realized they were both things I craved from Austin. I want him in any and every way he'll let me have him.

My heart thrashed against my ribcage as I gasped for air around Austin's mouth. A second and third orgasm shook through my system, both as mind-altering as the first, although they were more of a slow burn. One rolled into the next, and then a fourth overtook me as Austin pumped into me. I never *wanted it to stop. Me. Him. Us. I needed him to be with me forever.*

Memories ... They felt like memories. But it was as if I were watching a movie that had been recast and the script tweaked. I couldn't make heads or tails of it, even as I was swept away again.

Grinding my teeth, I swallowed convulsively. He was just so angry. I didn't expect that. "Yeah, um ..." I swallowed again. "With everything that's been going on, well ..." I stared into his deep brown eyes and knew I just had to tell him—I just had to get it all out.

Like verbal diarrhea, the words spilled from my mouth. "With everything that's been going on, I don't think it's a good idea if we see each other anymore. As boyfriend and girlfriend. I still want to see you as a friend. I mean, that is if you want to still see me as a friend. But I guess we're going to have to see each other anyways for work, but ..." I inhaled and exhaled. "But you know what I mean."

The muscles in Nixon's jaw ticked as he stared at me, not seeming surprised in the least. "I'm guessing it won't be a friends-with-benefits arrangement either."

I blinked. "What? No. Why would you say that?" I was not liking the emotional turmoil rolling off of Nixon at that moment. I'd expected hurt over anger. Unfortunately for me, he was definitely radiating massive levels of anger.

A bitter smile stretched his lips. "Yeah. I guess that was a stupid question because you're obviously interested in getting your needs fulfilled elsewhere." His eyes dared me to deny what he was saying.

Oh, fuck. He knows. *I wasn't sure how, but he knew about Austin and me.*

"It's not like that. I just—"

"Save it. I had my suspicions. Or rather, I thought I was being paranoid." He whirled around, his body rigid. *"I knew he wanted you. But I figured that part didn't matter. Of course he'd want you, he's Austin. I just figured as long as you weren't interested in him ... I thought after some time, he'd get over it, and you'd be more comfortable with us. That you'd come to care about me as much as I care about you."*

"I do care about you—"

He shot me a glare over his shoulder. "I said to save it. I saw you coming out of that room with him. I. Saw. You. But I was still willing to consider the possibility that nothing happened between the two of you, that at the worst, he put the moves on you and you turned him down. I was holding out hope that you wanting to talk to me was going to be about you admitting to me what he pulled. But the minute I saw you, I knew differently."

I froze. Why hadn't I even considered that possibility?

"What I want to know is, did you fuck him? Did you fuck him in that room? Did he make you promises that he'd be with you? That you're special to him?" He came at me lightning fast, grabbing my arms to shake me. *"Answer me."*

"I-I—No."

"No to which part? Spit it out, Sam!" Nixon shook me again, this time jarring me into a response.

"No! I didn't fuck him in that room!" Not a lie. I didn't fuck him in that room. I'd done other things. Definitely no need to

share that little detail, or the fact that I'd previously fucked Austin right down the hall from Nixon, for that matter.

His grip relaxed, barely. "Well, that's something. But he did talk you into breaking it off with me so you could, didn't he? He made you promises like I said?"

My gaze dropped, guilt tightening my chest. No, I hadn't fucked Austin in that room, but my mind flashed to other images of when we had been together. "It's not like that. He didn't tell me to break things off with you. He didn't promise to be with me. He offered me nothing. Absolutely nothing."

Hot tears slid down my face as I brought my gaze up to Nixon's again. "In fact, he won't be with me. He's afraid I'll die." My tears came faster with that admission, my breathing labored. "But I don't care. I want him. I'm so sorry, but I want him anyways."

Nixon let go of me, and I dropped to the floor in a heap. "I see." His voice was flat, cold. "So you were using me from the beginning. I never meant anything to you."

Standing quickly, I grabbed for him. I couldn't let him think that, I needed for him to know I did care about him, at least as a friend. "Nixon, please. You have that part wrong, too. I did care about you—do care about you. I was hoping that would be enough, and we could grow into more. I never meant to hurt you. I just can't pretend anymore. I don't want to hurt you more than I already have."

A harsh laugh escaped from his chest. "You're worse than he is. At least he told Jessica the score up front. It wasn't his fault she couldn't accept it. But you—you lied from the beginning." He turned, stalking towards the door.

I scrambled after him, not wanting to leave things like they were. "Nixon, wait! Please!"

He slammed the door in my face.

Why did Nixon have to see us together right before I broke things off with him? Why did fate have to kick me when I was down? I could only hope that after Nixon got over his initial hurt that we could maybe go back to being friends, but with the way things had just played out with him, I wasn't going to hold my breath.

The scene abruptly changed again.

I squeezed my eyes shut, not wanting to wake up, afraid that Austin's confession of feelings for me would be nothing more than wishful thinking or perhaps a dream.

An arm was draped over my middle, pulling me into a large, hard body, and I snuggled into its warmth. Please let me be in Austin's arms and not Nixon's. Please let me be in Austin's arms and not Nixon's …

"It's me," Austin's sleep-roughened voice answered my thoughts.

"Hey. Did I tell you that you could go creeping around in my mind?" I tried to sound chiding, but couldn't manage it with the smile curling my lips.

Austin rolled me onto my back, his eyes sparkling with mischief. "You were practically broadcasting what you were thinking. Besides, that's something you shouldn't mind sharing with me."

I nodded, pretending to consider. "Hmm … I don't know. If your head gets much bigger than it already is, you might not be able to fit through normal-sized doorways."

"And why would I need to get through any doorways at all? I could just lounge in bed all day while you cater to all my needs." He gave me a lopsided grin, causing my stomach to do a little flip-flop.

"Oh really? Is that what you think? That I'd be willing to do that." Snorting, I ran my fingers up the back of his neck and through his sexy, sleep-tousled hair, my eyes locking with his. A rush of heat bloomed in my middle, desire sizzling through my blood.

I cleared my throat, tension rising within me. I need to know. I need to ask. *"Why the change all of a sudden?"* I didn't have to explain further. He knew I was asking why he'd decided it was okay to be with me ... well, at least out in the open and for more than just sex.

His azure gaze darkened as he studied me. "I couldn't handle seeing you with him anymore, actually seeing you and him—" He shook his head as if trying to dislodge the image from his mind. *"And then, well, I love you, and you belong to me."*

Austin's explanation left a lot to be desired, but I understood what he was attempting to say. Plus, all need for talk flew out the window when his feverish lips met mine in a kiss that threatened to steal my breath away. Yes, this is right. Him in my bed, us together in the open, all of it ... so right.

I moaned, his hands seemingly everywhere at once, his need for me all-encompassing. And I reveled in my response, and the fact that it was mine, every single emotion I felt while with him belonged to me and me alone.

He pushed my arms above my head, restraining me with one hand as he pressed into me, sliding home. "You're all mine now." Austin's heated thought swam through my mind, branding me. And I couldn't disagree. I'd belonged to him since that first night at the after-hours club when we'd accidentally formed a link to each other. The connection was forged, forever changing our lives. But he was forgetting one thing—he was mine, too.

Taking him off guard, I wrapped my legs around his back, rolling us over to reverse our position so he was underneath me. I undulated my hips slowly, forcing my slower rhythm on him. "And you're all mine now," I thought, peeking at him through my hair.

A sudden orgasm crashed into me, sucking all coherent thought from my brain, and causing my pace to falter along with my grip on Austin's arms. Taking advantage, he quickly flipped me onto my knees, his fingertips biting into my hips as he held me in place so he could plunge back into me. I screamed in pleasure, his new pace blistering. One orgasm ran into another, all of them blending together.

Austin grunted a string of incoherent words, his release pulsing into me, hot and fast. While still inside me, he rolled us onto our sides with him curled around my back. I was happy and satisfied within his strong arms, content to languish there.

Austin smoothed my damp hair from my face, his raspy, post-coital voice breaking the silence. "What are you thinking?" His low laugh rumbled against me.

"What's so funny?"

"I never thought I'd ask a girl what she was thinking after sex, let alone care." He chuckled again.

"You could have just peeked." Why didn't he? Except for a

time here and there, he'd been so careful lately to not go into my mind uninvited, unlike when we first met.

"I know how much you hate it when I slip into your mind without permission." I felt his smile on the back of my neck. "I'm just trying to respect your boundaries."

I guffawed. "Respect my boundaries? Seriously? Is that what you called it when you kept trying to seduce me even after I said no? You ignored my boundaries completely and any façade that you gave a damn about my consent."

"That was different."

"How?"

"Your boundaries were fake, your consent given even if you wouldn't admit it out loud. I mean seriously ...You might as well have been begging me for it. These things play out differently with people like us." His lips stretched wider against my skin.

I snorted. "You shouldn't have been poking around in my brain to begin with." Although he wasn't completely wrong. There was a definite grey area when you could pick up on someone's feelings straight from their mind.

"It's true though. No point in denying it. You told me to leave you alone, but you never meant it. Not even once." His hand slid down my stomach, finding my clit and circling it slowly.

Heat flooded my middle.

"I also wasn't lying when I told you I'd be the best sex you'd ever have."

No ... no, he hadn't been lying.

Panic, anger, and confusion all raced through me in quick succession as my eyes fluttered open.

Chapter 9

An arm was draped over my middle, pulling me into a large, hard body, and I snuggled into its warmth. *Please let me be in Austin's arms and not Nixon's. Please let me be in Austin's arms and not Nixon's ...*

With familiar dread, I realized my thoughts mirrored the ones from my last memory ... or whatever it was. Confusion nettled, and yet I was drowning in a soul-deep yearning to be in Austin's embrace. Real or imaginary, sane or insane, I wanted Austin more than anything in that moment.

"Sam," Nixon rumbled, his voice drowsy. "You're awake." As his arm tightened around me, panic surged.

Wrong ... wrong ... wrong. This is all wrong.

Or is it?

Maybe I'd simply snapped, and the things I'd seen while in a drug-induced sleep were all part of a psychotic break. Quite possibly I couldn't tell reality from fiction anymore. Hell, I was beginning to question if I was actually awake.

But wait. The specialist that altered my ex-friends' memories of me from Club Elite, the same person could have tinkered with my mind as well. *But why?* For such an elaborate endeavor to be carried out it would require multiple people and for what? What would be the end game for hiding the details of my own life from me? None of it made sense. But ... but something inside of me was screaming for me to pay attention, to acknowledge the truth despite how crazy it might sound even in my own head.

Adrenaline spiked through my veins. "Oh God," I sputtered, flinging Nixon's arm from me, and scurrying from our bed. *I'm not supposed to be here.*

"Sam, what's wrong?"

"I don't ... I don't know." I backed up a few steps, wrapping my arms around my middle. I had no idea how to proceed. I just knew I couldn't trust Nixon or myself. *So who's left?*

"Tell me what's wrong so I can help you. Please, Sam, you're scaring me," Nixon pleaded.

Hysterical laughter exploded from my chest. "I'm scaring me the most. I don't know what's wrong. I just know nothing's right."

I dropped to my knees, cradling my head in my hands. "Help me, please," I whispered. "I just—please, I need help." But who was I asking? I didn't even have an answer to that simple question.

Nixon swooped me up in his arms, and I let him hold me, even though I received no comfort from it. "I've got you, baby. We'll fix all of this, I swear it."

The sharp sting of a needle bit into my arm, causing my eyes to flutter shut almost instantly. "It'll all be fine," Nixon said, his lips brushing my forehead.

Everything washed away into nothing.

"TELL *me where I can find Malcolm and the rest of your associates," I spat.*

"I can't," Renee gasped out as I tightened my grip on her throat. "What they'll do to me if I tell you is far worse than anything you could ever do."

I narrowed my eyes at her as she continued to struggle. Renee was a good couple of inches shorter than me, and a lot smaller, but she was stronger than she looked. "Are you sure about that?"

Wedging my arm under her throat to pin her against the wall, I stretched my fingers to grab the concealed knife from the sheath at my back. Her gaze flared with an edge of panic, and she twisted and kicked, redoubling her efforts to escape.

"I have no problem killing you, and no qualms about making it hurt in the process."

My vision blurred for a moment, and suddenly Renee was out of my grasp and running down the alleyway. She must have some kind of ability I don't know about. But it's not going to do her any good in the end.

Sprinting after her, I managed to catch her with ease with my longer strides, and I tackled her to the ground, her breath leaving her in a whoosh of air. We grappled a few minutes on the ground, before I rolled her onto her back, her strength leaching from her abruptly. Spotting blood on her forehead, I hoped she wasn't about to pass out because I needed her conscious for the time being.

"There's no point in fighting. I'm going to get the information I need one way or another."

A scream tore from my throat as a sharp pain registered in my right thigh. Glancing down, I spotted a knife embedded deep in my leg. I grimaced. No matter, I'll deal with it later. *Raising my mental shields, I dropped a wall down between me and the pain, allowing me to pull the knife from my thigh.*

Shit. Probably not the best idea. You're supposed to leave the weapon in the wound, dumbass. *And I knew that, had trained to react that way, but as it turned out, in the heat of the moment when a knife was protruding from your leg, it was extremely difficult not to just yank it out.* Who would have thought?

I watched in sick fascination as blood flowed freely from the wound, until dizziness caused my world to tilt. Collapsing onto my side, I turned my attention to Renee who was attempting to make her way down the alley again.

Nope. You're not getting away that easily. *Under the circumstances, it took me a few seconds longer than it normally would, but I slid into her mind easily enough, stopping her short. Whatever abilities Renee did have, her mind was a weak point. I smiled to myself.* "Show me," *I grated.*

"No," she hissed. *Fire lanced my abdomen, trailing upward towards my chest. Shock ricocheted through me as I realized that she'd cut herself open.* Shit. Shit. Shit. I'm not going to have a lot of time. *I scrambled to search her mind, even as she dropped to the ground.*

Her last thoughts were scattered and unfocused, littered with sadness and regret, and as she—we—drew her last breath, euphoria settled over me. For even though I was sitting shotgun on her ride to death's door, I would walk away more alive than ever.

It wasn't right. I knew it wasn't right, and I also knew if the wrong people found out about my activities, then my notice of termination would be signed.

But I couldn't bring myself to care. Because nothing made me feel more alive than experiencing someone else's death.

"Sam!" *Nixon yelled, his footsteps pounding towards me.* "Shit. I told you to wait for me. What the hell were you thinking?"

I met his angry gaze just as Renee took her last breath. Gasping, I arched up, letting the bliss burn through my veins. Nixon frowned, but I ignored his reaction and reached for him, wiggling my fingers. "Kiss me, Nixon."

Anger was replaced with worry in the deep lines of his face. "Sam, no. We need to get that leg taken care of before you bleed out."

"It can wait. Just kiss me, now." *I knew Austin would be pissed, but in that moment, I couldn't bring myself to care about him either. I needed this—needed to feel the passion of life after living through Renee's death.*

"Sam, no. Even if you weren't about to bleed out, the answer would still be no, because you're not fooling me. I know what you just did. It's the way Malcolm started."

"Don't you dare even think about drawing parallels between me and Malcolm. We could never be the same." I winced as he bent down and scooped me up in his arms. "Ever."

"I call 'em like I see 'em," he mumbled.

A delighted laugh ricocheted around in my head. "So you are starting to remember—just a little. It'll make our little game easier, and a lot more fun, if you truly remember who you are, and the darkness I helped to open inside of you."

"Who are you?" I mentally shouted.

"I'm Malcolm, of course. You might not remember me, but I know you recognize the name. And tell my boy Nixon that the prophecy of your death is not what it seemed. Its reality will be much, much better. For me at least."

MY EYES FLEW OPEN, and I fought back panic as I struggled to move.

But wait. I was drugged. I'll be fine. There's nothing wrong with me. At least physically.

"I can't let this go on anymore. All of what I did can't be for nothing," Nixon said.

Letting my eyes slide back shut, I pretended to still be unconscious so I could listen.

David replied, "We need her to catch Malcolm. We—"

"It could break her. Permanently," Nixon interrupted. "I won't let that happen. You know I love her, you know—"

"But will she love you when all is said and done? If she finds out what you did, she won't understand, no matter what you've convinced yourself of."

"No. She loves me. She'll understand. We've been together for two years now. What we have—"

"Is based on lies," David finished for him. "If we don't catch Malcolm, then you run the risk of him making her what she was on the path to becoming before, and you know who will eventually come for her."

"No. He would never take her life no matter what she might become."

"If not him, then someone else will, just like Maggie." Heavy silence hung in the room before David spoke again. "But if we use her to catch Malcolm, and soon, then there's hope to fix her, even if she breaks just a little."

A loud crash startled me as I struggled to keep up the illusion of unconsciousness. "Yeah. Fine. Okay. Just—" Another loud crash. "Fuck. I don't know if I'll be able to pick up the pieces this time. And I can't lose her, I can't—I won't."

I made a crucial decision in that moment. I wouldn't tell Nixon about my dreams, or memories, or whatever they were. I would play along as if I was feeling better to hopefully get the answers to my questions in the meantime. Nixon was lying to me, and I needed to find out about what. It didn't matter if he loved me, and was trying to protect me ... I still needed the truth.

"Nixon?" I murmured, pretending to just be waking up.

"Yeah, I'm right here, baby." His hand wrapped around mine as the bed dipped down with his weight.

I lifted my gaze to his.

He gave me a tentative smile, his eyes drenched in worry. "How are you feeling?"

"Better. I think. What happened?"

"You don't remember?" Nixon studied my face intently.

"No." I bit my lower lip as I stared back at him in my feigned ignorance. "Well, I mean I remember the murder scene ..." I shuddered at the memory.

He ran the back of his knuckles across my cheek tenderly. "Don't worry, baby, I'm going to take care of you."

My eyes slid shut under his caress. It was the same touch that had comforted me for years, and it still seemed to hold that power despite everything else.

What if I simply let go of whatever my mind wants me to remember? What if I just let it all go? I'd been happy with Nixon before. Why not again? Whatever was inside of me, whatever kind of darkness Malcolm claimed to have opened within me, Nixon knew about it, and he loved me anyways.

Maybe I needed protection from myself, and I just didn't know it. Perhaps Austin, if he really existed, was a bad guy. After all, I'd seen some pretty twisted interactions between the two of us in my mind. Nixon was my savior. It didn't matter that my heart seemed to beat for Austin alone. I would force him from my heart and mind to resume my relationship with Nixon. *I can do it. I have to.*

"Nixon," I murmured. "I love you."

Taking me in his arms, he whispered, "I love you, too, baby. Everything's going to be okay, I promise."

"Okay," I said.

Too bad I couldn't force myself to believe the lie even if I wanted to.

Chapter 10

"So, Samantha, let's talk about your feelings of inadequacy regarding your relationship with Nixon."

I pinched the bridge of my nose before letting my gaze fall to trace the intricate pattern of the carpet. "I feel that way because it's true."

How am I back here again? Sure, Dr. Gray helped me a lot over the years, but lately our sessions didn't seem to be doing any good at all.

"Okay. Let's try going at this from a different angle then. What triggered these feelings? Something set them off, and if you can figure—"

"Yes, I told you about my imagined affair, remember? That's an example of why I'm not good enough for Nixon. I'm sure he doesn't go around imagining I'm someone else when we're … being intimate."

"Everyone has fantasies, Samantha. You don't know what's in your husband's mind. It's not fair for you to ..."

Did Nixon have fantasies about other women when we were together? Conjuring an image of his face when he looked at me, I could picture with perfect clarity the love and devotion reflected at me from his eyes. I was positive he was never rewarded with the same response from me. And he deserved that, to have someone love him as much as he loved me.

"There's just something wrong with me," I blurted out.

"Why do you think there's something wrong with you, Samantha?" Dr. Gray tapped her pen on her notepad, waiting.

Because I can't stop thinking about Austin. And because I also can't stop thinking about being in that girl Renee's head when she died, if it even really happened. Regardless, real or imaginary, I wanted to do it again—feel death and walk away more alive than ever. Or maybe the biggest problem was that I couldn't tell the difference between real and imagined memories anymore.

But I couldn't say any of that, not unless I thought I could outrun the guys with the straightjackets. So I settled on something generic and vague instead. "There's something dark inside of me."

And if I was honest with myself, it began growing and spreading the second I felt Renee's dying emotions. Again ... Real or imagined, it didn't matter. Or maybe it began before that, the first time I'd gotten myself off while thinking about Austin. That's when my slow decline had truly begun.

"Samantha, I thought we talked about not using words such as dark or evil to describe how you're feeling. I know it's something that someone with your abilities associates with things, but as someone with no empathic abilities, the term dark is rather vague. I need to be able to understand you before I can help you."

"Well, I don't know what to tell you!" I snapped. "Because dark is how it feels. Like a seed of something foreign has taken root inside of me and is spreading its poison throughout me as it grows. Like if I don't stop it, I won't recognize who I am anymore." *Or maybe it's too late? What if the person that enjoyed being in Renee's head when she died is the real me, and this me is just a lie?*

"Okay, calm down, Samantha. I'm just—"

"Stop saying my name in that goddamn patronizing tone over and over again! I'm going to scream if you do it one more time!"

"All right, Sa— all right. I can see that you are not coping well with … everything. Maybe it's work or your relationship, but whatever it is, I'm recommending you get pulled from your current cases until we work through these emotions. I don't want to run the risk of you backsliding any more than you already have."

A loud buzzing sound took up residence in my ears, turning slowly to white noise. A moment later, a familiar voice wafted through my head. "I think this is a perfect time for my little gift. Enjoy."

My stomach flipped with the sensation of falling, and I blinked new surroundings into focus. I stood in a vaguely familiar apartment, the sounds of a woman's moans echoing through the small space. But it was the name she screamed that caught my attention.

"Oh, Austin! Yes, Austin!"

My heart seized, and I struggled to breathe. "I don't want to see this," I hissed into thin air.

"Too bad. I had to," Malcolm's bitter-sounding voice responded in my head.

That's when a young man, probably in his early twenties, tall, thin, dark hair—rather good-looking—came through the front door of the apartment, dropping the key from his hand when the same noises that were accosting my ears registered. Somehow I knew I was seeing a younger version of Malcolm. The disbelief and anguish on his face was plain, and I found myself trailing along after him as he slowly moved towards what I assumed was the bedroom. He stopped just outside the door frame, clutching at the wall, expression frozen in horror. Both of us stared into that room, unable to turn away from the small brunette ... and Austin.

"Maggie," Malcolm breathed in my mind.

That's right. Maggie, the girl who was somehow connected to Malcolm, and the reason why he was targeting me. My fists balled up with anger I tried to squash. "This isn't real, or it's just a memory, and it happened a long time ago. None of this matters. None of it fucking matters ..."

I repeated those words to myself over and over, that none of it mattered, and yet ... yet seeing him—seeing Austin's perfectly round, muscular ass, the one that filled all of my fantasies lately —seeing it move and bunch with effort as he fucked someone else ... My heart burned in agony.

"Why the hell are you showing me this?" I called out. So this was Malcolm's memory? "I just assumed you loved this Maggie, or you two were in love. I don't understand."

"Exactly," was the only response I got.

The young version of Malcolm, the one that was only a memory, seemed to be on the same page as me and turned to flee the scene.

Things wavered, and I was suddenly viewing a different memory: Malcolm cradling a petite brunette in his arms, tears streaking down his cheeks. Austin stood a few feet away, hunched over. Tension, guilt, and sadness twisted his face into one I almost didn't recognize.

"I'm sorry, Malcolm. So sorry. More than you'll ever know. But it had to be done. You have to know it had to be done."

A broken sob escaped Malcolm. "Why? Why would you do this to me?"

Austin flicked his gaze away as his shoulders sagged. "You know why."

"I love her! You know I love her! How could you do this to me?" Malcolm screamed, spittle flying from his mouth.

"You screwed up. You fell in too deep. You'll get over it and realize what you felt wasn't really love. She had to die. You know she had to die."

"No! I love her!" Malcolm couldn't tear his eyes from the small woman in his arms. "Maggie. Please. I love you. Maggie ..." Her name rolled off his tongue with reverence, devotion,

and clear and unconditional love. "I need her. Please, I need her."

My gut clenched, and I squeezed my eyes shut, not wanting to witness anymore. "I don't understand. Why are you showing me these things?"

"Because you need to know what he's really like. You need to know that everything I do to you is his fault. He took my Maggie from me, and I'm going to take you from him."

"I don't even know if he's real—if you're real! Just leave me alone!"

Maybe I was schizophrenic, and Malcolm was just one of my voices and Austin another. Of course, a little bit more than just Austin's voice was in my mind most of the time.

A bemused laugh filled my head. "Oh, I can assure you, every sick and twisted part of him is real. I'm going to make sure he gets you back before I rip you away from him again. And the best part will be when he realizes I've made you just like her. Just like my Maggie."

I needed more information. I needed to know more about Malcolm. If he was real, if he was actually speaking to me in my mind, then perhaps I could trace the origins and slip into his mind. It was worth a shot, anyways.

I pictured myself trailing an imaginary link, as if it was something tangible enough that I could physically touch it. There was a sensation of slipping and falling, as if I was on a slick patch of ice, and then I was blinking up at unexpected, and unwanted scenery.

His mind was hostile—angry and dark, the turmoil of emotions far exceeding anything that could be considered *normal. And even though I was cognitive that I wasn't physically there, the negativity of it threatened to suffocate me, my breathing shallow and raspy. But I persisted, the need to know who this person was, who the man who identified himself as Malcolm really was. So instead of giving in to my instincts to flee to the safety of my own mind, I began to push and explore, searching for the answers I craved.*

Malcolm. His name was Malcolm, but not really. I wasn't sure quite what that meant, and it wasn't necessarily important, so I moved on. Pushing deeper into the murkiness of the man's mind, it was clear that something was very wrong with him, and it was more difficult to sift through his thoughts than I'd anticipated. Everywhere I went, things were thick, sticky, bogged down by a simmering rage.

"You think I don't know you're here?" I heard a malicious— and quickly becoming too familiar—laugh.

"Who are you? I mean really?" I demanded.

"You're so gifted and yet so utterly clueless. It's a shame, really."

I ignored him, his opinion nothing to me. "Who are you?"

"How about I just show you?"

Ripped from his mind, I was thrown into a completely different scene. Blinking dazedly, I realized I was standing in one of the rooms I'd been in with Austin in one of my dreams. An unknown boy and a younger version of Austin were deep in conversation and didn't notice me at all.

"Of course they don't notice you. This is a memory. My memory."

"It just feels so real. I forgot for a moment." So the other boy

was Malcolm. When I looked closer, I did indeed see similar features between the boy and the man I'd observed before in the apartment with Austin, yet he seemed so normal in this memory. Nothing about him seemed to match the man's mind I'd just been in.

"Pay attention," Malcolm commanded tersely.

I turned my attention back to the memory in front of me and focused on the conversation.

"Malcolm," Austin said. "You'll do fine on this assignment without me. You're the only person here that could one day be as good as me."

"I don't know. We're almost the same age, but you've been training a lot longer than I have. I don't know if I can do it without you to guide me."

Austin smiled reassuringly. "You'll do fine. I have faith in you."

Malcolm smiled back, the admiration for Austin clear in his eyes. "If you think I can do it, then I guess I'm ready."

"He was like an older brother to me. He trained me. I trusted him." There was a tenor of sadness within Malcolm's voice that quickly morphed into fury. "And then he fucked me over."

The scenery quickly changed to a dim apartment. Malcolm cradled a petite brunette in his arms, tears streaking down his cheeks. Austin stood a few feet away, hunched over. Tension, guilt, and sadness twisted his face into one I almost didn't recognize.

It was the end part of a scene he'd already shown me. But now I was certain it was a memory—his memory. I tried to *study it with a new perspective now that I knew exactly what I was seeing.*

"I'm sorry, Malcolm. So sorry. More than you'll ever know. But it had to be done. You have to know it had to be done."

A broken sob escaped Malcolm. "Why? Why would you do this to me?"

Austin flicked his gaze away as his shoulders sagged. "You know why."

"I love her! You know I love her! How could you do this to me?" Malcolm screamed, spittle flying from his mouth.

"You screwed up. You fell in too deep. You'll get over it and realize what you felt wasn't really love. She had to die. You know she had to die."

"No! I love her!" Malcolm couldn't tear his eyes from the small woman in his arms. "Maggie. Please. I love you. Maggie ..." Her name rolled off his tongue with reverence, devotion, and clear and unconditional love. "I need her. Please, I need her."

"What happened? There had to be a good reason why he killed her. He didn't do it just to hurt you. Please, you guys were like brothers once, you said so yourself. I'm not even a part of this! Why are you pulling me into any of this?"

"You're more a part of this than you realize," he hissed. "I'm done. I don't know why I bothered to show you. Maybe I wanted you to see the type of person Austin really is, to see the type of person you'll be suffering for."

And just like that, he shoved me from his mind, and I landed with such force in mine, I jolted straight up, my body a livewire of tension.

"Oh my God," I gasped.

"What's wrong?" Dr. Gray sat on the edge of her chair, her notebook clutched tightly in her hands. "What happened just now?"

"I need to talk to Austin. I need to find out why it happened. Why? I just need to know why."

I shuddered with revulsion as I mulled over what I'd felt in Malcolm's mind. The endless depths of rage, the turmoil ... and yet he'd been different once. Maybe there was still good in him. Maybe—

No. I watched *Star Wars* one too many times as a kid because real life rarely ended the way movies did. Malcolm wouldn't be redeemed in the end the way Darth Vader had been, and if I thought that was the way it would go down, then I really and truly was insane.

"Austin? Is that the name of your fantasy lover? Why do you think you need to talk to him, Samantha?"

Jumping to my feet, I began pacing the room, nervous energy zinging through my system. "Malcolm. I was just in Malcolm's mind." I shuddered again. "It was ... it was horrible. I feel so ... so dirty."

Even though I hadn't physically left the comfort of Dr. Gray's office, it was as if I'd brought back some kind of contaminant from Malcolm's mind. It clung to me, seeping into my pores, dark and sticky, like tar.

"I need to shower." I stumbled towards the office door with bleary eyes. I needed to feel clean again, and showering was the only thing I could think of that might work.

Dr. Gray grabbed my forearm, and I shrugged her off. "No, I can't be here anymore. Please. I feel dirty—so fucking dirty." Every moment I wasted not getting to the shower made it worse. I glanced down at my exposed skin, surprised to not see physical evidence of what I was feeling.

"Let me help you," Dr. Gray insisted, grabbing for me again.

I shook my head, my gaze still locked on my skin, watching—waiting for the tar to ooze from my pores. "I can't. I can't be here anymore."

"I can't let you walk out of my office like this. I-I can call your husband."

With a sob, I dropped into a chair closer to the door. "Hurry," I pleaded. *It's coming. The tar. Soon I'll be covered in it.* I struggled to breathe. *I can feel it coming.*

"Okay. Okay," Dr. Gray said, fumbling around on her desk.

I dragged my nails down my skin. "Please. Please help me." *I'm contaminated. I need to get it off before it's too late. Before it kills me.*

"He's on his way, Samantha. Hang on."

"Make it stop!" I screamed, tearing at my skin. "Please make it stop!" The dark poison seeped from every pore, every organ, slowly killing me. *It's already too late.* "Make it stop!"

Dr. Gray murmured soothing words to me, but it was too late, I was beyond her help. *Austin.*

"Please!" I shrieked. "Make it stop!" *Please, Austin,*

please, I need you to make it stop. You're the only one who can make it stop. Please, help me!

I registered a loud bang in the distance, and then a commotion. "You can't be in here!" Dr. Gray exclaimed.

"No. Please. I'll fix her. Let me fix her." His voice was rough and thick with anguish, but there was no mistaking who it was. I'd know him anywhere.

Austin. He's come for me.

"Who the hell are you?" Dr. Gray demanded.

"It doesn't matter," he rasped. "I'm here to help her."

I felt myself being moved, and I whimpered, wanting to reach out to Austin, to touch him, to confirm the reality of him. It was impossible though, because I couldn't see anything but blackness swimming in front of my eyes—the disgusting black contamination that was killing me. The tar from Malcolm's mind.

"I'll make it okay. Do you hear me? I'll make it okay for you, Sammy. Just stay with me. Okay? Stay with me."

I was swallowed whole, my consciousness pulled into a fathomless pit of oblivion.

Chapter 11

"**B**aby? Can you hear me?"

Peeling my eyes open, I locked gazes with Nixon. Confusion ripped through me. *Am I still in that alley? No, that isn't right. Austin. Where is Austin?* But as I sucked in a breath of clean, untainted air, relief washed away all of my questions for the time being, because I was alive and ... normal. *Yes, that's right. I feel completely normal again.*

"What happened?" Pulling myself into a sitting position, I swung my gaze around Dr. Gray's office. *What am I still doing here?*

Nixon's forehead furrowed with uncertainty. "I was kind of hoping you could tell me."

"What ..." I followed Nixon's gaze to a sleeping Dr. Gray. She was curled up on the couch, her expression peaceful.

My heart took off at a gallop as I rifled through possible explanations for what occurred, but nothing I could come up with made sense. "I don't understand. I remember Malcolm, and then—" I clamped my mouth shut before I said Austin's name.

Nixon's eyes sparked with panic. "What does Malcolm have to do with this?"

I shuddered as revulsion swept through me. I didn't want to think about what I'd found in his mind. "He came to me, mentally, and then I slipped into his mind, to find out more information, but—" I swallowed the burn of bile as it crept up my throat. "It was ... it was like nothing I've ever— I don't know how to describe it beyond horrifying."

I tugged at my hair. "And I don't exactly know what happened after that. There was something—something followed me back. It was clinging to me." Rubbing my arms, I pushed away the memory of being contaminated. Real or not, I'd been convinced at the time that it was. "Or maybe I imagined it all."

"Clearly something happened," Nixon grated. "Dr. Gray called me to come get you. She was panicked." His fingers trailed along my forehead as he pushed some stray hairs aside. "I could hear you screaming in the background. And when I got here—" A muscle in his jaw twitched. "I found everyone sleeping."

"I-I don't know what to tell you." Again, I was playing the partial truth game with Nixon. Even though I wasn't convinced of Austin coming to my rescue—that it was reality—I couldn't fight the urge to keep his suspected presence to myself.

Nixon narrowed his eyes, suspicion playing across his visage. He knew I wasn't telling him something, but he also wasn't sure if it was worth the argument to push for whatever it was.

He stood abruptly, making his way to Dr. Gray with jerky movements. Leaning over her, he pressed his fingers into her neck, pausing to check the state of her heart rate. "She seems fine. She actually is just sleeping."

Good news. And yet from the tone of Nixon's voice, and the tension riding his shoulders, the entire situation left him anxious. "Come on. I'm getting you out of here." He stalked back over to me and scooped me up in his arms without any other preamble.

I glanced over his shoulder at Dr. Gray. "Aren't you going to call someone about her? Like David or something?"

"No. I'm not calling anyone about anything. I'm taking you, and we're running."

I whipped my gaze to his. "What? What do you mean by running?"

"I promise I'll explain everything, but not right now. There isn't time." Nixon made his way across the lobby of Dr. Gray's office building with me in his arms. But it was empty, no signs of even the security guards who normally sat at the front desk. *Something's not right.*

"Going somewhere?" David's voice boomed across the lobby, stopping Nixon mid-step.

Every muscle in Nixon's body tensed as he slowly turned. "You know I was."

"I thought we discussed this. It's not a good idea," David said, over-enunciating each word as if he were trying to explain a complex math problem to a first grader.

"Things have changed," Nixon's rumbled.

David shook his head. "Nothing important has changed, not really."

"Oh yeah? Who's going to stop me from taking her and leaving? You?" Nixon chuckled, the sound lacking any real humor.

"No. Not just me."

Dozens of men, all dressed in black ops tactical gear, rippled into view around us. I wasn't fool enough to not know that they'd been there the entire time. Someone was obviously keeping more than one mentally gifted person and said gifts, a secret from us. Although, I had to wonder how they could use their ability with Nixon being so close. Perhaps it wasn't a person after all, and instead was some new techy toy, which would ultimately make Nixon's void power useless.

"Neat trick," Nixon said, his eyes flaring with anger.

"Don't make this difficult, Nixon. And don't take this personally, Sam. We need you to catch Malcolm."

On the surface, David was the same, but the cracks in his public persona were showing. Fear shot up my spine, twisting my gut. "I don't want anything to do with Malcolm. Please, David, just let us go."

"I'm sorry, Sam. I can't let that happen. We need you."

"You're not who you say you are at all, are you, David?" I glanced up at Nixon, his impassive expression telling me that we'd both come to the same conclusion about him.

"It doesn't matter," David said, waving his hand in the air. "Take them."

Nixon dropped me to my feet and shoved me behind him. But what was he going to do? Take on all of these men by himself? *No. I can't let him get hurt trying to protect me.*

"Nixon." I placed my hand on his arm and stepped forward to stand beside him. "It's okay."

"No, Sam, it isn't—"

"Yes, it is." I took another few steps in front of Nixon before he could grab me. A handful of men swarmed me, roughly cuffing my wrists as they pushed me towards the door of the lobby.

"You can't do this," Nixon growled.

The sounds of a scuffle met my ears as Nixon shouted unintelligible words in a thunderous roar.

But I was done. I couldn't do it anymore. How could I fight when I didn't know what I was fighting for? I had so many unanswered questions. My life, my memories were all unclear to me. Before I could fight for myself, or anyone else for that matter, I needed to know who I really was. And I didn't care anymore where the information came from, just as long as I got it.

I'D BEEN in interrogation rooms plenty of times in my life, but my current issue was that Nixon and I were on the wrong side of the table with David in the power position. Plus, with Nixon being so close to me I couldn't use my ability to get a read on David, which I was guessing was kind of the point.

"Are you planning on telling us what's going on anytime soon?" Nixon growled, rocking forward in his chair.

David steepled his hands in front of him, smiling smugly. "Of course. Most of it you already know. We need Sam to catch Malcolm. I've informed you—"

Glass exploded inward, warm goo splattering across my face. I swiped at my eyes reflexively, my mind slow to process what was before me. David's head hit the table with a dull thud, pieces of his brain and skull scattered across the top. Bile shot up my esophagus as I stared at the gore dripping from my hands. When I finally managed to lift my gaze I—

Austin.

Dressed all in black, he stood in the doorway, his piercing azure gaze sweeping over me briefly before settling on Nixon. His lips pulled back into a feral grin. "I've wanted to do that for a very long time."

My heart stuttered in my chest before taking off at a gallop. "Austin." His name tumbled from my mouth like a prayer to a dark avenging god.

His gaze met mine, and I fell into the fathomless pools, drowning there. *He's real. He's real and he's here.*

"Let's get this show on the road." The guy I'd seen outside the murder scene and at Club Elite pushed in behind Austin, his amber gaze falling on me as well.

Austin nodded once sharply. "Right. Let's go." He reached out his hand towards me in an offering for me to take it.

My arm lifted on its own volition, straining towards him. Nixon grabbed my hand, holding it tightly. "What the fuck do you think you're doing, Austin?" Nixon ground out.

Austin quirked one dark eyebrow, flashing his teeth menacingly. "I've come for *my* wife."

"This is not the time for a pissing contest over Sam," Austin's companion said. "Bring Nixon with us and we can deal with him later."

"Fine," Austin growled. "Let's go."

Nixon paused for only a moment before he was on his feet and pulling me to mine.

"Wait. What's going on?" Still in shock, my brain simply wasn't processing things as quickly as it needed to.

Austin strode forward and tugged me from Nixon's grasp. Surprisingly, Nixon didn't resist. Austin leaned into me, touching his forehead to mine. His baby blues darted between my eyes, our breath intermingling. "You need to trust me, okay?"

I nodded numbly.

"I'm giving you back what was stolen." He grimaced.

"And I'm sorry because it's going to hurt." He touched my temple, pressing his fingers firmly into my flesh.

"No! You can't!" Nixon bellowed.

A white-hot light accompanied by searing pain ripped through my skull, stealing my attention away from everything else.

Chapter 12
PART 2

"I'm giving it all back to you, Chloe—my Sammy girl. I'm done waiting for you to be mine again." Austin's voice swam through my head just before an explosion of memories detonated in my mind. They filled in the cracks in my soul, piecing me back together, and answering the questions even I didn't dare ask. Jumbled and disconcerting as they were, when they settled, I knew I would finally meet the real me.

MARCH, *six years earlier ...*

BLINKING BALEFULLY from behind my dark sunglasses, I wistfully thought of my warm, comfortable bed. I'd fallen asleep about an hour before my alarm went off, and my entire body was protesting the prospect of heading back to work. *A girl has to pay her bills somehow, though.*

I sighed as I trudged into Club Elite, spotting our maintenance guy. "Hey, Mac. How you doing today?"

He looked up from mopping the floor by the VIP bar and eyed me from underneath his white bushy eyebrows. "Eh. Better than you it would seem."

"What happened back there?"

"Burst pipe. Nothing to worry about, already taken care of it, just cleaning up the aftermath."

"Okay, good. For a minute I thought something might be wrong, and the club might not be able to open on time, and as much as it would pain me, I would get to go home and go back to sleep for a while."

"No such luck today." Mac smiled before turning his focus back to mopping.

I busied myself getting the bar ready for opening, hoping I wasn't forgetting anything in my haze of no sleep. *Liquor? Check. Garnishes? Check. Bar mats? Check. Ice? Check. Bank? Check.* I was good to go, and not a moment too soon. I could hear Lucky clattering around in the DJ booth, letting me know it was almost noon. The club didn't open until then, but I had to be completely ready, as opposed to Lucky and the dancers who generally arrived at about five 'til twelve.

"Hey, Chloe," Lucky called from his perch in the DJ booth. "Ready to get this party started?"

"Yeah, not really." He looked about as bad as I felt. Apparently, I wasn't the only one who had a rough night.

And you know what they say about misery loving company—totally true in this case.

I adjusted the lights down to the appropriate level, which was what I liked to call 'stripper lighting'. It let you see just enough, keeping the flaws of the dancers hidden from even the most discerning eye. Good lighting was the key to any dancer's success. I don't care how hot you think a girl is, she has flaws of some sort—a scar, freckles, a touch of cellulite—and coming to a strip club was all about fantasy. No room for reality in a place like Club Elite.

"First up on stage today is the lovely Destiny," Lucky announced over our PA system. Why we bothered was beyond me. No one was even here yet. But then again, it was always better to be going than sitting around with our thumbs up our asses when customers finally did start showing up.

Weekdays in the afternoons were pretty steady with business, but on the weekend, it was like a ghost town until usually at least two. I'd tried countless times to talk to the owner about not opening until then, but he was stubborn. Way too old-fashioned and stuck in his ways. A pain in the ass really.

Light from outside spilled in for a brief moment, quickly fading as the door swung shut. I glanced up from my perch on one of the coolers, my gaze colliding with Austin's cool blue eyes. My breath caught in my throat. Why didn't it occur to me, even for a second, that he might come back to Club Elite to find me? Lack of sleep was making me short-sighted and just plain dumb.

Jumping off the cooler, I quickly surveyed the rest of the bar. I wanted to run—needed to, but I couldn't if I wanted to keep my job.

He casually strode over to the bar, and I forced myself to remain where I was. *Just breathe. In two, out two, in two … You're not going to lose this job because of him. And what do you think is going to happen? You're being overly dramatic. Stand your ground and woman up.*

Austin pursed his lips. "We need to talk."

"The only thing I'm talking to you about is what kind of drink you want."

His brow furrowed. "You don't understand—"

"I don't want to understand," I interjected. "Just please go and leave me alone."

Light spilled in from the front door, alerting me to another potential customer. I blew out a sigh of relief as the tall, muscular man made his way to the bar. He was a few inches taller than Austin, and he filled out his snug jeans and T-shirt quite nicely. His long, dark hair was pulled back into a low ponytail, accenting his sharp features and flawless tawny skin. As he neared the bar, he smiled, showcasing straight white teeth.

Then he turned his attention to Austin. "Hey, man. Did you tell her what's going on yet?"

Shit. He knows Austin.

Austin scowled. "I was trying to, but she doesn't want to listen."

"That's because you're too intense sometimes. Let your buddy Taryn take care of this one."

Taryn turned his attention to me. "Hey there, Chloe."

Crap. How did they know my name? It wasn't like I was wearing a nametag. Did Austin hear it at the after-hours club? Or did I give it to him? I couldn't remember anymore.

"You're going to have to come with us if you want to live."

What the fuck? I backed up slowly. "Leave. Now."

"Yeah, I don't think that's helping. I'd feel her panic a mile away."

"I'm not the empath here. You are. Besides, I've always wanted to say that to someone."

Empath? "Who are you people?" Was it possible that they were like me?

Austin glanced at me, assessing, before addressing Taryn. "Do your thing. I was hoping it wouldn't be necessary, but we don't have time for this."

Taryn grinned, and it was like the sun coming out from behind a cloud. "Look at me, sweet girl," he said.

My eyes lifted to meet his dark amber gaze.

"I'm going to show you something that isn't going to be pleasant."

Intense pain spiked through my skull, and suddenly I was standing outside my apartment building.

Fumbling with my keys, I tried to get the main door to my apartment complex open. He was there. I could feel him. He'd been hiding, lurking in the shadows, content to merely watch.

But something changed, and now his hatred was a living, breathing thing, strangling my senses and making it difficult to focus.

He wanted to make me suffer. Not just me, but all of those like me. Whatever that meant.

My hand shook as I tried to push my key into the lock. His heavy boots clomped the pavement behind me, but I didn't dare look back.

As I opened my mouth to scream, a strong hand slid over it, cutting off my oxygen supply. I twisted sharply, using my elbows and legs. Sudden pain tore through my side, causing spots to dance in front of my eyes. Still, I gave everything I had left to the fight.

Burning spasms ripped at my flesh, slowing me down. He's stabbing me. *Darkness pushed around the edges of my vision, and realization slammed into me.* I'm going to die.

And that pissed me off like nothing else ever had before.

Insurmountable rage filled me to the brim even as I blinked amber eyes into focus and found myself back in the bar. "What the hell was that?"

My pulse thumped inside my head and my vision blurred. As if I'd been torn open, emotions poured into me clearer than I'd ever experienced before, almost as if I could read minds.

Austin's emotions were louder than the rest, begging for my attention. And in the instant, I was hit with the knowledge that he would play an extremely important role in my life. I just ... knew. I bit the insides of my cheeks as the pounding in my head worsened.

"It was too much for her. She doesn't have a grip on her abilities even on the best of days," I heard Austin say. "We'd better handle this one quickly."

Abruptly everything cut off. The bliss of being alone in my mind left me wobbly, and I stumbled forward. Strong hands steadied and then lifted me. I managed to mumble a few protests but lacked the ability to put up a physical fight.

"Shhh ... sweetheart. I have you. Everything's going to be fine now."

Warmth and safety wrapped itself around me like a blanket. I allowed my eyes to slide shut as I snuggled into Austin's arms. "You're going to be someone very important to me," I murmured.

"What's she saying now?" Taryn asked.

"Nothing that matters," Austin replied.

Lie. "Why are you lying to him?" I mumbled, unsure if the words made sense outside of my head.

"You need to rest. You're confused right now, but when you wake up, you'll be safe, and we'll explain everything."

Annoyance swelled up within me. "Don't patronize me. I'm confused about some things but not that. You're going to be important to me." Exhaustion tugged at my consciousness. "And I'm going to be just as important to you."

"I know." It was the last thing I heard Austin say before everything faded away.

Chapter 13
MARCH, SIX YEARS EARLIER ...

know."

"I Austin's words bounced around in my skull as I slowly swam back to consciousness. Was he acknowledging that he was lying to Taryn, or patronizing me? Or was he admitting that he knew we were going to be an important part of each other's lives?

Why is it bothering me so much? Damnit. What does he know?

The absence of pain in my head was a short-lived relief as adrenaline surged through my system. I had no idea where I was or how I'd gotten there. Cracking my eyes open, I was greeted by the bland atmosphere of a hotel room. A rather large man, with dark hair, stood gazing out the window with his back to me. *Where the hell is Austin? And why did it matter with everything else that was going on? Pull it together, Chloe.*

"Austin had some things to take care of. I'm Nixon," the guy said. He turned towards me, a pleasant smile adorning his handsome face. Was there a meeting of *Hot Guys R Us* nearby that I didn't know about?

I swiped a hand over my face, frowning. "Did I ask where he was?"

"No, but I don't have to be an empath to pick up what you're feeling. If you ask me, he's running scared. From you," Nixon stated, mirth dancing in his dark eyes.

Scared? Of me? My curiosity was officially piqued. "What do you mean he's scared of me?"

Nixon crossed the room, lowering himself to perch on the edge of the bed. "You've intrigued him." Nixon shook his head, his smile widening. "The man is a serious player. He gets more action than he knows what to do with most of the time, but besides the physical, his interest has never lasted beyond introductions."

"And I care because?"

"Because you've managed to do something that no other woman has done before: intrigue him. He's been in your head, and instead of being put off by what he saw, he wants to know more."

"Lucky me." I rolled my eyes. "And thanks for the warning. He doesn't need to run from me because I'm not going anywhere near the mess he obviously is."

"Yeah, that's what they all say. But in the end—"

"In the end," I interrupted, "I'll let those other girls have him."

When Nixon's gaze met mine, I felt his attraction flare.

Guess my ability to pick up on people's emotions is back online. Nixon was definitely the type of guy I usually went for, but ... but Austin.

Fuck. But Austin indeed. Despite the warning from Nixon, and my outright denial, I was intrigued by Austin just as much as he apparently was with me. That night at after-hours when he'd touched me, something happened —something I couldn't quite put into words. A connection was fused while our minds and emotions intermingled, and ... *Even now I can feel his presence within me. It's just there—unbreakable as far as I can tell. And I know it's the same for him.*

I cleared my throat. "So enough about Austin. Do you plan on telling me what the hell is going on? Yeah, sure, I may seem to be taking this all in stride, but that's only because I've been a freak my entire life. Strange things aren't unbelievable to me, but still ..." I raised my eyebrows, waiting.

Nixon shook his head as if to clear his present thoughts to make room for new ones.

I hope they're less lusty.

"First things first," he said, rising from the bed. "We need to do a makeover."

"And what exactly is that supposed to mean?"

"Exactly what it sounds like."

"But ... why? Seriously, are you fucking with me? Because I'm pretty sure there are more important things to concentrate on at the moment. Like, I don't know, just a stab in the dark here, but how about we worry about the serial killer who wants to kill me."

"You being on the killer's radar is exactly why you need a makeover. We don't need him to accidentally spot you. He won't find another girl to focus on until he realizes you're out of his reach for good. Let him think he just needs to figure out your new pattern. We don't want him to know we're on to him. It'll be the perfect opportunity to catch him while not having to worry about your safety at the same time."

"When you guys find him, what are you going to do with him?" I wished I could get my hands on him. I wasn't usually in favor of violence, but after the vision Taryn shared with me, I wasn't opposed to it under the circumstances. After all, turnabout is fair play. I wanted the man who wanted to kill me dead.

"We'll kill him, of course."

I nodded. "Good. I wouldn't want it any other way."

Nixon snorted. "A woman after my own heart. An eye for an eye and all of that."

If getting a makeover in a roundabout way led to the death of our friendly neighborhood serial killer, I was willing to suck it up. I shrugged. "All right, I guess I need a makeover then. What do we need to do?"

Handing me my jacket, Nixon said, "Oh, this is going to be fun."

I grumbled a string of obscenities under my breath as I slipped on my jacket. My life always tended to stray into strange territory because of my ability, but this situation took the cake.

AFTER WHAT SEEMED LIKE AN ETERNITY ... and a day, I finally headed back to the hotel with Nixon. I'd been given a beauty overhaul, which turned out to be less traumatizing than I thought it would be. After my cut and color, there was no way the killer would recognize me at a glance, or even a second or third one, especially since my own reflection shocked the hell out of me.

My long, all-one-length, platinum blonde hair had been chopped off to just past my collarbone and dyed strawberry blonde to boot. Quite a shock at first, but as weird as it sounded, I felt more like me. Of course, that was probably because it was dyed back to my natural color, the first time since my teens. The woman Nixon had taken me to see was a miracle worker, managing to minimize any damage to my tresses.

On the threshold of the hotel room, the hum of Austin's presence sprung to life within me, and my heart quadrupled in time. Without thinking, I reached up to smooth my hands over my new do, wondering what he would think.

No. Nope. It doesn't matter what he thinks.

Nixon cast me a sideways glance. "Don't worry, he'll love the new you."

Amusement swept over me, coming from Nixon, and it had me wondering exactly what he meant. I pondered the short list of possibilities as he swiped the keycard to the room. I hesitantly trailed in behind him, letting his large body block me from Austin's view.

"It's about time you two got back," Austin rumbled. "I was beginning to—"

Nixon stepped out of my way.

Austin froze, his gaze darting over me. My cheeks heated under his scrutiny.

Austin whirled towards Nixon and he snapped, "This is your doing, isn't it?"

Nixon's eyes glinted with mirth. "I don't know what you're talking about, man. She chose the color. I had absolutely nothing to do with it. Although I really wish I had."

Austin stalked over to stand in front of me, his anger flaring. "Why did you pick this color?" He touched a strand of my hair before dropping it as if it had burned him. "Did you do it on purpose?" His eyes bore into mine, searching.

"I don't know what you're talking about. This is my natural color. I mean, I've been bleaching it for years, but—"

"Natural?" His nostrils flared, and his jaw muscles feathered. "Fuck."

He studied me another moment, attraction spiking within him, before he stalked past me, careful not to touch me again in any way. He mumbled something about having an errand to run before he slammed out of the hotel room in a swirl of dark emotions.

I don't get it. What did I do? Baffled, I turned to Nixon.

"What's wrong with him? Why did he get all weird about my hair?"

Nixon's smile threatened to overtake his face. "Oh, well, he has a weird thing about redheads. Always has." He turned, muttering to himself, "And he thought he was in trouble before."

"Oh." I still didn't understand. Not really. It did explain why he accused Nixon of putting me up to picking the color though.

"Yep, he always claims it'll be a redheaded woman who will one day do him in. Funny, I didn't know precognition was one of his gifts. Thought it was just one of Taryn's."

"Oh," I said again, not sure if there was an appropriate response to give to the guy I barely knew. Although it was nice to be wanted by someone as attractive as Austin, even if I didn't do anything about it.

"Okay, so now what?" I asked, intent on changing the subject. "I got my makeover ... what's next?"

"You're just going to have to sit tight while we take care of business."

"You've got to be kidding me!" There was no way I was going to sit back and do nothing while Austin, Nixon, and Taryn hunted my would-be killer. I needed to do something. "There has to be something I can do to help besides sitting around twiddling my thumbs."

"Afraid not." Nixon gave me a sympathetic smile. "I'm going to go track down Austin and Taryn so we can get a move on. Don't want to have to leave you here for too long."

"I'm not staying here." I glared at Nixon. "Who put you guys in charge anyways?"

"The people we work for put us in charge, that's who. And you aren't part of the team."

"Team? What team? Who exactly do you work for?"

Nixon suddenly busied himself with absolutely nothing, swinging his gaze around the room to touch on everything except me. He might as well have started talking about the weather as convincing as he was being.

"I have a right to know, don't I? It's my life that's on the line here."

"When and if our employers deem you worthy of that information, they will answer all of your questions. Until that time, if it happens, it'll be on a need-to-know basis." Nixon gave me another sympathetic smile. "Sorry, I don't want to lose my job."

"This is complete bullshit." I stalked towards Nixon, not exactly sure what I was going to do—maybe try to shake it out of him?

Stopping a few inches from Nixon, I shot him a death glare.

His lips twitched up. "What do you think you're going to do? Scare it out of me? Good luck with that one."

I slid closer to him, leaving almost no space between us. Softening my expression into one similar to the dancers at Club Elite when they were trying to part men from their money, I trailed my fingers down his arm while batting my eyelashes. "Tell me. Please," I cooed.

Nixon stilled, tension thrumming through his body,

sudden attraction to me swelling up within him. "Shit," he grated between clenched teeth. "You're good, baby. I'll give you that."

"So you're going to tell me then?" Rising to my tiptoes, I threaded my hands through his thick, dark hair. I warred with the urge to do more, his emotions starting to affect me. If I didn't back off, it wouldn't be long before his desires would be indiscernible from mine, and then the player would get played.

I licked my lips, and Nixon's eyes followed the motion intently.

Maybe half a heartbeat passed and then his mouth slammed into mine.

I only resisted for a millisecond before getting completely caught up in the moment. It had been so long since anyone had touched me in a sexual manner, and Nixon's mouth was clever and quite skilled. He knew just when to deepen our kiss and when to back it off. A moan erupted from me as his hands slid down to cup my ass, his pelvis grinding against me with need.

Like a bucket of ice water being dumped over my head, my desire was yanked away abruptly, leaving me cold and bereft, although Nixon didn't seem to notice. Pushing at his chest, I managed to disentangle myself from him just as the door slammed.

That's when I knew. *Shit.* Austin cut me off from Nixon's desire. Apparently, *none* of it had been mine. My cheeks flamed with a mixture of shame and embarrassment.

"What the fuck, Nixon? You know what you're doing is wrong."

Nixon turned towards Austin lazily, as if he was dazed. "Wrong?"

"Yeah. Wrong. She's a very powerful, *untrained* empath. Do I have to spell it out for you? Why didn't you use your void ability? You need to have it up all the time around her."

"Stop. It wasn't his fault," I said in the general direction of Austin, unable to meet his gaze.

"Did you even consider that she might actually want me? Not every girl is going to pick you," Nixon interjected. "You aren't God's gift to women as you seem to believe. Maybe she's just smarter than those other girls."

Austin stalked over to stand in front of me. His proximity forced me to look up and acknowledge his presence. "Did you want him? I mean, did you want him all on your own?"

God's gift to women, huh? Oh, I knew his type, and I wasn't going to fall victim to his bad-boy wiles. "Like I said, it wasn't his fault."

Surprise briefly played across Austin's face, which made me want to twist the knife a little deeper.

"I'm sorry. I'm just embarrassed that you walked in when you did."

Austin's eyes narrowed as he reached to touch my arm. I instinctively knew he would be able to tell I was lying if he made contact with any part of my skin, so I sidestepped him. "Don't touch me," I snapped, my nostrils flaring.

I wanted Austin, not Nixon, but I didn't *want* to want him. And I wasn't the type of girl who could convince herself that someone like Austin would change. He'd use me until he got bored, and I would be the one hurt in the process. He was the type of guy who could get into a girl's system like a drug, worsening her cravings each time he touched her. Eventually, he would end things, move on to his next victim, and leave her forever wanting, never fully satisfied with another man.

I simply wasn't willing to chance involvement of any sexual kind with Austin. I'd never fallen for a guy in that way, but I'd dealt with the aftermath of friends who had, and it wasn't pretty. That old saying 'It's better to have loved and lost than never to have loved at all' ... Total bullshit. I say it's better to not know what you're missing.

"I won't touch you. I'm sorry, I—" Austin scowled at me, his feelings of frustration so strong I could practically taste them. "I didn't mean to try."

His lie beat against my senses. He most certainly did mean to try to touch me. He still ached to do so. "That's a lie. Don't say you're sorry with a lie."

"Oh, man. Having another empath to call you out is going to be awesome," Nixon interjected. "You better watch your back, Austin. She hasn't even been trained yet."

Austin turned to address Nixon. "She's not going to get any training, at least beyond being able to block out people when she wants to. She only needs to get control of that."

"I think once the higher-ups get a load of her, they're going to be interested in training her for the team. No one's had as much raw empath talent since you."

"No. They don't need her, they already have me. Besides, I'm more than just an empath. I'm—"

"You're what?" I jumped in. "What other skills do you have? How do you know I don't have them, too? I haven't been trained. Maybe I might be interested in working with people that understand me, people who—"

"No. Not going to happen," Austin growled.

"You might not have a say in it, man," Nixon said. "If they want her, and she wants to do it … End of story."

My blood boiled. Why the hell was it any of his business what I did? Was it just sour grapes because he thought I'd chosen Nixon over him? "Why the hell do you care what I do anyways?"

"No," Austin said through gritted teeth. "I won't let it happen." Dark, angry emotions pushed at me.

I gasped. *Is this what he's feeling? Why?*

"Please. Stop," I cried out, the room spinning. "Why are you doing this to me?" The floor came up to meet me, and a metallic tang filled my mouth.

"Austin! What the hell are you doing?" Nixon yelled. "You're hurting her!"

"What's meant to be will still happen," I whispered, not sure why I said it. Austin's rage rampaged through me threatening to split my head open. "It's too late."

"No!" Austin roared. "I don't accept that! The future can change!"

"It already has," I croaked before screaming out in agony.

I'm dying. Make it stop. I'm dying ...

It all halted abruptly, the relief so great I let myself sink into the sweet oblivion of complete darkness.

Chapter 14
MARCH, SIX YEARS EARLIER ...

Whispers, voices that I couldn't quite make out, eased me back to consciousness.

Where am I? What happened?

Panic jolted me straight up, vibrating through my system. "Austin!"

I needed to see him immediately. *No. That's not right.* I rubbed my temples. *I need to run in the opposite direction of wherever he is.*

Yet, something was itching in the back of my brain, a piece of vital information I couldn't quite reach that had to do with Austin. And that elusive puzzle piece triggered my give a damn about him. *Shit.* Caring about Austin in any way beyond human decency would not end well for me. *What is it about him? Beyond the fact that he's the most attractive man I've ever laid eyes on.*

"He's not here. Don't worry," a vaguely familiar voice spoke softly.

I blinked Nixon's blurry form into focus. He was sitting at the end of the bed that I was sprawled across. "Where's Austin?" I rasped.

"You don't need to worry, hon," a feminine voice responded.

Swinging my head around, the room tilted. Nixon hurried to my side. "You feeling okay?"

"Yeah, I-I'm fine." I swallowed around the boulder in my throat. "Just moved too fast, I guess, and got dizzy for a second."

The owner of the feminine voice stepped into my view. She was medium height, probably about 5'4" or 5'5". Her pale skin was flawless, practically glowing in the dim lighting. Her features were finely structured and framed by a long mane of fiery red hair. Her tight yet casual clothing showcased impressive curves that gave me a slight tinge of irrational jealousy.

"Who are you?" I croaked.

"I'm Jessica." A sweet smile curled her lips. "Don't worry, Austin is out trying to track down our latest target. Nixon brought you in after what happened so I could help you."

"Brought me where? And what did I need help with?" Turning my head, slowly this time, I scanned my surroundings. Although no longer in the hotel, the new room still had a sterile feel to it. White walls, dark wood furniture, muted neutral colors on the bedding, and curtains.

"Austin isn't used to having another empath as strong

as you around, especially an untrained one. He didn't mean to hurt you. Really, he didn't. He is a lot of things, but cruel isn't one of them."

Staring into Jessica's cool, grey eyes, I immediately knew I was meeting one of Austin's victims. Fresh jealousy of a different sort flared, burning my insides.

Wait. Don't be fucking ridiculous.

There was no reason to be jealous of Jessica. Austin wasn't mine and never would be. If only I could get my rational mind to beat my irrational emotions into submission.

"Anyhow, Nixon immediately brought you here for me to heal you. Of course, you would have healed on your own eventually. I just sped up the process."

Do not think of Austin and her together in any way. Do not think of them kissing. Do not think of them naked in bed together ... their sweat-drenched bodies writhing—

Stop. I said to not think about it, damnit.

Be nice. Be nice to her because she seems nice and you have no logical reason not to be. "So you're a healer?"

She smiled pleasantly. "Yes, that's me, a healer." She obviously didn't have any empath skills because she wouldn't be smiling at me if she knew the internal battle I was currently waging with myself.

Nixon drummed his fingers along the bedframe. "When you're feeling better, some of the higher-ups want to meet with you. Natalie was already in to see you when you were unconscious, and she was quite impressed with your untapped abilities." Nixon grinned at me. "And let me tell you, babe, Natalie isn't impressed very easily." His grin widened. "You might get to join the team after all. Austin is going to flip his shit. Again."

Jessica frowned. "Why is Austin so opposed to her joining the team? I never did get around to asking you, Nixon."

"Because he's an arrogant asshole. He didn't like me kissing Nixon and couldn't comprehend why any woman would want anyone besides him. He probably just doesn't want to be constantly reminded that I don't, and never will, want him."

I shook my head, internally chastising myself. I just couldn't resist letting Jessica know that Austin wanted me, as if the information had inadvertently slipped out or was relevant to the topic. *Did I hit my head and wake up in high school? Stop acting like an immature brat, Chloe.*

A blush crept over Jessica's cheeks. "Oh ... well—"

"He's not so bad," Nixon interjected. "He's one of my best friends, and everyone knows I have impeccable taste. Although someone does need to knock him down a few rungs once in a while." Nixon chuckled. "Thanks for that by the way."

"Yeah, no problem."

Hopefully, Nixon would let the whole kissing thing go. It wasn't as if Nixon was unattractive. It was just that ever since Austin and I accidentally forged the link between us, I wanted him far beyond the physical. I craved ... I craved something and I wasn't even sure what it was, simply that I could only find it with Austin. *Maybe I'm going crazy. At least that would give me an excuse for wanting Austin.*

Clearing my throat, I said, "I'm feeling better now. How soon can I meet these higher-ups like Natalie?" And get some questions answered.

"I thought you might want to get showered and eat something first," Jessica offered with a helpful smile.

As if on cue, my stomach gurgled. "Yeah, I am pretty hungry. The rest can wait until after the meeting."

Nixon caught my gaze and smirked. "Maybe not."

"What?" I self-consciously ran my hands over my hair and down my face. "Oh, come on. What are you trying to say?" One of the problems of being an empath was picking up on people's emotions but not knowing the cause.

Nixon sighed. "I didn't realize you thought it's only been a few hours. You've been unconscious a bit longer than that."

"A bit longer? How much of a bit?"

"Two days," Jessica said.

"Two days! You've got to be fucking kidding me!" I mentally cursed Austin to hell and back.

"So, I guess you're going to want that shower now?"

"Why, yes, Nixon, aren't you Captain Obvious?" I snapped.

Nixon rose from the edge of the bed, raising his hands in surrender. "Just trying to be helpful."

"I'll show you where the bathroom is," Jessica offered.

Go away already, Jessica. I don't want to be mean to you.

"And while you shower, I'll go pick up a change of

clothes for you. I can also put in an order for what you want to eat on my way out, that way your clothes and food will be here when you return."

"Umm ... yeah, that would be great. Thank you." I mustered what I hoped was a genuine smile for her.

"Let me know if you're weak and need any help showering," Nixon added.

"She'll be fine, Nixon. Now get out of here and stop sexually harassing her. You can come see her later, as I'm sure you'll be back sniffing around in no time."

"Hey. Not fair," Nixon yelped as Jessica hustled him out the door by pulling him by the ear. "I was just trying to help. Don't blame me if she slips and falls in the shower."

"Okay, I won't," Jessica said with false sternness. "And you were only trying to help yourself into her pants."

Nixon broke away from Jessica's grasp long enough to throw a wink in my direction. "Can't blame a guy, can you?"

Jessica gave him another shove before closing the door. "Sorry about him," she said with a laugh. "He's completely harmless, I swear."

I sighed. "Yeah, I know he is. I just hope he didn't get the wrong idea from our kiss. I like him, but just as a friend. I kind of got swept up in his emotions."

A frown graced Jessica's beautiful face for a brief moment before it was replaced with a brittle smile. "Poor Nixon. He has a knack for finding his way into the friend zone with girls. I'm not sure why."

"Yeah, I'm not sure why either. I mean, he's hot—really hot."

"So you're not attracted to Nixon or Austin then?" Jessica's gaze flitted around the room as if she didn't care what my answer would be. But her emotions didn't lie. She was concerned about the interactions between me and Austin. She wanted to believe that I wasn't attracted to him, but didn't quite.

"No, not attracted to Nixon." My stomach growled, and I took the opportunity to change the subject. "Thank you so much for helping me out because as you can tell I'm starving." I rubbed my belly demonstratively and gave her a self-deprecating smile. "What kind of food options do I have to order from?"

"Umm, pretty much anything you want." Her emotions were still swirling with worry and jealousy.

"Great!" I exclaimed, causing Jessica to jump. "How about five-cheese ziti al forno? Or any kind of pasta with no meat sauce and lots of cheese. I'm not that picky."

She nodded. "No problem. Come on, I'll show you where the bathroom is."

We fell into an awkward silence as I trailed along behind her, neither of us wanting to talk about where our minds were: Austin.

Coming to the end of the hall, Jessica halted, motioning to the open door in front of me. "Well, here we are. Extra towels are in the closet by the sink, where you'll also find an array of products to choose from. Hopefully, there'll be some in there that you'll like. When you're all finished, just head back to the room you were in, and hopefully your food and clothes will be waiting for you."

"Okay, thanks." I turned to head to the bathroom.

"What size are you?"

"Huh? Oh, size. Sorry." I smiled sheepishly. "Six in jeans. Medium or large for tops, depending ..." I glanced briefly down. It depended on how tight the top was across my chest since I wasn't lacking in that department.

Understanding lit in her eyes. "Yeah, okay. I know what to look for." She sauntered back down the hallway, leaving me to my own devices.

I quickly shut and locked the door behind me, letting out a sigh of relief. After flipping on the shower, I made quick work of stripping and gathering toiletries, while I waited for the water to heat. Once naked and under the hot spray, I raked my gaze down the length of my body. I didn't have show-stopping curves like Jessica, although I wasn't completely unfortunate. At 5'10", I was slender with moderate curves and a girl-next-door kind of appeal, or so I'd been told. But unlike Jessica ... *Stop. The grass is always greener and it will get you nowhere to compare yourself to other people. Life isn't a competition. Or it shouldn't be.*

Of course, my thoughts moved on to Austin next.

Again, I couldn't help but ponder the question: What is it about him? I conjured up a mental image to dissect. He was tall and well-built, but lots of guys were. And sure, his shockingly blue eyes that contrasted so dramatically with his nearly black hair drew me into their depths with such ease. And full, perfectly formed lips made me wonder what it would be like to kiss them ... but none of that was anything special. He was just another hot guy in a sea of hot guys.

My mind meandered back to focus on his lips, despite me not giving it permission to.

Hmm ... what kind of kisser would he be? Would he be aggressive? Yes, he would be. He was the type of guy who took what he wanted, not with force, but with finesse, yet it would be passionate, harsh even. He wouldn't hold back either. He had the kind of confidence that made him know his touch would deliver pleasure.

I bit my lower lip. *Shit.* I was no longer contemplating what it would be like to kiss Austin in a general sense, but how he would kiss *me.* I also wondered how he would touch me, if I let him. My imagination was spinning out of control, and I fell into a full-blown sexual fantasy starring none other than Austin.

I struggled to shove him—and what he would do to me —out of my mind, even as I imagined him pushing into my hot flesh from behind. I practically purred. *Oh, God, he would be so good. I know it.*

And why would you deny yourself that or anything close to it? my id demanded.

Because you don't do casual sex, I responded harshly.

And that's exactly what it would be with him. Casual, definitely no commitment.

Finishing up in the shower, I stepped out, drying myself off with agitation. *Get it together. You will not sleep with Austin. The connection you think you feel with him is all in your head.* It was probably a little trick he used to get his harder-to-seduce conquests like me to finally give in to him. But I wouldn't fall for it. No way, no how.

Unlocking the bathroom door, with a towel wrapped snuggly around my middle, I dashed down the hallway to my temporary bedroom, shutting the door quickly behind me.

A startled gasp burst from me, and my pulse thundered against my eardrums. I wasn't alone. Austin sat on the corner of the bed, his azure gaze snagging mine.

He rose hesitantly, taking a few steps towards me, his posture slightly hunched. "I didn't mean to startle you." His gaze flicked away and back, remorse settling into his lipid pools. "I just wanted to see for myself how you were doing. I didn't mean to hurt you. I-I'm sorry."

I steeled my emotions against him the best I could. "As you can see, I'm fine. Why are you here? I mean really?" There was internal turmoil leaking from him, but I didn't have any real clues as to the cause of it.

The corner of his mouth hitched up. I was suddenly very aware that I was in nothing but a towel, and I swallowed a few times in an attempt to return the moisture to my throat. A flash of my shower fantasy sashayed across my brain.

"It might take some getting used to, having another empath around." He took another couple of steps, drawing closer. His smile slipped away, his lips pressing into a thin line. "Chloe," he inched closer, ever so closer, "just let me touch you. It would be so much easier for the both of us." His hand hovered over my shoulder, waiting.

"Touch me?" I swallowed again. I was caught in the intensity of his gaze. Goose bumps erupted across my flesh. "What purpose would that serve?"

"It would just be easier for the both of us to get an understanding of each other. Without words getting in the way."

"I'm not having any trouble understanding you. You apologized, and I accepted. If it's too hard for you to explain the rest, well then, okay. I'm not about to go through what happened the last time you touched me."

"That was different. I wasn't expecting you to be an empath. I can control it this time."

A part of me was curious. The smarter part of me wanted to run like hell. "Okay," I heard myself say, as if a separate person was controlling my mouth. *I never listen to the smarter part of me. This is a mistake. He could peek at things you don't want him to see. But then again, I can do the same to him.*

The moment his fingers slipped across my shoulder, I fell into his mind, and yet was still very much aware of my own. Random thoughts and emotions took shape in front of me in the form of fast-moving pictures, almost like I was watching a movie. They rolled backwards from the present, revealing bits and pieces of the innermost parts of Austin that I was sure he would never willingly share.

I witnessed him experience anxiety, guilt, and regret the last couple of days as he waited to see if he'd truly harmed me. Which was nice, in a way, but not terribly interesting.

I wanted to know why he'd freaked out to begin with, inadvertently putting me in harm's way. I pushed, searching for that bit of information, but instead, my shower fantasy scene rose up in front of me.

Liquid heat permeated every molecule in my body as I watched us together. It was ... we were—

Embarrassment washed away everything else when I finally realized that Austin was pulling the images from my mind, rifling through them with smug satisfaction.

"How dare you!" I gasped, stumbling away from him.

A lecherous grin pulled his lips wide. "I think someone is confused about who was thinking about who naked. I certainly wasn't the offender."

Backing away from him, I searched the nearby area for something to throw.

"Do you want to know?" he asked, his gaze dipping to my mouth.

"Know what?" I squeaked.

"What it's really like to kiss me."

We began a silly little dance of me backing up and him stepping closer, until I was flush against the wall, his large body caging me in. I closed my eyes in an attempt to escape, but his spicy scent curled around me, and my senses were engulfed with his essence, his heat. I shivered in horrified delight.

"And what it's really like to have me inside you ... fucking you."

"Oh God," I gasped. I wanted to deny it but couldn't. He'd seen my true desires and a lie would be useless at this point.

A few seconds passed, my heart thrashing against my ribcage, and his hot breath fanning across my face. I silently willed him to leave, but of course, he didn't.

Cracking my eyes open, my gaze met his heated blue depths, his pupils blown wide. I'd never thought of blue as anything other than cold, but looking at him—staring into the fathomless blue depths—I knew blue was the color of fire and I would most definitely get burned.

A fine tremor ran over him as he inched away. "But I won't do it unless you say it out loud. I won't let you blame me when you want an excuse later, even though we would both know it wasn't true." He smirked. "I know your type."

Ha! He knew *my* type. I glared up at him with defiance. "Not going to happen, because I know *your* type."

His smirk dropped into a scowl. "My type? You know nothing about me."

"And that's the way I intend to keep it."

A sharp knock on the door drew my attention. "Hey, it's Jessica with your food. Is it okay if I come in?"

Austin noticeably tensed, which added fuel to my anger. He obviously didn't want to be caught in my room by her. Therefore, I did.

"Sure, come in," I called, smiling saccharinely sweet at Austin.

The door creaked open slowly, revealing Jessica with a

tray of food balanced in her hands. She made it a few steps into the room when she registered Austin's presence, and then swung her gaze to me in nothing but a towel. Shock and hurt flushed her face and rolled through me. "What are you doing here, Austin? I thought Natalie told you to stay away from Chloe."

Austin's jaw muscles jumped. "Jealously doesn't suit you, Jessica. What I do is no longer any of your concern." Austin stalked towards the door, his body rigid.

She slammed the tray down on the desk. "How could you say that to me? After everything … after everything—"

"Just sex," he interrupted. "I told you not to get attached, Jessica, but you didn't listen. Not my fault."

"So what? You're just going to find someone new to play with until you get tired of her, too? Is Chloe your new intended victim?"

"Jessica, you're forgetting something. A victim has to be unwilling."

Jessica whirled, pushing past Austin and falling into a run as she hit the hallway. Austin left without another word. Stunned, I blinked a few times before deciding it was probably a good idea to shut the door.

As I reached for the doorknob, Nixon appeared. "Hey. Just coming to see how you're doing after your shower. I'm supposed to take you up to your meeting when you're ready."

"Oh, yeah. That's right." In all the confusion, I'd temporarily forgotten. "I just need to get dressed and eat, and then I'll be ready." I paused, my thoughts still on what had just transpired between Austin and Jessica. "What's happening between Austin and Jessica—seriously? I mean, beyond the fact that they had sex."

He snorted. "They've been at each other's throats for a while. Austin broke things off with her about six months ago, and she still hasn't gotten over him, obviously."

"Yeah. Obviously."

"Things have gotten nasty because she gets jealous if Austin even looks in the direction of another girl, so that's a lot. But you get to be the first that might be on the team."

I rolled my eyes. "Lucky me."

"Just stay out of the drama and you'll be fine. Austin and Jessica are both my friends, and it's a real shame things turned out this way." He grimaced. "I warned her before she started up with him, but she wouldn't listen." He eyed me with meaning. "But with her being a healer, I suppose she thought she could heal some of his issues."

"Issues? What kind of issues does he have … besides the obvious?"

"Austin's pretty screwed up about women. But with good reason, I suppose. When he was young it was just him and his mom, and they were pretty tight. Then when he was about fifteen, he watched her die." Nixon shrugged his shoulders. "He blames himself for not being able to protect her."

"But he was just a kid. What could he have done?" *Poor Austin.*

"He used to get visions, well, up until his mother was

killed, and then ..." Nixon motioned with his hands. "Poof. Gone. He had a vision about her death, but she wouldn't listen. He felt, or still feels, I guess, that he should have done something, stopped it somehow. The whole thing fucked with his head pretty badly. You see, when he got there he wasn't too late. He was just in time for her to die in his arms."

"Shit," I whispered.

"Yeah. He's had one other vision since then, a few years back, but he won't talk to me about it. It shook him up pretty badly. He mutters in his sleep, sometimes, about history repeating itself, and how he can't watch *her* die, too."

"Her?" Icy fingers crawled up my spine.

"Want to know my theory?"

I nodded my head enthusiastically.

"Okay. I think he saw the death of the girl he's destined to fall in love with."

I quirked an eyebrow at him.

"Pretty far-fetched, I know, but hear me out. He goes through women pretty quickly. It's like he's always searching for something, yet at the same time, he's petrified of finding it."

I chewed on my bottom lip. "Yeah, that does kind of make sense. It's like he yearns for that love but also knows if he finds it, he might have to watch her die, like he did his mother. It's like if he doesn't find her, then he won't love her, but he can't help himself from wanting it on some level."

"Exactly."

"Still doesn't explain why he goes through women so fast."

"Sure it does. Look at Jessica for example. She's intelligent, funny, and absolutely gorgeous. He knows she's not this woman from his vision—even if she did dye her hair red—so he hopes she'll be enough, but after a while, she isn't. He yearns for more, but ..."

"Okay, okay. I get it." And unfortunately, instead of scaring me away from Austin, it was having the opposite effect. It was all so cliché—I was a cliché. But humans stuffed full of emotions all had the same tendencies because of them, me being no different in that aspect. It was difficult to ignore the urge to fix Austin, to want to heal him from the trauma he'd experienced. It didn't matter if thousands of women had tried and failed, there was a part of me that thought he would be different with me. That those other women didn't love him enough or understand him in the way I could. After all, we did form a bond—

Well shit. I'm going to be just as bad as Jessica, aren't I? Maybe when Austin eventually breaks my heart, we can start a club.

No. I can't let it happen. I won't. Austin is off-limits. Find a way to deal with it—him.

I shivered, which reminded me I needed to get dressed. "Well, I need to put some clothes on, and I'm famished so ..."

"I can wait."

"Um, no. I don't think so, buddy. No free show for you today."

"Really? I promise not to touch." Coming from someone else, I would have been offended, but not when Nixon said it. What *was* it about his personality that made him fall into the friend zone?

"That's still a no, I'm afraid."

He turned to leave, halting halfway to the door to give it one last-ditch effort. "I can help if you're still feeling weak. I mean you haven't eaten yet and that fork is awfully heavy."

"Get out," I said, laughing.

"Fine, but just like before I don't want to be blamed if you injure yourself."

I pointed my index finger at the door. "Don't worry, you warned me, so your conscience should be free and clear."

"Yeah, yeah," he muttered good-naturedly as he shut the door behind him.

Finally. I was afraid my stomach was going to start eating itself soon. That I was functioning at all was a small miracle. I quickly dressed in jeans and a long sleeve T-shirt.

Inhaling my food, I barely tasted the scrumptious manicotti. A few minutes later, I sat back, sighing heavily as I rubbed my belly. Having showered, dressed, and eaten, I was beginning to feel more like myself. And now that I could think straight, more questions were beginning to push their way to the surface. Like: Where was I? Who employed all these people with unusual abilities? Could I maybe work for them? If not, did I still have a job at Club Elite? How did Austin and Taryn get me out of there to begin with? Were my parents and friends freaking out because I was missing?

With too many things swirling around in my mind to focus on, I chose to dry my hair and put on some makeup instead. *Makeup, really? Who are you trying to impress?* Ignoring the niggling feeling that I wanted to look good for Austin, I put minimal effort into my appearance as protest. *Yeah, because that's going to change how he makes you want to climb him like a cat in heat.* When I was finished obsessing about not obsessing, I headed for the door and the impatient man on the other side.

I was greeted by what was quickly becoming a familiar smile from Nixon. "Ready for your meeting, babe?"

"As ready as I'm going to be." I self-consciously fidgeted with my clothes.

Nixon rolled his eyes. "You're not one of those beautiful girls who doesn't know they're beautiful, are you?"

My cheeks heated. I didn't take compliments well because they usually felt false to me. Most of the time, the person giving me one wanted something in return, so it was hard to see beyond it to believe they were sincere. *Empath problems, the struggle is real.* "I can't be one of those girls because I'm not beautiful. Pretty, sure, but not like …" I choked on my words, not wanting to compare myself to Jessica. Or anyone for that matter.

"Good, you are. So maybe I have a chance with you after all." Nixon aimed a wink in my direction.

"Nixon," I chided. "You're hot. You can do way better than me. Besides, I have tons of baggage. You'd probably run for the hills the first chance you got once I started unpacking."

He beamed. Again, I found myself wishing I could be attracted to Nixon instead of Austin. "You think I'm hot? I'll take it."

Of course, he would latch on to that part and ignore the rest. "So who's this person you're taking me to meet?" I asked in an attempt to change the subject. I would find out soon enough without him telling me, but I had no interest in talking about the prospect of an *us*.

"Her name's Natalie. So what kind of baggage do you have?"

I sighed. He heard the rest after all, and wasn't going to let me change the subject. "I have low self-esteem. It's probably because every guy I've dated has cheated on me. I suppose I'm lacking in some department. Wish I could figure out what it was so I could fix it."

"They must have been stupid to cheat on someone like you. If you were mine, I'd never want anyone else."

"You can't know that. You might even believe it would be true … but you can't know that. No one can give any other person any real guarantees."

I could feel Nixon's gaze burning into the side of my face. "Wow. Yeah, okay. You're right. You do have baggage.

Almost as bad as …" He let his voice trail off, but we both knew he was talking about Austin.

He snorted. "Empath issues, I guess."

Was it true? Was my baggage almost as bad as Austin's? I didn't trust anyone. Not really. I mean, I believed people were basically good, and made promises they thought they could keep, but no one could truly guarantee anything, especially when feelings were involved. I had friends swear to be there until the bitter end only to ditch me a few years later because I did something weird. And I had boyfriends declare their undying love for me only to find their way into someone else's pants the moment I got to be too much for them to handle. I found out the hard way how promises like that worked: they didn't. I never had someone close to me die in my arms and feel responsible for it, but when it came to emotional walls …

Well, shit. I don't know if I'm anywhere near as fucked up as Austin, but I'm definitely living in the same neighborhood.

"Here we are." Nixon's deep voice broke into my self-analysis.

We stood in front of huge, natural wood, double doors. It took me a second to process that we'd already arrived since I'd been distracted by our conversation.

"Come in," a feminine voice called just as Nixon raised his hand to knock.

He opened the door, holding it open for me. Hesitating, I turned to Nixon, who gave me a reassuring nod. As soon as I was in the room, the door clicked shut behind me. I pressed my sweaty palms together behind my back.

"Have a seat, dear. I promise I won't bite."

A petite, black woman sat behind a large oak desk, the size of it making her appear childlike in stature. Her short-cropped, silver hair was cut into one of those vogue European styles that only women with perfect bone structure and high cheekbones could pull off. Despite her obvious age, she only had a few creases in the usual places; around the eyes and on her forehead. Her makeup was artfully done to complement her large, brown eyes, and she wore a hunter-green suit. She was tiny but intimidating.

Fidgeting, my gaze flitted around the room. She was studying me, and unsure if she had any abilities of her own, I was terrified of what she would pluck from my subconscious.

A soft, throaty chuckle filled the room. "You empath types are all so jumpy when untrained. You should have seen Austin the first time I met him."

I sat down in the chair opposite her, the massive desk between us. Clasping my hands in my lap, I fruitlessly tried to will myself to calm down. "Hi. You must be Natalie. Nice to meet you. I guess in this situation it would be more proper if I knew your surname, but I—"

"Oh, nonsense. I don't like the formality. That's why I don't have my name on the door or my desk. I prefer to just be called Natalie." She paused, and I met her gaze as she studied me intently for a moment before continuing.

"I came to see you when you were unconscious, to find out what I could about your abilities. I already guessed from Austin's reaction that you were quite strong, and I found that to be true. But you have almost no control and tons of untapped power. You have absolutely no idea what you can do."

I spoke before thinking. "Why would that freak Austin out? Apparently, everyone around here has some kind of ability. Why does mine bother him so much?"

She smiled. "Ah, I can see Austin has already gotten under your skin. Not unusual. But no one has managed to get to him like you have, and so quickly to boot." Her smile grew. "It has finally begun, and he knows it."

"What does he know? What has finally begun?"

"If I were to tell you anymore, it could change the path of things, and that isn't my wish. You will find out soon enough if what I think is true."

"Great. Just what I need, one of those 'you must go left to go right, wax on wax off, you can only see clearly when you close your eyes' people. Yet another cliché come to life." Slapping my hand over my mouth, my eyes widened. I hadn't meant to say any of that ... out loud. *Shit.*

"It's one of my gifts, dear. People just blurt out what's on their minds in my presence if they're not careful. And it's impossible to lie to me or in my presence."

"I'll make sure to be careful then." I slapped a hand over my mouth again. *Crap, I didn't want to say that out loud either.* I didn't want her to think I was hiding anything, but then again, weren't we all to some degree?

"You'll get used to it. Luckily, I understand people's true natures very well and am not easily offended." She reached for a mug on her desk, taking a sip of the contents. "You will begin training immediately. One such as yourself can't go walking around like you have been without any control. I'm surprised you've stayed sane this long."

"Who says I'm sane?" I grumbled.

Natalie continued as if I hadn't spoken. I supposed she was used to people saying things like that since they couldn't help it. "You will get to know the members of our team, and once you're trained, you will be given the choice to stay on or go back to your old life. Of course, if you decide to leave, you will not be permitted to retain any memories of us. It's for our and your safety, of course."

"You would take my memories of everyone and everything here? How?" I did *not* like the idea of someone kicking around in my brain. They could break something irreparable, and I quite possibly wouldn't even know it. Worse, I would.

"It's one of Austin's gifts."

My gut twisted. "You mean he could just wipe my memories clean? Why hasn't he taken Jessica's then?"

"She would know he took them. We can't permit Austin to wipe clean everything to do with us because she's part of the team. If she were suddenly missing time, she would know who took it from her mind and would want to know why. It would be much worse if he did alter her memories. Believe me, he's wanted to."

"But with me?"

"We would have him erase all of this and provide a cover story to explain your missing time. A car accident, for example. We would leave the knowledge of how to use your abilities intact, just not how you obtained that knowledge. It's been done before."

"Oh. I really don't like the thought of anyone messing around in my brain. Hopefully, that won't need to happen. So how does this training thing start?"

Natalie's eyes glinted with something I couldn't quite read. "We usually pair someone to be trained with a mentor, someone who has the same inclination as they do with their abilities. Sometimes, it's hard to find a match, and we've had to make do with what we've had, but in your case we have Austin."

"Of course. Just my luck," I said. "Maybe I should just go sleep with him now and get it over with." *Shit.* I was going to have to try harder around Natalie to keep my internal dialogue … internal.

Natalie's laughter filled the room, even as I slouched in my chair. "Austin's going to have his work cut out with you."

She seemed entirely too pleased with the situation. It was almost as if she was intentionally throwing me in his path. Which didn't make a whole lot of sense. "I'll let Austin explain how we work and introduce you to the rest of the team as needed. Most of them are out on assignments at the moment."

"I thought Austin was supposed to stay away from me after what happened. And shouldn't he be out hunting the psycho that made me his next target?"

Natalie strummed her nails against the desk. "Things have changed. I've sent another team to hunt down your would-be killer. Austin's abilities will better serve our facility as your mentor."

"Great. But not so much." *Huh.* Natalie's gift allowed sarcasm as long as it was clarified.

"Nixon will escort you back to your temporary quarters, and I'll have a chat with Austin to let him know what I decided. Afterwards, I'll send him to you so you can get started." She bit back a smile.

I had the distinct feeling I was missing the punch line of some private joke. "Okay. Thanks, I guess." Again, I wished I could have kept my sarcasm as inner monologue, but Natalie didn't seem to notice or care.

Scurrying towards the door, I glanced back at her over my shoulder. She was seemingly engrossed in some papers on her desk. I idly wondered why I hadn't spotted a computer or laptop, or anything of higher tech in her office. I, myself, preferred not to rely on a lot of modern technologies simply because of the tendency of such equipment to go wonky around me. It made me wonder if it was the same for every one of my ilk. Now that I considered it, I hadn't even so much as spotted a cell phone on Austin, Nixon, or Jessica. *Hmm ... interesting.*

As I pulled the door open, Nixon jerked up quickly from where he had been trying to eavesdrop.

He turned, walking back in the direction we had come from, and I fell into step beside him. "Well? What did she say?"

I chuckled. "I guess that means your eavesdropping attempts were unsuccessful?"

"I wouldn't be asking if they weren't."

"Yeah, well, she told me that I needed training, but from the expression on your face, I'm guessing you already knew she was going to. But surprise, surprise, Austin is going to be my mentor."

"What?" Nixon stopped short, his brow furrowing as he stared at me. "You ... are you sure Natalie said that? I mean after everything that's happened? Maybe you misheard her. Maybe she said Austin will *not* be your mentor."

"Oh, I'm sure, all right." I grimaced. It made me wonder again—was Natalie trying to put me in Austin's path?

Nixon tapped his chin. "Well, she must know something we don't." His eyes slid over me. "Huh," he muttered to himself.

"Huh, what?"

He started walking again, and I jogged to catch up with him again. "Nothing. It's nothing. I don't know if I should be worried about you or him."

"Why would you worry about Austin?" I was the one who was going to have to be on constant guard so I didn't do something stupid.

"No reason." Nixon's expression shuttered, his emotions a jumble.

"Fine, don't share," I grumbled.

And then, just like that, his emotions went from tumultuous to cheery. It was the emotional equivalent of the sun bursting through rain clouds. Having someone like Nixon around would be very refreshing to an empath like me. Maybe that's why Austin seemed to like him so much.

"I'm guessing Natalie is going to send Austin down to get you once she breaks the news to him. She usually likes to jump right in with new people's training."

"Yep, that's pretty much what she said."

He shook his head slowly. "I can't wait."

"For what?"

"For the fireworks, of course. It's going to be great entertainment for the rest of us." He left me at my door with my mouth hanging slightly ajar. "I better let everyone know to start battening down the hatches for the oncoming storm of fireworks," he called over his shoulder with a laugh.

Annoyance zinged through me. "Don't mix your metaphors, Nixon. Are we going to cause fireworks or the damage of a storm?"

He didn't respond as he clomped down the hallway, but I could see the telltale sign of his shoulders shaking. He was still laughing. *Fabulous. Not a good sign.*

Chapter 15

I awoke to the soft light of dusk filtering through the gauzy curtains in my temporary room. Warm arousal spiraled through me, conjuring an image of Austin slowly removing his clothes before sensuously sliding into me. He rocked back and forth slowly, languorously, until I shuddered my release. *Mmm ... yes. That would be nice. And it would serve as foreplay for later when he wouldn't take me so gently ...*

"Should I come back later? Or do you want me to join you?"

Sucking in a sharp breath, I met Austin's heated gaze briefly before rolling onto my back. *Ignore him. He's an empath. Of course he's going to pick up on my arousal. But he doesn't know I was thinking about him. So no big deal. I am a fully grown woman with sexual needs after all.*

I chose not to answer his inappropriate question. "Sorry, I fell asleep. I guess I'm still tired."

His eyebrows lifted as if to say he knew what I was doing. But how could he? It was just his arrogance assuming I was fantasizing about him.

"You being here means you talked to Natalie then?"

"Mmm hmm ..." Austin prowled closer, his gaze scalding me with its liquid blue heat. "Training starts now." He pounced on top of me, pinning my arms over my head and using his body weight to keep me captive.

"What kind of training is this?" I squeaked in alarm. "I'm not training to be a prostitute."

"Keep me out. Try to keep me out when I'm this close," he growled.

"What?" He couldn't possibly mean what I thought he meant.

Understanding dawned when he slid into my mind. He wanted me to learn to keep him from digging through my brain when he was touching me. However, something like a finger on my hand would have been sufficient. He was taking advantage of the situation, hoping it would get him somewhere.

And it most certainly would.

Deposited on the floor.

Abruptly standing, I used the element of surprise to offset the extra weight he had on me. He crashed to the floor in a heap. Laughter bubbled up in my chest, but before it could escape, he swept my feet out from under me. Joining him on the floor, our legs tangled awkwardly. He grabbed my arm, sliding back into my mind.

"No! Stop!"

"Then make me," his mental voice mocked me, the smugness of it bouncing around in my skull.

I pushed at his presence, but it was an effort in futility as he began to pick through my brain.

"Let's see who was sparking that delicious lust of yours when you woke up just now."

He went slowly, giving me a chance to fight him. But as much as I tried, my efforts continued to be fruitless, and I watched in horror as an image of my most current fantasy of Austin and me popped up in vivid detail.

He mentally chuckled. *"I knew you were thinking about me. Why bother denying it? Just let what's natural happen."*

"Natural? You've got to be fucking kidding me! It's not natural to be used up and thrown away, and I won't let it happen to me. I know what kind of guy you are. And despite my fantasies, I know it would be nothing but sex."

He let go of my mind, and I stared at him defiantly, even as my body cried out to do just what he'd suggested, to give in. To demand that he take me right there on the floor. I yearned to arch up to meet him.

"It would be nothing but sex," I repeated out loud.

His nostrils flared. "What's wrong with no strings attached sex? If you know that's all it would be, you would be going into it with your eyes wide open."

"There's nothing wrong with no strings attached sex. But I'm not wired that way." I licked my lips, watching his gaze follow the movement. "I can't do casual sex, and I would end up hurt. I don't want to be hurt."

Releasing me, he stood, his visage a mask of

indifference. "It's your loss then. Because we both know it would be good."

"*My* loss? If we both know it would be good, then wouldn't it be *our* loss?"

"I've had lots of good sex and will continue to, with or without you. But you on the other hand …" His eyebrows rose.

Clenching my fists, I fought the urge to punch him. *Arrogant asshole!* "Are you trying to say that you would be the best I ever had, or that my sex life has sucked in the past? Or both?"

An image of Austin taking me from behind, me pressed up against the wall, affronted me. I gasped, knowing he was putting it in my mind. I managed to push the image away, battling it with my anger. It was immediately replaced with me shuddering my release while riding him. *His*—these were *his* fantasies. And what exactly was he trying to say with them? That's what I could expect if I let him fuck me? Because that's all it would be—fucking. No love, just raw, primal fucking.

Two can play this game. I'd never pushed images into another person's mind before, and I didn't stop to contemplate that fact. I was caught up in the moment, letting my anger fuel abilities that I hadn't known were there. I wanted to hurt Austin, piss him off, therefore I pictured the first thing I was certain would do the trick— Nixon and me together. It took more effort than I wanted to admit to imagine having sex with Nixon, but I somehow managed.

"I know you don't want him," Austin growled. "Don't lie to me and yourself."

I chose not to dignify his statement with a reply in words, but instead threw an image of me on my knees in front of Nixon, his head tilted back in pleasure. Anger from Austin fizzled all around me. I grinned.

"Don't tell me what I do or do not want. You don't know me, Austin. And trust me, you *never* will."

An emotional wall slammed down between us. "You don't know me either, Chloe." He tipped his head in acknowledgment. "Well done putting images into my mind. Bravo." He clapped slowly. "It took me much longer to learn that little trick. I think we've done enough for now." He turned abruptly, stalking from the room. "Sleep well tonight, Chloe."

"Asshole." Slumping onto my bed, I punched a pillow. I hoped not every 'training session' was going to turn out like that. Austin seemed determined to antagonize me as well as get into my pants. I wondered which one he wanted more.

"Seems like you two are off to a good start." Nixon peered into my room. "Mind if I come in?"

"Sure, why not?" I grumbled.

"Well, don't act too happy to see me." He chuckled. "Want to tell me what happened? Austin seemed pretty pissed off. He didn't even acknowledge me just now." Nixon settled himself on the edge of the bed and crossed his arms, waiting.

"The same thing happened that keeps happening with

us." I sighed, flopping back to stare at the ceiling. "And sorry, by the way, it might be my fault ... again that he's annoyed with you."

"Yeah? How'd you manage that, considering I wasn't even here this time?"

How was I going to tell him without going into details? *Crap.* I really hadn't thought that one through. "Umm ..." I grimaced. "He put images in my head of me and him ... together."

"Uh-huh. And?"

"He really got me riled up so I shot back with the first thing I could think of that I knew would piss him off." *Crappity, crap, crap, crap.* I didn't want to tell him, but it was a little late to hide it. Plus, I kind of owed him an explanation since I'd caused the tiny rift between him and Austin.

"And that would be?" Nixon prodded.

I heaved a long sigh. "You and me ... together. You know ..." My entire body flushed with embarrassment. You would think bartending at a strip club would have jaded me to sex talk of any kind. And it was true, about other people's sex lives. Mine? Not so much.

"So he put images of you and him having sex inside your mind to try and seduce you, and you got pissed off and put images of us having sex in his mind?" Nixon burst out laughing. "Oh, yeah, that would definitely piss him off."

"Shut up. It's not funny. How am I supposed to train with him when we can't be in the same room for more than five seconds without something like that happening?" My lower lip trembled, settling into a pout much to my chagrin. I was simply too drained to hide my reaction. "You're right. We're going to cause some major damage around here if I don't figure something out."

"Well, babe, you have one of two options, as I see it. One, you just sleep with him and get it over with—"

"How about no?" I interjected.

"Or two, sleep with me so he'll back off." Nixon waggled his eyebrows. "Personally, my vote is for option two."

"Yeah, still no. I'm not sleeping with either of you." I smiled at Nixon. "Although if it makes you feel any better, if I had to choose, I would pick you."

He gave me a mock wounded expression. "That hurts. I'm only trying to help."

"Help your way into my pants." I laughed. "I just can't complicate my life any more than it already is if I plan on becoming part of the team."

"He won't give up then. And neither will I, for that matter."

I could feel his determination. Underneath all Nixon's joking, he was legitimately attracted to me.

"At least if you pick me, I'll stick around to give us a real go. I would be stupid not to. Besides," humor flooded back into his system, "I don't have women issues."

I needed to tread carefully because I felt, just for a moment, what was hidden beyond Nixon's joking. He buried his true emotions ridiculously deep to conceal them from empaths, which he probably picked up from being friends with Austin.

"It's all too much right now. If I have a minute to stop and think about everything, I mean really think about everything, I might just have a nervous breakdown." I sagged into myself a bit. "Nixon, I know this isn't what you want to hear, but I could really use a friend right now." And that was the truth. I didn't want to deal with any of it—not Nixon, not Austin, not my training, and not the psycho who planned on making me his next victim.

Instead of disappointment like I'd been expecting, Nixon gave me a genuinely warm smile that reached his eyes. "I'll be whatever you need me to be. No pressure. I just want you to know that I'm at your disposal in any capacity you deem necessary."

Again, I found myself asking why I couldn't be attracted to Nixon. He was such a good guy. And hot, he was definitely hot. So why no chemistry? *Aaaah! Fate must hate me.* "Thanks, Nixon."

He lumbered to his feet, heading towards the door. "I think maybe you should get some rest. Tomorrow Austin will be back, I'm guessing bright and early, to pick up right where you left off. The guy is nothing if not persistent."

"Good idea," I mumbled.

"Lunch tomorrow?"

I stared blankly at him, not quite grasping the words through my haze of exhaustion.

Understanding bloomed in his eyes. "Good night. I'll see you tomorrow."

I blithely waved at Nixon. "Night," I managed, my mouth not wanting to cooperate with me any longer.

As soon as the door clicked shut, I slumped onto the bed and pulled the comforter around me, not even bothering to see if Jessica had brought me pajamas. My mind grasped at broken threads of thought, too exhausted to muddle through and yet not quite able to let go completely. After who knows how long, I finally fell into blissful slumber.

Chapter 16

T *hat's it. I'm never sleeping again.*

Rolling over, I stuffed my face into my pillow and screamed, warring emotions intertwining to form frustration and anger. During my not-so-delightful nocturnal slumber, my dreams, or rather nightmares, had been full of Austin as per usual, but with one disturbing addition: Jessica.

The images of them together, naked and ...

I screamed again into my pillow, wishing there was a way to scrub what I'd seen from my brain. Was it my insecurities playing out in my subconscious? Austin did, in a sense, reject me by making the no-strings-attached sex offer the only option he was willing to give me. But insecurities or not, rejection or not, why did I have to dream about the two of them together in such graphic detail? The worst part was, that despite everything, jealousy punched through my chest, leaving a gaping hole of smoldering flesh. I didn't want to think of him with her, he belonged to—

Nope. Don't even think it.

A soft knock at my door had me sitting up in bed. I eyed the door warily. *Please don't let it be Austin or Nixon. I can't deal with either of them right now.*

"Come in," I called with false cheer.

A smiling Jessica glided into my room amidst a cloud of contentment. "Good morning, Chloe." She set a tray down on the desk. "I brought you some food since I figured you wouldn't be much in the mood for socializing after what happened last night. Natalie said to be ready for another training session with Austin in an hour."

Completely baffled, I stared at her. "Thanks. I appreciate you bringing me breakfast. You didn't have to."

My stomach twisted into a knot, bile creeping up my esophagus. Something about her mood was setting me on edge. "Are you sure Natalie said Austin would be training me? He made it pretty clear last night that he wanted nothing to do with my training."

Jessica's smile faltered. "Oh? I hadn't heard that. But yes, I'm sure."

The knot in my stomach turned into a hot burning poker, scalding my insides. I needed her to leave. "Okay, well, I just wanted to make sure. I guess I misunderstood. Things have been a bit stressful lately. Thanks again for breakfast."

Jessica stared at me blankly for a few seconds before

turning to leave. "Let me know if you need anything else, Chloe," she called over her shoulder as she left.

Okay, that was just weird. An image from my nightmare of her and Austin rose unbidden in my mind, and I doubled over to dry heave. *What the hell is wrong with me?* I pressed my palms into my eyes, rubbing.

"You know what's wrong," my mind whispered. *"Stop pretending you don't."*

I clutched my head in my hands, screaming out in frustration. I wished I could just lie down, fall asleep, and wake up somewhere else as someone else.

Strong, warm arms encircled me in a comforting embrace. "I'm here for you, baby, I'm here." Dealing with Nixon was not something I thought I could do at the moment, but maybe he was exactly what I needed. He could be my friend and nothing more if that's what I wanted.

"I'm sorry," I croaked into his shirt.

"Don't feel bad. Who wouldn't get a little stressed under the circumstances? I think you're doing better than most would." His warring emotions pressed at me. He wanted to simply comfort me, but having me in his arms was making him aroused as well.

I twisted my fingers in his shirt, wanting to pull away. Now that I knew he was turned on, the idea of simple friendship became too complicated. *Sometimes knowing people's emotions is a curse. If I didn't know I could pretend ... but I do. Fuck.*

Liquid heat thrummed through my system, pooling in

my middle. *Crap.* Nixon's feelings were seeping into me, and I was too emotionally distraught to shut them out.

I breathed in and out through my nose, attempting to center myself. I couldn't count the number of times I'd gotten carried away with ex-boyfriends because of their emotions, and then afterwards I felt violated in a strange way. None of them forced themselves on me, but as an empath I didn't realize how being swept away by someone else could leave me feeling empty, alone, and even dirty.

Had I been ready to lose my virginity to Donnie Sullivan? No. He'd been ready to take it, though. Almost every sexual encounter I'd ever had, with the exception of Austin, left me twisted up inside afterwards. Well, okay, Austin had left me twisted up, too, but for a completely different reason.

I wanted to go into sex knowing I was being propelled by my own feelings, and not someone else's. Which was why I knew it was a mistake when I kissed Nixon. As usual, I just couldn't help myself. If I'd been completely repulsed by Nixon, then resisting his emotions would have been easy. The problem was resisting guys I actually liked.

Nixon groaned as I slipped my tongue past his lips, his emotions driving the both of us. We stayed like that, frantically kissing each other for what seemed like an eternity before everything started moving too fast.

I was on my back. Wait. I was on my back naked, arching up to meet Nixon as he slid into me. A tiny voice in a distant part of my mind cried out to stop, that I didn't want this with him, but a much louder voice screeched that I did—desperately.

Nixon moved in and out of me with skill, and it felt good ... really good. But even as my body trembled and shook with my release, it was as if I stepped outside of myself to observe that I wasn't fully present for what was happening. And when it finally came to its inevitable conclusion, and Nixon spilled within me, I was left satisfied and yet numb. The contradiction jarring.

Nixon cupped my face in his hands, gazing down at me with reverence. "You're so beautiful, you take my breath away." He dipped his head to kiss me, his thumbs stroking my cheeks. I fell into the kiss, wanting to deny or maybe escape what I'd done. The regret was already building.

But why? Why do I need to feel that way at all? I could give it a real go with Nixon. Give him a real chance. I liked him as a person, and he was attractive. He also knew what he was doing when it came to sex, that much was clear from how he'd somehow managed to give me an orgasm despite my tumultuous state. Other successful relationships had started with less, I was sure.

What about Austin? The thought pressed at me, causing my heart to fist. *No. He doesn't matter.* He'd made it crystal clear last night that although we both felt the connection between us, he wasn't going to let things go any further than sex.

Nixon wanted more, and I didn't have to hide that I was an empath. There was an actual possibility of a real long-lasting relationship with him. Nixon was the smart choice. The right choice. And I decided to pick him instead of the hurt waiting for me if I chose Austin.

"Baby," Nixon murmured, kissing his way down my neck. "I wish we could stay like this all day. I've wanted you like this since the first moment I saw you." He paused to take my nipple in his mouth, and I gasped. "But you have to train again today."

"Yeah, I do." *With Austin. Oh, joy.*

"You don't have much time to get ready before your session. It's a shame, really." Nixon lavished attention on my other nipple, causing me to temporarily lose focus. "It was too fast this time. It only made me want more."

Struggling to sit up, I disentangled myself from him. "They'll be plenty of other opportunities for us to be together—later." I bit my lower lip, trying not to react to the fresh wave of lust emanating from Nixon.

"You're right, baby." The smile that spread across Nixon's face threatened to blind me. "I'll be back to take you to where your next session with Austin is. I'll leave you so you can get ready with no distractions from me." He quickly dressed and left.

What am I supposed to do now? I was going to give things a go with Nixon, which lessened the pressing guilt about having sex with him. But how was I going to lie to Austin about it? He would feel the hesitation, the doubt, plus he would sense the attraction I still felt for him. Would he respect Nixon's new claim on me, or would he force me into a hard place? Because I was already pressed up against a rock. *Guess I'll find out soon enough.*

I glanced at the tray of food Jessica had brought, deciding I was no longer hungry.

———

THIRTY MINUTES later I was on my way to meet Austin for our training session. Nixon was chattering away about God knows what because I couldn't manage to focus. All I could think about was how to bypass Austin's empath abilities. Basically, how to lie without it seeming like a lie.

"Well, we're here. Want me to stick around?" Nixon's brown eyes twinkled. "You know, to keep you guys from killing each other?"

"No. I'll be fine." I forced a smile.

"All right, babe. Have fun." He leaned in to give me a kiss, which he deepened briefly before pulling away. "Oh, hey, man. I was just saying good-bye to Chloe. We should catch a bite to eat later. We have a lot to talk about."

Austin stood a few feet away, Jessica clinging to his arm even as his gaze drilled into mine. My heart dropped to my feet. *Not a dream. It was real. It happened. He fucked Jessica last night. Did he put those images in my mind on purpose? To punish me?*

Who are you kidding? You already knew. You were just in denial. It's the real reason you let Nixon's emotions carry you away. It's why you let him fuck you. To even the playing field ... to escape.

But why? Why is Austin with her again all of a sudden? It doesn't make sense.

"Yeah, apparently we do have a lot to talk about," Austin said flatly. "I'll come find you after my session with Chloe."

Nixon graced him with a slight smile, which amped up when he looked at me. "Cool. I'll see you both later then."

I glanced at Nixon's retreating form before gluing my eyes to the floor so I wouldn't have to see Austin's good-bye kiss with Jessica.

"I'll see you after you meet with Nixon?" Jessica asked in a sickly-sweet tone.

I fought the urge to retch.

"Yeah, sure."

The sounds of them kissing singed my ears.

Austin at least had the decency to wall off his emotions, but he forgot about Jessica's, and hers were soaring. I bit my lower lip until a metallic tang filled my mouth.

"Ready?" Austin muttered.

Blinking, I realized that Jessica was already gone, and I was standing there like a jackass staring at the floor.

"I guess."

I followed him through the door behind us, where he situated himself at a tiny table at the center of the small room. I stopped short as Austin's cool gaze met mine.

"You two are pretty close all of a sudden." He paused for a moment, as he seemed to wrestle with something internally. "He's a good guy."

I took a few more steps towards the table but couldn't bring myself to be any closer to him just yet. "Yeah, I know. That's why I decided I'm going to give him a chance—to give us a go."

Closing the remaining distance, I sat cautiously in the empty chair across from him. "What about you and Jessica? I thought you didn't want anything to do with her anymore. Well, at least the way she wants."

Austin's jaw muscles jumped. "I figured, why not? The sex is good, and I can have it whenever I feel like it. But I'm still not going to give her what she ultimately wants." He studied me as I felt him pushing at me mentally. A bitter smile quirked his lips. "I see Jessica and I aren't the only ones getting laid around here."

My cheeks heated as my temper flared. "Fuck you, Austin! Fuck you! What the hell kind of game are you playing?" I stood, shoving the flimsy aluminum chair across the room.

Austin drew his large frame up from the table with alarming speed, catching me by my wrists. "No games," he growled. "It all got very serious last night. Too much is at stake."

"Yeah, it got so serious that the only thing you could do was fuck Jessica."

Despite the situation, being so close to him did crazy things to my hormones. I swallowed hard, trying to combat the sudden dryness of my throat. "What you did—to comfort me last night—was that before or after you fucked her? And why the hell would you send me those dreams? You're one sick bastard!"

"But you still want me, don't you?" His gaze bore into mine with challenge.

Before I could respond, or even process his words, he was on me, and his tongue swept in to take control of my mouth. A shockwave of pleasure rocked my system, and I was carried away, our connection electrifying.

No! What are you doing? Stop!

Jerking away, I slapped him across the face with all the strength I could muster. "You asshole! You fucking asshole! You don't get to kiss me after you fucked her. Especially not when you're probably going to fuck her again."

I raised my hand to slap him, but he caught my arm that time, eyes brimming with fury. I withdrew my attack, spinning on my heel to leave. "Nixon's your friend. Your best friend. And I'm with him now. If you don't care about Jessica's feelings or mine, then maybe you'll care about his."

"You forget, I know the real reason why you're with him now. Why you accepted his advances so suddenly."

Trembling violently, I demanded, "Why do you even care? Why, Austin? Why do you care?"

His lips—the same lips that had just been pressed passionately against mine—pulled into a sneer. "I don't. Not really. I guess I had at least hoped I would get to have you first."

His words landed like a punch to my gut, and I fought

not to double over as if they were an actual physical blow. I was sure—so sure, about our connection, and about the things I felt from him. How was I so wrong? How could I, as a friggin' empath, not get it right? Could he fake feelings? I had no idea about his abilities, or anything else apparently. Because I was a fool—a complete fool when it came to Austin.

Trembling with barely controlled rage, I screamed, "You're nothing but a huge fucking asshole!" A dark, twisted knot formed in my stomach, ripping from my body. "I hate you! I fucking hate you!"

Austin dropped to his knees, clutching his head and gritting his teeth in agony. In the same instant, the emotional barrier he erected came crashing down. Pain. He was in so much pain. The physical was almost nothing compared to the emotional agony seething within him.

The revelation had me stumbling back as my anger receded. The wall in his mind immediately reformed, and his visage softened, easing with the loss of pain.

A scowl in place, he pulled himself to his feet. "That was highly unexpected." One dark eyebrow rose in question. "That ever happen to you before?"

Flustered and unsure of how to act, I inched forward. "Are you okay? I didn't mean to hurt you like that. And no, that's never happened to me before."

Austin rolled his eyes with condescension. "I'm tougher than that, sweetheart. I was simply unprepared for your sudden attack. Hate's a pretty strong emotion to feel so soon after meeting me, don't you think? Maybe you hate that you want me, and that's why you're really pissed."

"Stop. I just tend to get swept away with my emotions and say things I don't mean." Like I owed him an explanation. "And I'm not your fucking sweetheart."

"You're not sweet, that's for sure. Although I bet you could be if you tried, especially—"

I raised my hand. "Don't. I know you're just going to hit me with some kind of sexual innuendo I don't want to hear. I wonder why you're trying so hard to piss me off today."

Austin's jaw muscles rippled. "Tell yourself whatever you need to feel better. The only thing that ever could be between us is sex, and since you won't let that happen, then there's nothing between us. Nothing. No connection, nothing special like you imagined. Nothing."

"Yes. Nothing. You've made yourself perfectly clear." I narrowed my eyes, needing to antagonize him in the same manner he relished doing to me. "Too bad there's nothing special between us because the things we could have done together … Mmm …" I let my gaze roam up and down his body, pushing images at him of exactly what I was thinking. "But I'm not into casual sex. So your loss."

I turned away, pausing with my hand on the doorknob. "And I guess Nixon's gain."

Two can play this game, Austin baby. And although he scored first and was up a few points, I was about to show him what a comeback looked like.

Chapter 17
APRIL, SIX YEARS EARLIER ...

ake it 'til you make it flashed through my mind when I saw Nixon lounging on my bed, obviously waiting for my return. If I could feign enough feelings to convince him to be in a relationship with me, and if I continued sleeping with him, surely deeper feelings would follow. I mean, most girls got sex and love all mixed up together, right? I could grow to have genuine feelings for Nixon if I kept sleeping with him. *Probably. I hope.*

"I knew you'd be back early from your session with Austin." Nixon threw me a cocky grin.

I snorted. "Why? Did you have a premonition or something?"

As if he'd need one. Austin and I were at each other's throats most of the time, the cause of it generally lost on everyone besides the two of us. Not that I wanted to

AVA WIXX

educate anyone on the subject. And it seemed Austin
didn't either.

"Nope. Don't need one of those to know the two of
you can't be in the same room for very long without
things getting violent."

"If only Natalie could figure that one out," I grumbled.

"So how bad was it?"

As long as I left out a few details, I could tell him the
truth. "Let's just put it this way ... he pissed me off to the
point where I hurt him with my anger. I didn't even know
I could do something like that."

"Really?" Nixon grinned. "Maybe Austin isn't such a
bad mentor after all. He did unlock a new skill. Congrats!"
He shot off the bed, taking me in his arms.

I allowed myself to sink into his embrace, to feel the
warmth and comfort that his arms offered. "Thanks.
Although I'm not sure hurting someone with my mind is
something to congratulate me about." *Wrong. Wrong. He's
not Austin. You should be in Austin's arms, not Nixon's.*
Shoving away the voice of insanity in my head, I
continued to let Nixon hold me.

Slowly, Nixon's emotions seeped in to divert my
attention.

"What are you nervous about? Do you have something
to tell me that you're worried I'm not going to like?"

There, underneath his seeming calm, lurked a massive
pool of anxiety. He tensed around me.

"Just tell me, please."

He stepped away from me and dropped his gaze.

"Natalie wanted me to tell you ..." He paused, letting his eyes skitter around the room.

"Oh for God's sake, just spit it out already. All this stalling isn't going to change what you have to tell me, is it?"

"No."

"Well then, out with it."

"All right." He cupped the back of his neck and grimaced. "She wanted me to tell you that she's sending Austin to see your parents this afternoon."

My chest tightened. "Okaaay, and why would he be doing that?"

"He's going to plant the thought in their minds that you're dead."

"What?"

"He's also going to be paying everyone at your old work a visit." Nixon suddenly found his hands very interesting.

Coward.

"This is some kind of joke, right?" I forced a laugh even though I knew he would never be so cruel.

Nixon's eyes lifted to meet mine, regret swirling within them. "It's the way it has to be. We've all been through it. It's for their protection as much as it is for yours. We went over this before ..."

"I know, I just—" I wrung my hands while pacing in front of him. "I thought I would have a chance to say good-bye, and I thought Austin would just erase me or something. Not make them think I was dead. How is putting them through that any better?" I couldn't bear the thought of my friends and family suffering because of me. "Plus, I just started training. I didn't think it would move this fast. I thought I had time to think about this. I just thought I had more time for everything."

"They already think you're missing. Giving them closure would be better. And with the way you're being targeted, I would think you'd want them protected."

"I do want them protected. I do. But me dead? Why can't he just erase me?" It would suck if my parents never knew I existed, but it was better than the alternative, for them at least.

"Austin could erase you, but it's more difficult, and he'd be drained for days. Natalie worries when he does it. He only uses that ability when there's no other option." He cleared his throat. "Plus, the physical evidence would need to be altered, too. And not just with your parents. School yearbooks and all that kind of stuff."

"So he gets drained for a little bit, so what? Maybe if I ask him, he would do it anyways." Hoped flared to life in me. "And the rest is possible. I could do it. After all, I know where to look for everything."

"He's already gone, I'm sure. Your parents are a few hours away from us, right? He probably left right after your session, as soon as Natalie told him to do it."

No, no, no, no, no. Without thinking of the consequences, I reached out to Austin, searching for the warmth of his presence lingering in the void. I didn't know what I was doing exactly, but that had never stopped me before. And just like that, something within me clicked, and I slipped into Austin's mind.

"Chloe," he murmured, surprise skittering through him.

"Austin. Please, don't make them think I'm dead. Erase me. Please, just erase me." Opening up my own mind, I let him see and feel my anguish and how I couldn't handle hurting my parents with my supposed death. *"Erase me, please."*

"I can't."

"Austin, please."

"I'm sorry, I can't." A wall came crashing down between us.

My eyes snapped open, and I cried out in frustration. *Why won't he do this for me?*

Nixon wrapped me in his arms again.

"What's it like?" I croaked.

He situated me in his lap as he sat down on the bed. I pressed my face into the crook of his neck, letting his scent surround me.

"I won't lie, it's hard. But you have to take comfort in knowing you're protecting them—your friends and family."

"How long's it been for you?" I mumbled, exhaustion pushing at me. Connecting mentally with Austin the way I just did was more taxing than expected. "I mean, since your family first thought you were dead?"

"A few years." He gently stroked his fingers through my hair.

"Don't you miss them?" I fought to keep my eyes open,

but they slid shut despite my best efforts. "How do you deal with it?"

"Of course I miss them. Every single day. But they're safe. That's what matters. And that's what I remind myself all the time."

"I thought I wanted this, to be a part of this place, to feel like I belonged somewhere, but I'm not so sure anymore."

"It's a little late for that."

"Yeah, I know."

Nixon continued stroking my hair for another few moments, and then he settled me under the comforter on my bed. "You need to rest. You've had a rough couple of weeks, and things aren't going to get any easier anytime soon." He ran his knuckles gently over my cheek.

I grabbed his hand without opening my eyes. "Stay. Please. I don't want to be alone."

His pleased emotions slithered through me. "Yeah, sure." He slid into the bed, cradling me in his arms, his warm body comforting.

"Thanks," I mumbled, not even sure if my words were discernible.

Chapter 18
MAY, SIX YEARS EARLIER ...

"She means a lot to you, doesn't she?" Austin rumbled.

"Yeah. There's just something about her. It's just, I don't know—there's something special about her beyond what she looks like," Nixon said, as he mimicked Austin's earlier touch, running his fingers from my temple to jawline. "I could fall for her."

Emotional turmoil rolled off Austin in waves, and I wasn't quite sure what to make of it. He wouldn't be Austin if he was easy to figure out though. "I'm happy for you. I'll leave her alone from now on. I'll respect what you feel for her."

"No! Don't respect it! I want you! Don't give up on what we could have! Please, Austin!"

I managed to make a strange gurgling noise in the back of my throat, but I couldn't open my eyes or do much of anything else. I tried again to shove my thoughts directly into Austin's mind, but my abilities were temporarily burned out and I was a helpless lump of flesh.

"He'll give you what you need," Austin said in my mind. *"I just want you to be happy, Chloe. To live."*

I tried to tunnel back into his mind using the pathway he'd used, but I was met with a brick wall. Another gurgling sound bubbled up in my throat, my body utterly useless to me.

"Is she okay?" Nixon asked, worry evident in his tone. "Is she trying to wake up?"

"Yeah, she's fine, or she will be. Chloe is nothing if not stubborn. She drained herself that's all, so I'm going to give her a little mental push to sleep."

"No! You bastard! Don't you dare!"

But of course, he didn't listen to me, and before I knew it everything was slipping away.

MY EYES POPPED OPEN, my gaze immediately alighting on Austin, who was watching me from a chair beside my bed. Anger sizzled through my veins as his words replayed from just before he forced me to sleep.

"I'm happy for you. I'll leave her alone from now on. I'll respect what you feel for her."

I attempted to sit up but realized something prevented me. My gaze dipped to Nixon's arm, which was draped around my middle, and I cringed. Austin had stayed, forcing himself to watch over me even as I was cuddled up with his best friend. Why?

"Austin," I murmured. He had to know—had to see it in my eyes. I wanted him, not Nixon. If he just admitted out loud what he felt for me then we could be together. "Please."

Sadness settled into the hard lines of his face, and he rose abruptly, leaving the room without a word.

My heart ruptured within my chest, his actions all the answer I needed. He truly was giving up on me—on the possibility of us.

"Hey," Nixon mumbled. "How you feelin'?" He pulled me into him, his hot lips pressing against the back of my neck.

His spike of arousal washed over me, and I tried to push it away, to block it as best I could, but I was utterly drained which left me completely defenseless.

Turning into him, I choked back a gasp as his deep chocolate gaze bled into scorching blue. Long, brown hair shortened into a mess of inky locks. Bronzed skin lightened to pale, and slightly angular features shifted into much sharper angles.

Austin's eyes glinted with lust, and I moaned my encouragement as he ripped my pajamas from my body, plunging roughly into me.

Yes, yes, this is what I want.

Wrapping my legs around his waist, I pulled him closer as I scored my nails down his back, drawing blood. His grunts of satisfaction filled my ears, surely as my screams filled his.

The sex was fast, rough—almost brutal—and yet passionate. It was everything I'd imagined my first time being with Austin would be like and simultaneously better. *Because it's mine. Everything I'm feeling is mine.*

I bit into his shoulder to muffle my scream as my release tore through my system, my body convulsing almost painfully. Moments later he collapsed on top of me, panting.

"That was … Mmmm," I hummed, words to describe it escaping me. How could something so brief, be so intense … so perfect? It only made me want more—need it.

"Yeah, it was, wasn't it?" Nixon murmured in my ear.

I tensed. *Wait. Did I—*

No. I didn't somehow convince myself that I had sex with Austin, did I? *Shit. It wasn't real. It was all a figment of my imagination.* But it felt like more. Maybe not reality, but not quite nothing either.

My heart and mind yearned for Austin, felt connected to him, and not the man who was my boyfriend. The man who I'd actually just had sex with and was still semi-hard inside of me.

I am so fucked in the head.

"You all right, baby? I mean, it wasn't too soon after everything that happened?"

I squeezed my eyes shut and shook my head. "I'm fine. Just a little tired still."

Nixon rolled off of me. He removed the used condom,

discarded it, and then tucked me into his side, his fingers playing idly in my hair. "You need to get some more rest then, especially after what we just did, because I'm feeling a little tired myself." He punctuated his statement with a yawn.

What I really needed was to find a way to get my head screwed back on straight. My mind raced with possible solutions but only one was even slightly reasonable. "I can't. I need to talk to Natalie. You know, about everything."

Nixon propped himself up on his elbow. "Yeah, maybe you should talk to her about everything that's been going on with you, get a game plan going for what you should do next. Want me to go with you?"

I was already out of bed and pulling clothes on. "No. I —" *Shit.* I couldn't tell him I wanted space right after we had sex, it would hurt his feelings. But I needed to be alone with my own thoughts and emotions for a bit, even if that time only consisted of however long it took me to track Natalie down.

"You're tired. You just said so. Stay here and sleep, and I'll see you when I get back." I turned to leave, but before I could, Nixon was out of bed and swiveling me back around to face him.

His forehead was creased with worry. "Did I push you? I mean with my emotions? I don't know how to act around you sometimes, Chloe, and I don't want to hurt you."

I conjured a weak smile. There was no way in hell I

could tell him that he had hit the nail right on the head. "I'm sorry if I can't be what you need right now."

He blinked down at me, his eyes widening. "What I need? You're the one who's been going through so much lately. I'm the one who should be making sure you're getting what you need."

"What I need is to not talk about this anymore right now, okay? I'm going to go find Natalie, and you're going to stay here, or not, whatever you want." I knew my words came out harsher than I intended, but I couldn't handle a long, drawn-out talk with Nixon right now. I was trying, trying so hard, to make it out of the room without hurting his feelings any more than I already had, but he wasn't making it easy.

"Yeah, sure." He let go of me, the very hurt I was attempting to spare him evident on his face.

"I'm sorry," I whispered, hurrying out of my room.

Sprinting down the hall, I ran head-first into none other than Austin. He almost tipped over as he grabbed my arms to keep both of us from falling.

"I-I'm sorry," I stammered.

As he straightened himself to his full height, I met his stormy gaze. My mind flashed to our recent imaginary tryst, my cheeks heating.

Jerking, I tried to move away from him, but he crowded in around me, his presence suffocating. "Austin, what are ..."

His nostrils flared, the only warning that his control had snapped. He shoved me against the wall, his hand gripping my throat tightly, as his lips seared mine. I grunted in dismay even as I met his desperate tongue with matched fervor.

His hand flexed against my throat as he ground against me, my leg already hooked around his waist. His touch burned and soothed, excited and calmed my inner turmoil because maybe us being together was a betrayal and a mistake, but it was my betrayal and my mistake, all of what I was doing my choice with no outside emotions cluttering my mind. And I wanted this—him like I never wanted anyone or anything before.

"I need you, Chloe." Austin's heated breath skated over my flesh as he kissed his way down my neck.

"Yes," I moaned, throwing my head back to allow him better access. "I need you, too."

"We need to go somewhere." He'd somehow managed to get my shirt up, capturing my nipple between his teeth. "Can't do this here."

"Your room," I rasped.

"No ... Jessica," he said around my other nipple.

Irrational anger caused my gut to clench. Then I remembered Nixon. He was waiting for me in my room. Guilt replaced every other emotion.

I pushed at Austin's chest. "No, Austin, we can't. What about Nixon? He's your best friend."

Austin's voice was low and gruff with unspoken promises of pleasure. "I need you."

He offered me no other explanation, no argument, no rationalizations, just that he needed to be with me, plain and simple. And I wanted it—oh how I wanted it. I wanted him in any and every way he would let me have him.

What little will I had to resist melted away as he stumbled, with me wrapped around his waist, into a nearby room. He yanked my shirt off and deposited me on a desk. Leaning back, I clutched the edge of the scarred wood as Austin tugged my pants and underwear off. The cool air skated over my overheated flesh, causing goose bumps to erupt.

Austin paused, his gaze running over me from head to toe, as if he was planning what to do with me next. I swallowed, my throat suddenly as dry as the Sahara.

"You're so beautiful," he said, echoing Nixon's words the first time we'd been together.

I forced my mind away from the guilt that knowledge brought with it.

He shucked his clothes quickly, coming to stand between my quivering thighs. It was my turn to give his naked body the once over. He was exactly how I'd imagined him—perfect. I knew it was ridiculous to even think, but to me he was. Austin was absolutely perfect in that moment. His long, lean muscles gleamed with a fine sheen of sweat, his toned abs flexing under my scrutiny as I drew my gaze down the line of his body … lower, lower, and lower until it snagged on his massive erection.

I gulped. I knew he was large, I'd felt him before, but seeing him standing there in front of me, completely naked and ready to go … it was both intimidating and awe-inspiring.

I abruptly hooked my legs around his back, causing him to pitch forward. Grabbing his hair, I pulled him down until he was mere inches from my face, our breath intermingling. My lips curled up at the corners as I said, "Fuck me, Austin. Fuck me now."

His eyes flashed as a pained sound erupted from the back of his throat, his nostrils flaring. I threw my head back when he plunged into me. His fingers bit into my hips as he pulled out and slammed back in, falling into a brutal, demanding rhythm. The desk inched its way across the floor, the metal legs scraping loudly, blending with our moans and grunts. *Oh, yes. Yes, this is what I want—need.* I'd never had rough sex before, but then again, I'd never been running on my own emotions during sex before either.

Austin gripped the sides of my face, forcing my head down. "Look at me, Chloe," he growled. "I want you to look at me when you come."

As if his words gave me the permission I needed, my body exploded in pleasure, and I screamed. Austin held me steady even as I tried to thrash my head, his gaze capturing mine for the entirety of my unraveling, followed shortly after by his. His eyes held a single-minded intensity that spoke of possession, passion, and in that moment, we completely belonged to each other—and each other alone.

A silence fell over us, even as our hearts thrummed in our chests like hummingbirds. I kept my breathing shallow, afraid if I moved, I'd break the trance, this one perfect moment when nothing else mattered but us.

Austin moved first, gliding his thumb over my bottom lip. I nipped at him playfully, which caused him to dip his head to deliver me a long, sensual kiss, much different from the ones he just gave me minutes earlier.

Threading my fingers into his hair, I pulled, eliciting a grunt of approval from him. As our kiss deepened, I felt him grow hard inside of me again. I rocked my hips in encouragement. The slow, steady rhythm he built was the opposite of what we'd just done, but I realized they were both things I craved from Austin. *I want him in any and every way he'll let me have him.*

Squeezing my eyes shut, my muscles coiled and then spasmed, my heart pounding out of my chest. But Austin didn't stop, not yet, and my pleasure continued with each deliberate thrust. I clawed at his back, arching up when he finally spilled his release, pumping slowly, as I clenched around him. I never wanted it to stop. Me. Him. Us. I needed him to be with me forever.

"Fuck!" I shoved at him, horror dawning. "We didn't use a condom." I covered my mouth with my hand. "You just came in me twice and we didn't use a condom." Dizziness assaulted me as panic surged.

"So?" Austin's confused gaze darted over my face. "You have an IUD. I saw it in your mind. You can't get pregnant."

"No, I can't get pregnant unless something goes wrong, but I'm not ... that's not—"

Austin pulled away from me, his features pinched in offense.

"Don't you dare look at me like that. I mean— Oh, my God! Did you use one with Jessica? Did you fuck her and then me without—"

My gut roiled, and I doubled over. "I think I'm gonna puke." Retching, I fumbled for my clothes, pulling them on with jerky movements.

Stupid, stupid, stupid. There wasn't a single moment that couldn't be considered stupid since I'd run into Austin in the hallway. Not only did I cheat—I was now a cheater—but I could now—

"Are you fucking kidding me?" His eyes flashed with anger as he pulled his clothes on. "That's what you really think of me? That I would do that? Fuck her without a condom and then you?" He ran his hands through his hair and tugged. "Jesus fucking Christ. I'm not a fucking scumbag. I don't even—"

He leaned into me, speaking through clenched teeth. "And you're going to stand judgement on me when I know you just came from fucking Nixon."

My face and neck heated. "I tried to stop you. I—"

"Yeah, okay." He narrowed his eyes. "You gave me the cursory, 'Oh, we can't do this! Oh, Austin, no! What about Nixon?' But we both know you only did that to try and save yourself some guilt later. You don't give a shit about Nixon, just like I don't give a shit about Jessica. We're both using them, for different reasons maybe, but in the end, it's all the same."

"That's not true! I care about Nixon! You know I care!"

"Then that's even worse. You care about him and you still did it. You just cheated on your boyfriend. You just cheated on your boyfriend—twice—while he waited for you down the hall in your bed. Why don't you wrap your sanctimonious mind around that one?"

I raised my hand to slap him, but he caught my wrist before I could connect. "What the hell was all this about then? Tell me what just happened between us!"

His anger visibly drained from him, his visage paling. "It was about weakness—my weakness and yours."

He let go of my wrist, his fingers dancing along the side of my face. "I let myself take what I don't deserve. My need for you overrode the fact that I know we can't be together."

"So that's it. You fucked me twice in …" I glanced around to see exactly where we were, "in some empty office. And what? Are you planning on going back to Jessica? Do you expect me to go back to Nixon and pretend none of this happened?"

"I don't know. I just— This can't happen again." He turned away from me, scrubbing a hand along his jaw. "I-It was just so real, and I wanted … needed it to be real. At least once. Which is why we can't be together. You're the one person who isn't even an option and you're the only one I want to keep." He let out something between a growl and a snort. "The fucking irony is almost too much."

Alarm bells clanged within my skull. "What felt so real? Tell me exactly what you're talking about."

Austin expelled a long sigh. "When I was with Jessica … I don't know, she became you. It was so real, and like I said, I needed it to be real. For her to be you. I just wanted you. I needed to have you at least once."

My eyes widened. "This happened when? Just now?" My heart thrashed against my ribcage as I waited for his answer.

He narrowed his eyes as he studied me. "Yeah. Why? What's going on?"

I waved my hands around frantically. "Me too! But with you—with Nixon." I started pacing. "I knew it felt like …"

"More," Austin finished for me. "Fuck."

Whirling back in his direction, I said, "That ever happen to you before?"

"No. You?"

I shook my head and rolled my eyes. "No."

He glowered at me. "That can't happen again, either."

I clicked my tongue. "I didn't do it. You must have."

He quirked one accusatory eyebrow at me. "You're the one with untapped, untrained abilities, not me."

"Fuck you, Austin."

His lips pulled into a sneer. "I believe you just did. Twice."

My stomach knotted as I stared at his expression. "So you're going to go back to being an asshole to try and run me off?" I crossed my arms over my chest. "Well, I'm not buying it anymore. Oh, you can definitely be an asshole, that is an undeniable fact, but—"

I closed the scant distance between us and rested my palm gently against his cheek. "I know you feel it."

His eyes fluttered shut and he turned to press his nose into my hand, inhaling deeply. "I feel it. I won't deny it anymore ... or maybe I just can't."

His eyes snapped open, snagging me within their icy depths. "I've felt it since that first night. I want you, Chloe. No, I *need* you, so much it fucking hurts." He shook his head fiercely. "But it doesn't matter because you're the one I've been running from since my last premonition. I just didn't know who you were yet."

"That premonition doesn't have to come true and you know it," I whispered. "Do you think I *want* to die?"

"No," he grated. "I won't risk it."

Frustration burned through my veins. "He still wants to kill me regardless. But you knew that already, didn't you? So what's this really about?"

"It defies rational thinking how much I already care about you, someone I barely know. I don't understand how you can mean so much—be so important to me so soon. And if you're under my skin like this now, if we're together ... if I let myself ... "

He moved several steps away from me, anguish etched into every line on his face. "I want what we could have together. So goddamned much. But we can't ... I can't risk you dying." He sucked in a few ragged breaths, snagging my gaze with his once more. "The one who dies has it easy, you know. The one who's left behind is the one who truly suffers."

"You're a coward then. You won't give us a chance because I might one day die. Would you give up the small amount of time you had with your mother so you didn't have to deal with the pain of her loss? We could all die at any moment, but not everyone runs around being afraid of any real connections because of it!"

"I couldn't save her," Austin ground out. "I will save you."

Great. I had to fall for a guy with mommy issues and a side of hero complex to boot. "What was the point of all of this then? Of being with me like this? Huh? Tell me! Why couldn't you just leave me in peace?"

He turned to leave, pausing to say, "Haven't you figured it out yet? There won't be peace for either one of us, Chloe."

He pushed through the door, leaving me in that small room, where I crumpled to the floor in a heap. Choking back a sob, I swiped at the tears tracking down my cheeks. *Why won't he see reason? Instead, he's going to let us continue on this path leading to mutually assured destruction.*

"No one ever said men were easy to manage, dear, but it can be done."

Startled, I lifted my gaze to meet Natalie's.

"What are you doing here? And why the hell are you smiling?" Damn Natalie's gift, although I was too emotionally drained to care at the moment.

"I'm smiling because it was only a matter of time before we all ended up here, and I've been waiting for things to play out like I knew they would. I'm also smiling because I find the predictability of you and Austin amusing."

"Yeah, well, I'm glad my misery amuses you."

"My dear, nothing about your misery amuses me, and that's why I'm here—to help you." She frowned, regarding me with dismay. "Lord knows I tried to fix it from Austin's end, but he's too stubborn and has entirely too much baggage to contend with."

I snorted. "Like I don't have baggage."

"Not as much as Austin. You, my dear, I can work with." She grinned. "Now get yourself together because you're coming with me. We have a lot to talk about."

Chapter 19
AUGUST, SIX YEARS EARLIER ...

Several months had passed since Austin had officially turned me into a cheater. Of course, I knew it was my fault just as much as it was his, but I preferred to let the blame sit squarely on his shoulders. But thankfully, outside the two of us, only Natalie was privy to the gruesome details of our indiscretions, and none of us were talking.

I'd fallen into a fairly comfortable routine that consisted of training, spending time with Nixon, mostly of the naked kind, and avoiding Austin as much as possible.

My training was progressing nicely, and I had picked up some nifty tricks to employ for everyday use. One that I found to be particularly helpful was the ability to turn off all emotions at will. Not only mine but those around me. It would enable me to think coolly under pressure when in the field if I needed it.

Although not meant to be used regularly, I ignored the guidelines since it enabled me to spend naked time with Nixon guilt-free. I simply let his lust run the show with our amore sessions, and then I switched everything off when the act was finished. It wasn't a permanent fix, but it worked for the time being, so I wasn't complaining.

"Chloe, you need to stop doing that."

"Doing what?" I glanced at Nixon as I pulled my clothes back on.

"Completely shutting down after sex."

I blinked at him blankly. I wasn't surprised that he noticed. After all, it was like night and day the way I went from hot and passionate to cold and emotionless. He wasn't stupid. I just wished he didn't care.

But Nixon wanted a real relationship with me, and that meant he wouldn't let something like this go. I couldn't tell him the truth though—that I secretly considered him nothing more than a friend with benefits, even though I continued with the pretense of being his girlfriend.

I expelled a long breath. "My mind is on my training."

Nixon frowned. "If it was only that then I could accept it, let it go. I know what you've been through, what you're going through. But, Chloe ... it's not. It's more. Just tell me what I'm doing wrong."

Normally, if I hadn't shut down emotionally, his question would have pulled at my heartstrings. Fortunately, I felt nothing at the moment. "I told you, I just have other things on my mind right now. I need to get back to training."

"All you do is fuck me and train. And yeah, that's what it feels like. You're making me feel fuckin' needy, Chloe, but damnit, I want more. I thought that's what you wanted, too."

"I do." *With Austin,* my mind managed to whisper despite me being shut down emotionally. I mentally tightened down to prevent anything else from slipping in.

Nixon pulled his large frame out of my bed, taking my face in his callused hands. He studied me intently while I waited for him to tell me what he needed to say. "It's like you're not there." He dropped his hands. "What are you doing?"

Nixon worked for the same people I did, his best friend was Austin, but he didn't truly understand all the intricacies of being an empath, let alone some of the added talents I seemed to have in common with Austin. Even if I tried to explain them to him, I still didn't think he would get it. Not that there was anything wrong with that. We simply had different gifts. I was sure if he tried explaining his visions and void abilities I would be at a loss as well.

"It's just something I learned to do—for training. It keeps my head in the game, so to speak."

Nixon eyed me warily. "What exactly are you doing, Chloe? Who taught you how to do this?"

"Natalie explained to me how to do it. She says it helps Austin out in the field, and that it could help me, too."

His eyes widened slightly. "Shit, Chloe. You can't shut down like that all the time. It's meant for the field when you need to turn everything off. I've seen Austin do it. He says if he uses it too much, he needs to open up completely to feel anything at all. He compares it to using uppers and downers to function. After a while, you'll get caught in a Catch-22 situation."

Okay, so maybe he did know a little bit more than I gave him credit for, but I still wasn't concerned. "I'll be fine. It helps me train." Among other things, like keeping me from feeling any unpleasant emotions I didn't want to deal with.

"I'm guessing Natalie doesn't know how far you've taken it." Nixon tilted his head, studying me again. "I think we need to talk to her about this. It's not good for you to shut down completely. Or maybe you could get Austin to help you?"

I quirked an eyebrow at him. "Now why would I do either of those things? If it's not broken, then don't fix it. This is helping me, Nixon. Please don't worry."

"But I am worried."

"Then you're just going to have to get over it." I waved him off as I headed out the door, not bothering to wait for a response.

A FEW HOURS LATER, after working on some self-defense moves with the resident personal trainer, Rob, I was at the gun range reloading the clip on a Glock 9 mm. I frowned at the paper target dangling in front of me. Most of my shots made it onto the paper, but none would have been a death shot if my target had been living flesh. I needed to do better. I had to train harder.

"Not bad, for a beginner," Austin's low voice rumbled from behind me.

I quickly double-checked my emotional barrier before turning around to acknowledge him.

My cool gaze slid over him with appreciation despite my lack of emotion. "Not bad isn't good enough," I said as I met his penetrating blue eyes.

His gaze dropped to blatantly sweep me from head to toe. "Well, apparently Natalie doesn't think so because she sent me to let you know she thinks you're ready for your first mission." He stared at me expectantly, obviously waiting for some kind of reaction.

"Great. What are the details?" I set the Glock down to give him my full attention.

"You, me, and Nixon are going after a serial killer. Natalie's getting the file ready for us to study before we head out. Once we do that, then the three of us will settle on a course of action."

"Okay," I responded flatly. I turned to load a new target before sending it down the range. Picking up the Glock, I readied myself for more practice.

"Look at me, Chloe," Austin demanded.

Of course, I chose to ignore him. Only a few heartbeats passed before a hand came around to relieve my possession of the Glock just before I was spun around into Austin's iron grip.

"Nixon wasn't exaggerating, was he? I thought maybe you were just ... I don't know—" His eyes darted back and forth between mine. "But he was right. You've shut down completely."

"It's no one's business but mine."

"You can't keep it up, Chloe. It'll only make whatever emotions you're trying to hide from worse when you do feel them. I would know."

"Well, I'm not you. I can and will keep it up. Like I said, it's no one's business but mine." I had to clamp down even harder on my emotional barrier.

"I won't let you do this to yourself," he growled.

His fingers pressed into my temple, and my emotional wall was blasted apart, splintering into millions of pieces. I screamed as all of the unwanted emotions slammed into me like bricks raining from the sky.

"Shhh," Austin murmured. "Just let me see ..." His consciousness rifled through my mind, finding and studying each of the memories I didn't want to deal with and their accompanying emotions. But there were so many, most of them mundane and innocuous, he could easily miss the ones I prayed would stay hidden.

He faltered, pulling away abruptly, shock playing across his features. "Chloe—" he choked out, encircling me in his arms.

I squirmed within his embrace. "No. I don't want to hear it. You had no right to do that ... any of it. And whatever answers you think you've discovered, you can keep to yourself."

"Never once? Never once before me?"

It was something I never thought I'd have to say out loud to anyone, let alone to the guy I'd secretly fallen for, the shame already building that he knew. Would he think differently about me now that he knew that besides him, I'd never had a sexual experience that I fully wanted? That even now, after I had sex with my boyfriend—his best friend—I had to emotionally shut down so the guilt and disgust wouldn't overwhelm me. Austin knew I wanted him, and that Nixon was my second choice, but I was positive he hadn't guessed the rest.

Fuck. Maybe I have more issues from being an empath than I ever thought possible.

"No," I said hoarsely. "Never once before you. Or after. Even with the way we left things."

I tried to blink back the tears that were threatening to escape my eyes, but my control was shot. Austin had ripped me wide open. "What about you? Haven't you ever …?" I wasn't quite sure how to ask the question, or if I really wanted the answer. How did I ask him if he ever felt dirty after any of the girls, any of the many, many girls he'd slept with?

"No, for me, sex is sex," he said softly. "Until … it isn't. Until it's more."

"Oh," was all I could manage.

Of course. Did I actually expect him to understand, or to maybe have experienced it himself? Maybe. Or perhaps

I simply hoped that every time he had sex with Jessica, he felt as bad as I did because he knew it was us who belonged together.

"It doesn't matter. It's none of your concern," I said flatly.

Austin stepped into me and cupped my face. Even that simple contact, now that my shields were gone, sent shivers down my body. "It does matter, and I'm making it my concern."

Anger bloomed, burning through my veins. "You don't have the right to be concerned about me, Austin. I have my life, and you made it quite clear that's all that matters to you."

Regret clouded his eyes. "You shouldn't have to feel that way. I thought at least with Nixon—"

"What?" I interrupted. "That at least with Nixon what? And I don't feel that way, not anymore. That's the point, isn't it? Problem solved."

"But it's not solved. You slapped a band-aid on a bullet wound. Let me help you." Austin's voice broke low, his body swaying closer to mine. "Please let me help you."

"Hey. There you are, Austin." Jessica's much too pleasant voice landed between us, and Austin pulled away, annoyance flashing across his face. "What's wrong? Why are you crying, Chloe?"

Taking a step back, I swiped at the offending tears with the back of my hand. "It's nothing, really. Austin was helping me with some empath stuff, just a silly side effect,

I guess." I tried to smile but I was afraid my face might crack.

"We'll finish this later," Austin said brusquely before stalking away.

Jessica lingered, making no move to follow him, her smile dropping into a glare aimed straight at me. "What the hell do you think you're doing?" she snarled.

I struggled to put my emotional wall back up, but it was futile. Austin had left it in rubble, and now I had no choice but to feel the full brunt of Jessica's anger.

"What are you talking about?" I finally managed to squeak out. My head was pounding, and a cold sweat trickled from my pores.

"You know exactly what I'm talking about." She tapped her foot rapidly against the floor while I continued to stare at her blankly. She let out an exasperated sigh tinged with fury. "Austin. I'm talking about what you're trying to do with Austin."

"I think there's been some kind of misunderstanding." She obviously didn't know that Austin and I had sex, otherwise she wouldn't be acting quite so calm, relatively speaking. Besides that doozy, there was nothing else for her to be upset about.

"Oh, for Christ's sake! I know you're trying to steal him from me." She put her hands on her hips and continued to glare at me while waiting for a reaction.

Laughter bubbled up from my chest, threatening to choke me. "You've got to be fuckin' kidding me," I gasped out.

"No. I'm not. I see the way you look at him when you think no one is paying attention."

Clutching at my middle, I sucked in ragged breaths. I sounded borderline hysterical. "And exactly how do you think I look at him?"

"I don't know … like you want him, like you're undressing him with your eyes. And then every time I come across you two alone together, there's this sort of tension—and I know it's you trying to seduce him. He's happy with me." She was quick to tack on the end.

"If he's so happy with you, then even if I laid down in front of him naked and begged him to fuck me, he wouldn't."

Her mouth dropped open. "What? Of course he would fuck you. He's a guy."

"No. I refuse to believe that. If a guy truly loves a woman, he would turn down an offer like that, no matter what you think."

"So that's your excuse. He'd say no if he loved me?"

"That's not what I'm saying at all." I sighed. "I'm with Nixon." I was the queen of lying without lying. I wasn't currently trying to seduce Austin, and I was with Nixon. Let her draw her own conclusions beyond that.

"Are you saying that you wouldn't fuck Austin if he offered to right now?"

I quirked an eyebrow at her. "So which is it, Jessica? Am I trying to seduce Austin, or do you think he's going to offer his services to me and you're afraid I'll accept?"

She stomped her foot like a child throwing a temper tantrum. "You're not answering my questions."

I fought back a smile. "No, I'm not. Because first you come in here demanding that I stop trying to seduce your man, and then you imply he's going to offer sex to me, and I'd better say no. This whole conversation is ridiculous, and I've now lost brain cells for having participated in it. So no, I'm not going to dignify your questions with the type of responses you're expecting." I punctuated my sentence by spinning on my heel to leave.

"You're just like him, you know that? Never a straight answer. Maybe I should let you have him, so you guys could drive each other insane," she called after me.

"Let me have him?" I muttered under my breath. "As if."

As I came around the corner, Austin, who had obviously been eavesdropping, snagged me by my wrist and yanked me into a nearby room. His large frame caged me in against the closed door.

"You already drive me insane," he rasped, dropping his head to nibble on my ear.

The proximity of him, combined with my emotional wall being completely down, caused my gut to clench and my blood to boil with desire. I knew he was carefully shielding his own emotions to make sure everything I felt was all me. It was almost sweet coming from someone like him.

"Austin, no," I murmured in tones that were all yes. "What happened to respecting what Nixon and I have?"

He pulled away to snag my gaze, pinning me in place with just his eyes. "Let me do this for you. Let me help you."

"What are you talking about?" I whispered. "Do what?"

"Sex, Chloe. I'm talking about sex. Let me ... just let me." His mouth unerringly found my nipple through my shirt, and as he clamped down, his thoughts seemed to shatter as well.

I let him kiss, nip, and fondle me for another few moments before reality set in. He wasn't saying anything was going to change. He wasn't saying we were going to be together. No, he was offering me what he had before—sex. Just sex and nothing else.

No. Not this time.

Shoving at him with everything I had, I took him by surprise causing him to land in a heap in front of me. "I said no. If you want me, then you can have me. All of me. But I'm not going to let you fuck me in whatever side room you pulled me into this time. I won't cheat on Nixon again."

Austin pulled himself to his feet, eyes blazing. "You don't even want to be with him. You want me. You need me."

"I don't want to hurt him. Your best friend! You keep claiming you don't want to hurt him either, by the way. Which I don't think I can believe anymore. And yeah, it's true, I want you more than I ever have anyone before. But I don't need you! I don't need anyone! You're the one who's keeping this from happening ... from us happening.

You. Not me. Remember that when you're taking that cold shower later. Oh wait, you won't need one because you have Jessica."

"Chloe, don't do this."

"Don't you get it? I didn't feel all those icky feelings after I was with you because all the necessary emotions are there on my part for you. But because of that, I can't just have sex with you, Austin. I need more than that from you. It has to be all or nothing for you and me. So what exactly don't *you* want *me* to do to you?"

"Fine. If that's the way you want it. I just figured—"

"Figured what? That I would accept any little scrap you threw my way? That I'd consider myself lucky to get you any way I could?"

My face heated at the memory of me thinking just that the last time I'd been alone with him. But now? Now I would have all or none of him. I couldn't handle the limbo he was offering me.

"I'm done with this conversation." I paused with my hand on the doorknob. "And when I'm able to put my emotional walls back up, don't you dare attempt to pull them down again, or you'll be sorry."

"I already am sorry," he croaked as I stepped out of the room, letting the door click shut behind me.

Chapter 20
FEBRUARY, FOUR YEARS EARLIER ...

"Nice of you to join us." Nixon's sharp tone cut through the silence.

"Sorry. I was sleeping," I mumbled, gaze locked on the table in front of me.

"With who?" Bitterness dripped from his words. Apparently, he was taking our breakup harder than I thought he would. "Because we all know you're not the type to sleep alone."

Normally I would have responded with a snide remark, but I kind of deserved his ire. After all, I'd treated him like complete shit. *I'm not a good person and I can't even pretend to be in this situation.*

"Don't fucking talk to her like that," Austin growled.

Nixon barked a humorless laugh. "Yeah, of course you'd defend her."

"And why exactly is that?" Jessica cut in, her tone shrill.

"What? You haven't figured it out yet? Austin and Sam have something going on between them. I saw them coming out of one of the empty offices together."

"That doesn't mean anything," Austin interrupted.

Nixon leveled his gaze at Austin. "Don't lie to me, man. I know."

Guilt flashed through his eyes. "Fuck. I'm … sorry. I never wanted to hurt you, you have to know that. You're like a brother to me."

Nixon snorted. "Yeah, brother, okay. But it doesn't matter because you can have her. She's nothing but a lying, cheating slut anyways."

Austin's fury ripped through the room, his chair clattering to the floor as he stood abruptly. "Don't you ever talk about her like that again. I fucking mean it. It's not her fault you weren't enough for her."

Nixon's head snapped back as if Austin had landed a physical blow, and he jumped to his feet. "And what, you think you are?"

Austin's jaw muscles feathered before a sneer twisted his lips. "Yeah, maybe I am. I mean, she couldn't get enough of me earlier when her sweet lips were wrapped around my cock before I—"

Nixon launched himself at Austin, the two of them hitting the floor in a flurry of fists and elbows.

What the fuck? Seriously … there was entirely too much testosterone in the room. Austin had zero reason to go there, and in such a crass manner to boot.

Suddenly Jessica was in my face, screaming unintelligible things. Even though I couldn't understand her exactly, I did get the gist of it, and it was clear that she thought I was a slut and a homewrecker. Color me surprised.

"Yeah, yeah. You think I'm a slut. Maybe you and Nixon can take out an ad announcing it to the world. Now get the hell out of my way so I can break up their stupid fight."

Jessica was like a little gnat buzzing around my head, and I shoved at her with annoyance, causing her to stumble backwards. Taking the opportunity, I scrambled around her to get to Austin and Nixon, who were currently beating the crap out of each other on the floor, both of them having gone feral.

Without any sort of plan, I headed into the fray. I was instantly rewarded with an elbow to my face, which knocked the back of my head into the nearby wall.

Stars danced in front of my eyes as I slid down the rough surface, clutching at my jaw. "Who knew elbows could be so hard?" The stars expanded to darkness, which pushed around the edges of my vision.

Strong arms snatched me off the floor, cradling me against a warm body. "Back off," I felt rather than heard Austin rumble. "You've already done enough."

"Shit. I didn't mean to. No matter how pissed I am, I would never hit her on purpose. You have to know that. I would never hit her," Nixon said.

"Yeah, I know. I didn't mean for this to happen. No matter what you think, I would never go after someone you were into unless I had real feelings for her."

"Then why?"

"I thought I could protect her … from me, and that she would be better off with you," Austin grunted. "But I couldn't stay away. I guess I'm too selfish for that. I want her more than I've ever wanted anyone."

"So she's the one?"

One what? Were they referring to Austin's old vision again? I fought to stay conscious so I could finally get some answers.

"Yeah, and it's already too late. I'm in love with her."

There was a moment of tense silence before Nixon spoke again. "It's fucked up, all of it. But under the circumstances, I guess I understand." Nixon laughed. "Who was I kidding? Anyone can see the two of you deserve each other."

Austin snorted out a rough laugh in response, and I wasn't quite sure how to take that.

"Austin?" Jessica's shrill voice cut through the newly found peace between the guys. "What does Nixon mean? What are you saying?"

A few heartbeats passed before Austin responded. "I think you know, Jessica."

"Put her down, you bastard, and talk to me." Choked sobs filled the air. "You can't do this to me again."

"I'm not doing anything to you again. I never made you

any promises. It was always sex—just sex—from the beginning."

"Noooo!" Jessica wailed. "Lately I could feel something different. You started to feel something, too! I know you did!"

"For her. I was feeling it for her."

"What are you saying?" Jessica screeched.

"Every time we've been together since Chloe—I mean Sam, came here, I was imagining you were her."

Austin was the only one who could remember my old name since he erased it from everyone's mind when I assumed my new identity. It was sometimes weird how he slipped up and no one called him on it. But none of that mattered. Austin had just come clean about his feeling for me.

I managed a groan as my grand response. Warm lips touched my forehead. "Shhh ... Sam."

The tenderness in Austin's voice caused my heart to flutter and I fought to open my eyes.

"Noooo!" Jessica screeched again, followed by some loud noises, and then Nixon let out a grunt. "I've got her." He grunted again. "For now. You better take Sam and leave."

"Yes. I suppose the meeting will have to wait. I see no other way around it," Natalie's voice cut in.

I forgot she was in the room with everything else going on. Then it all clicked into place. The honesty fest was courtesy of Natalie's gift. *Duh.* I'd have to thank her later.

"Going," Austin said.

"I'll be here when you wake up." Austin's voice was a soft caress in my mind as sleep pulled me all the way into unconsciousness.

Chapter 21
FEBRUARY, FOUR YEARS EARLIER ...

"I-I— Sam ..." Austin cupped my cheeks with his large hands, thumbs stroking my skin. His ragged emotions rolled over me briefly before he shut them down. But I already knew what they meant.

My anger flared. "Oh no you don't. You're not pulling away from me again."

Dropping his hands, he backed up a few paces, the stark panic in his eyes confirming my suspicions.

I ground my teeth together. "I won't let you. I'll let him have me. I'll walk out of this room right now and let him kill me without a fight if you pull away from me again. And then that'll truly be your fault."

A lump formed in my throat as I rolled my words over in my head, realizing I meant them. I wasn't sure when Austin had become more important than my next breath, but he had.

He shook his head, gaze darkening. "I was stupid to think I could have you. I was—"

The corners of my eyes burned. "You're stupid if you think you haven't had me body, heart, and soul since the beginning. You can't stay away any more than I can. If you try, that's what'll kill me."

Stalking forward, I shoved at him as hot tears sprung free, spilling down my face. "Stop lying to yourself. Stop making me lie to myself." I sucked in a ragged breath. "If he eventually kills me, then at least let me have you now. Don't deny me that." Teeth chattering, and body trembling, I shoved at him again.

Austin wrapped strong arms around me, and I sunk into his embrace. "You're the most pigheaded person I've ever met." His lips moved against the top of my head, his mouth curving into a smile. "It's one of the reasons I love you."

"So you're going to stop being stupid?"

He snorted. "I'm not the one threatening to let Malcolm kill me."

I tilted my chin up, staring him down. "Austin," I hissed.

"I don't think I could stay away from you again if I tried. You've done something to me. I used to be able to have no strings attached sex, but even the thought of it now ... "

He shook his head slowly. "I can't go back to the way I was before ... how I was before you." His lips brushed mine softly, almost timidly, and then he claimed them with burning need. My hands crept up to wind themselves in his hair, as his slid down to cup my ass.

The kiss ended much too soon, and Austin pulled away from me, determination gleaming in his eyes. "I'll just have to find him before he gets to you. I'll find him and kill him."

His fingertips brushed along my cheekbone. "I won't let anyone hurt you again. *Ever.*"

He snatched his jeans from the floor and plucked his phone from the side pocket. "I'm going to let Natalie know what's going on so we can figure out our next step. Go shower, you'll feel better." He nodded towards the door, dismissing me.

A nice hot shower did sound appealing, but I wasn't about to let myself fall prey to Austin deciding what was best for me in every situation. Our relationship wouldn't stand a chance if I let any more of his bullshit fly.

Glaring at his back, I decided to bring up the issue later when he wasn't distracted. I grumbled under my breath the entire way to the bathroom, warring with myself about following his shower directive. I did want a shower, but I didn't want to be told to take one. Therefore, if I didn't take one just because he told me to then I was cutting my nose off to spite my face. Although—

I jumped as warm hands slid around my waist from behind. Austin's breath tickled my ear, his voice low and rough. "We have just enough time to take a shower, *together*, before the meeting I just set up."

Remaining stiff, I fought my body's response to him. "Well, I've decided I don't think I want to take a shower now." So much for not cutting my nose off to spite my face. *I have zero chill sometimes.*

Austin chuckled, his hands skimming low on my abdomen. "Chafing at being told what to do? I thought you liked it. Or is that just during sex?"

"That's different," I murmured.

One of his hands dipped below my waistband to circle my already engorged, slick flesh, the other wrapping around my throat. I moaned. He chuckled again. "Get in the shower, Sam, so I can fuck you into submission. Just the way you like." He punctuated his sentence by curling one long finger inside me.

My lashes fluttered as I leaned back into him, both loving and hating how his words made me burn. Unable to speak, I let him crowd me into the bathroom, shutting the door behind us.

WHEN WE EMERGED from the bathroom sometime later, my attitude about following Austin's orders had softened. What could I say? The man had a body that *had* to be obeyed.

Swaddled in nothing but a towel wrapped around my middle, I laughed as Austin's towel-covered lower half pressed me into the wall just outside the bathroom. His hands slid over my still-damp arms as he dipped his head to deliver me a thorough kiss. I pushed him away playfully. "Stop. I'm not going to be able to walk for a week. Seriously! Besides, we have a meeting to get to."

Being with Austin made me feel like the rest of the world didn't exist, like nothing mattered but him. Not even feeling someone's death.

His lips slid along my jawline as he murmured against my flushed skin, "I can't help myself. I'm addicted and I'll never get enough."

My heart fluttered with joy. "Later," I gasped as he bit my nipple through the towel.

"Now," he growled.

"Aren't you tired?" I pushed at him again. "I mean most men would be completely spent by now."

"Making up for lost time." His fingers slid under the edge of my towel.

A creak from down the hallway caught my attention just in time to spot Nixon dip his head back into the doorway he'd just emerged from.

"Austin. Stop." *Shit.* I didn't want to be cruel to Nixon by rubbing our relationship in his face.

"It's fine. He was just watching us."

"What?" I squeaked. "Why didn't you stop?"

"I was a little preoccupied."

Fine. I'd been a little preoccupied as well. Still ... I swatted at his arm. "So? What'd you pick up on?"

"He's begrudgingly happy for us. He was thinking he's never seen me like this with anyone, and that it was good to see you not shutting down after sex for once. He's still a little bitter, but he'll get over it. Eventually. He also recognizes that us being together is about more than attraction and sex—for both of us."

I stared at my pruny toes. "Oh." I would never get enough of hearing Austin admit his feelings for me.

Austin intertwined his fingers with mine, tugging me along after him towards my bedroom. That's when it occurred to me ...

"I've never seen your room."

Austin's brows crept up his forehead. "Yeah, so?"

"You don't think it's a bit weird that I've never seen it?"

"You haven't seen it because I was trying to keep you out of my life."

"But that's not the case now." I pulled my hand from his. "Has Jessica seen it?" I didn't know why I cared, but I did, and unfortunately, I was pretty sure I already knew the answer.

"A few times."

"Did you two ever ..." I sighed. *Why am I doing this to myself? Morbid curiosity? Jealousy? It doesn't matter. None of it matters.* And despite knowing that I still asked, "Did you two ever have sex in your room?"

He shot me a cagey glance. "She's a part of my past. No good can come from talking about any of it."

Grabbing his arm, I pulled him to a stop just outside my door. "I know she's a part of your past. And I'm okay with that, as much as I can be. I just don't want there to be something you shared with her, or any other girl, that you haven't with me. I want—need to feel special."

He glowered. "You are special to me. You fucking know that."

"Mmm hmm ... and you still haven't answered my question. Have you or have you not had sex with Jessica in your room?"

Without a word, he turned and entered my room, yanking me in behind him.

I exhaled loudly. "Fine, then. If you don't want to answer, then I'm going to have to assume the worst and you can suffer the consequences." I crossed my arms over my chest. "I'm burning your sheets."

He shot me a look of disbelief. "Seriously? You think I haven't already put new sheets on my bed? You think I would—"

"You're a guy and sometimes guys don't think about stuff like that." I narrowed my eyes at him. "Tell me I'm wrong."

His nostrils flared. "Trust me, will you?"

"I do trust you, Austin, or I wouldn't be here. It's just, well ..." I raised my brows.

Our relationship had been messy from the start and there were things better left unsaid even if we both knew them. Like the fact that both of us had been having sex with other people. I'd been cheating on Nixon, and although Austin hadn't technically been in a relationship with Jessica, that didn't make the situation any less complicated.

But if we stood any kind of chance at a real future, I was going to have to let all of that go. I gave him a teasing smile to lighten the mood. "Besides, when did you have time to change your sheets? You've been with me pretty much every second since the meeting."

A sly smile replaced the scowl on his face. "Around the same time I put new sheets on your bed."

Whipping my head around, my gaze landed on the brand-new set of sheets already stretched over my mattress. "Seriously? When did you do that?"

"When you were sleeping. I couldn't stop picturing you and Nixon—" He cleared his throat, letting the rest go unsaid for both our sakes.

"Yeah, mmm hmm …" I flicked my gaze to the floor.

"Neither one of us has exactly been sleeping alone lately."

"Yeah, I guess not."

I turned to pull some clothes on, trying to ignore the massive pit opening in my stomach. The things we'd done, how we'd treated Nixon and Jessica … we'd acted like shitty human beings. Maybe we didn't deserve to be happy.

Austin's arms encircled me from behind. "It was my fault this all happened. And maybe I don't deserve to be happy, but you do."

"I thought you weren't going to poke around in my mind without my permission anymore."

"It was unavoidable, you might as well have been shouting your thoughts at me." He lifted my hair to kiss the back of my neck, sending chills down my spine. "The past is the past. We can't change any of it. You're with me now, and that's all that matters from this point on."

Austin spun me around in his arms, his azure gaze locking with mine. "Feel better now?"

"Yeah, I guess." *Not really.*

Austin's brows drew together. "Don't, Sam. Please. It's different when you're an empath. The ease in which we can use other people's emotions to cover up the ones we don't want to feel ... the temptation is fucking strong. No one understands what we go through."

Smoothing my wet hair out of my face, he tucked me under his chin, his voice dropping lower. "And things were different with us, too. With our connection and my vision. There was no way things weren't going to be messy."

I'd done him a disservice by not considering that he might have been doing the same thing as I was by using other people's emotions. He did understand me like no one else ever could, our connection unique and undeniable.

"I love you," I murmured against his chest.

Was our love an excuse to hurt people? No. But Austin was right, what was done was done, and for the sake of our love, we needed to move on.

Sinking into his embrace, I inhaled his spicy scent, wanting to hold on to him forever. And I had every intention of doing just that ... no matter the consequences.

Chapter 22
FEBRUARY, FOUR YEARS EARLIER ...

Hovering outside the conference room, I shifted from foot to foot. "Maybe we shouldn't walk in together?"

Austin raised his eyebrows. "And why exactly *wouldn't* we walk in together?"

"Oh, I don't know, because Nixon and Jessica are in there ..."

Austin clenched his jaw, his piercing gaze studying me for a moment before he responded. "I refuse to walk on eggshells for them. It's all out in the open now, and they're just going to have to deal with it." Grabbing my hand, he entwined our fingers and reached for the door.

"Wait." I yanked on his hand. "I'm not saying we *should* walk on eggshells, it's just that I don't want to be cruel."

Austin tightened his grip on my hand and sighed. "I get what you're saying, Sam, and you might think me callous, but I don't give a shit if I hurt their feelings. With the way things are, with Malcolm and everything else, I'm not wasting a single fucking moment with you."

He skimmed his fingers over my cheek tenderly. "I'll protect you with my life if I have to, but what if that's what it takes in the end?"

My oxygen thinned and I struggled to breathe. "No. I couldn't ... I just couldn't, without you."

If he died—if I lost him—I couldn't even bear the thought. Icy claws of dread dug into my spine as I stared at him. *This can't be healthy, loving someone this much, let alone how soon I feel this way about him.* But there was no denying I did. Not anymore.

"What the fuck, Sam?" Austin rumbled. "Don't say something like that. You will go on if something happens to me." He took me by the shoulders, leaning into my space, his eyebrows two angry slashes on his forehead. "Promise me right now. If something happens to me, you will find a way to go on."

I shook my head.

"Promise me, or I'll do something we'll both regret."

"Like what?" I squeaked.

"It doesn't matter. Just make the goddamn promise."

I'm not sure what I saw in his expression, but I was suddenly terrified of what his retribution would be if I denied his demand. "I promise," I whispered.

"Good." He nodded slowly. "Now let's go."

He pulled me into the conference room behind him. I kept my head down, careful not to make eye contact with anyone as he led us to the table. Austin pulled a chair out for me, which I quickly settled into as he scooted a second seat next to mine, taking my hand in his again.

The emotions in the room were stifling, and I contemplated shutting down completely just to avoid dealing with them. But somehow that seemed cowardly. I'd made my bed, and it was time to lie in it.

"All right, now that we're all here, let's get started," Natalie's voice broke the silence.

Austin cleared his throat. "Before we get started with that, do you think that Jessica could heal Sam's face?"

What the hell? The man had absolutely no sense sometimes.

"Austin," I hissed. "I don't think—"

"Yeah, Jessica, it would make me feel a hell of a lot better if you healed the visible reminder that I hit her, even if it wasn't on purpose," Nixon added.

"Unbelievable." Jessica's voice trembled. "You two can't be serious."

"Things are the way that they are, Jessica. Nixon has accepted it. I think it's about time you do, too, so we can all move on with our lives. It's not like we meant to hurt either one of you," Austin stated calmly.

"Accept it? Accept it?" Jessica's voice rose in both pitch and volume. "I can't and I won't just accept you and her suddenly being together. A few days ago, you were mine. Days!"

Austin exhaled loudly through his nose. "How many times do we have to go over this? It was just sex. I've never been yours."

"So what, you expect me to believe you have real feelings for her? Just like that? She's done something to you. Maybe it's an untapped ability and she's entranced you or something. She could be—"

"Stop. Just fucking stop." Austin's voice had gone glacial. "Don't attack her because I'm not the man you wanted me to be for you. We were done before she even started training. And I'm sorry I hurt you—used you to try and avoid my feelings for her. But it's time to move on and forget me."

"F-Forget you?" Jessica sputtered. "I love you." She stared at Austin intently as if she expected her declaration to change something.

"And I'm sorry for that, I really am. But I love Sam."

"You *love* her? You can't ... you can't be serious."

Austin gave her a small nod as he squeezed my hand. "You know with Natalie here I can't lie."

Jessica's head swiveled to Natalie as if she had forgotten she was there. "No. How can you love her? We-We were building something."

"No. *We* weren't. *I* was building something with *Sam,* from the first moment I saw her, maybe before."

Before? What does that mean?

"Before? What does that mean?" Jessica echoed my thoughts.

"It means I felt her presence in my heart before we ever met. She's the one I've both been searching for and running from since I—"

He swallowed, his Adam's apple dancing in his throat.

"Some part of me recognized her from the moment I laid eyes on her. And it scared the shit out of me. But in the end, I couldn't stay away. I'll never be able to stay away."

"How were you building something with her?" Nixon grated. "Did you guys hook up before that night? More than once?"

Oh, shit. Why did Nixon have to ask that now? Austin grimaced, his eyes burning with guilt. "Yeah. We did."

Nixon's nostrils flared. "When? How far did you go?"

"You can't be serious! We're not together anymore, Nixon. Let it go," I interjected with an edge of panic. If this came out, then there was absolutely no way in hell that Nixon would ever forgive us. The tentative peace would be destroyed forever.

Nixon ignored me and addressed Austin again. "*Tell me.* You'd want to know if it were you. I have every right to know."

Austin stared at him for a moment before he shot me an apologetic look. *Shit.* I closed my eyes, waiting for impact.

"From the beginning—that first week she was here. We didn't have sex right away, but we did … other things."

"What?" Jessica screeched, but no one paid her any attention.

"The whole time?" Nixon asked flatly.

"No." Austin ran a hand through his hair. "She didn't want to, I mean she wanted me, but she didn't want to cheat on you."

"But you did anyways, didn't you, Sam? You fucked

him when you were with me. You didn't just cheat on me once and then end it like you made me believe." He shook his head slowly, his gaze flaring with anger. "I can forgive him, but not you. You fucked him, and then came back to me as if nothing happened. Or is that when you started shutting down your emotions? When the guilt got to be too much?"

"Nixon, I ..." I what? It was true. All true. What could I possibly say in my defense? "I'm sorry." I bowed my head to break eye contact with him.

"Yeah, I believe you're sorry, mostly because you can't lie with Natalie here, but what part are you sorry for? For cheating on me? For lying to me? For using me? For getting caught? Which part are you sorry for, Sam?"

"All of it," I whispered, wishing the floor would open up and swallow me whole.

"It's my fault, Nixon. I pushed her into everything. Not intentionally, of course." Austin's lips pulled back from his teeth. "And I let her flail around with her untrained empath abilities, knowing exactly what could happen. You and her in bed together is what happened. I know you don't understand completely, but when I got back with Jessica, it left Sam unshielded from your feelings of lust. She couldn't control it. It's been that way for her with every guy she's ever been with before—" Austin snapped his mouth shut, grinding his teeth together.

"Before you? Is that what you didn't want to say? And what makes you so different? So special?" Nixon growled, his anger growing and spreading around him, pushing at my skull.

"I'm an empath, too. I understand. *Truly* understand. And I have the skill to shield her so she doesn't need to. I can let all her emotions be only hers when we're together."

"I'm a void, I can do that, too. I can—"

"But you didn't," Austin interjected. "You fucking didn't."

Jessica rounded the table, coming to stand directly in front of Austin "Truly understand? Does that mean—you can't possibly mean ..."

Austin grimaced. "Yeah. It means I let myself open up to your lust to pull me under."

Despite everything else going on around us, his admission caused my heart to swell. *Yep, I'm a horrible person.*

"You didn't want me? Not really?" Jessica's voice cracked as her body seemed to shrink down into itself.

"I did want you at one time. How could I not? You're beautiful on the inside and out, you have to know that. But you're not Sam. What I feel for her, what I've felt for her even from the beginning has always been ... more."

Nixon's fist hit the table, and I flinched, my gaze lifting to his which was obviously his goal. "Am I hearing this right? You never wanted to sleep with me? Is that it, Sam?"

"Nixon, please." A rogue tear rolled down my cheek. "It's not like that, I mean it is, but I ... you're so amazing, Nixon. Any girl would be lucky to have you, and I wanted to want you, I just—" More tears spilled from my eyes,

AVA WIXX

dripping down my cheeks. "What Austin and I have is different. I never wanted to hurt you."

Nixon turned back to Austin. "Let me get this straight, none of this would have happened if you weren't such a fucking coward when it came to Sam."

Austin snagged my gaze when he responded to Nixon. "Yeah, I'm the one who fucked everything up. It's all my fault."

Nixon let out a demonstrative sigh. "I don't know what to think or feel about any of this anymore. I'm so fucking pissed at both of you and yet I can't say that I blame you for acting the way you did. And yeah, I guess I'll never understand what it's like to be an empath, but—" He sighed again. "This is all so fucked up."

Austin's lips curled upward. "You got that right. Story of my life."

Nixon returned Austin's smile. "I should hate you. I should hate both of you." He speared me with another hostile glare. "But for some reason, I don't." He shook his head. "I guess I just need time."

"Now that all of that's settled, finally, we need to get down to business," Natalie interjected before anyone else could say anything. It's funny how she just kind of blended into the background anytime the truth bombs started dropping.

"It's not settled," Jessica whispered, her voice so low I almost didn't hear her. "Not yet."

We all turned in her direction.

"I need to leave."

"Probably a good idea," Natalie stated. "I'll fill you in on what you missed when you've calmed down."

"No," Austin said while studying her. "She means our entire operation."

What? Jessica wasn't exactly my favorite person at the moment, but I didn't want her to leave the entire operation because of me. It's not like I wanted to turn her whole world on its side.

"If you think that's what you need to heal, dear," Natalie replied evenly. "Then I'll send someone for you when this meeting is over, and we can talk about your options."

Jessica nodded once before she rushed from the room without another word.

As soon as the door clicked behind her, Nixon said, "Like I said, this is *allllll* fucked up."

"Be that as it may, we have more important things to attend to now." Natalie swept her gaze across the remaining three members of our team. "For instance, Malcolm targeting Austin through Sam. It seems Malcolm knew Austin's feelings for Sam from the beginning. He wasn't fooled just because the two of you weren't officially together. Tell us exactly what happened."

Twenty minutes later, Austin and I had filled in both Nixon and Natalie about the dreams Malcolm had sent me—or visions rather.

"Sam's out from now on. Malcolm knows how we run things. He also knows where to find her. There's no way we can let her go back in on the case," Austin said with vehemence.

Nixon slapped his palm down on the table. "Damn straight. I may be pissed but I'm not letting anything happen to her while I'm on the clock."

"Hold on a minute. Don't I get a say in this?"

"No," Austin and Nixon said in unison.

"I'm not completely helpless. I've been training for months! I'm not backing out now."

"They're right, though," Natalie said. "It's too risky. It has nothing to do with what we think of your skill level or training prowess. You've been exposed. We'd pull even a seasoned agent in your position out."

I grimaced. "But it's not fair. People are dying because of me, and I can't even help stop the bastard who's doing it."

"We'll catch him. Make no mistake about that." Austin's barely controlled rage rolled through me.

"Damn straight," Nixon added.

"Please, just let me help. You can't expect me to sit back here and wait, doing nothing while you guys go after him."

"You won't be 'doing nothing'," Natalie stated patiently. "You'll be training, getting better, so when the next person like Malcolm comes along, you'll be ready."

"You're right. I won't be doing nothing ... I'll be worrying," I mumbled. "I'm just not the stay-home-and-wait kind of girl. Even before I started training, I would have wanted to be involved." I turned my best puppy-dog eyes in Austin's direction. "Please. Let me go with you."

"No, Sam. I'm not putting you in that kind of danger."

I hit the desk with my fist and cringed at the stab of pain. "What about you? You're going to be in that kind of danger. I can't sit back here and worry."

Austin's fierce gaze softened. "We have more training and experience. Besides, Malcolm isn't targeting us."

"Yes, he is! It may be through me, but he's still targeting you. If he gets the chance to go directly to the source and just take you out, who's to say he won't jump at the opportunity?" I wouldn't be able to go on without him, no matter what I'd promised him.

Austin cupped my face in his large, callused hands, forcing me to look up at him. His gaze shone with a determination I'd never seen in them before. "He won't take me out. He doesn't want me dead. That would be too easy. He wants me to suffer the same way he did when he lost Maggie. That's why he's going after you. He knows the worst thing he can do to me is hurt you."

I pulled away from him, letting out a frustrated growl. "I can't just wait here for you!"

Austin tilted his head, studying me for a minute, before turning his attention back to Natalie and Nixon. "We need to come up with a new plan. Before we can get to Malcolm, we need to take out our original target. Maybe I can—"

Natalie interrupted Austin. "Sam, maybe it's best if you

go. I don't want you to be here for the rest of this. It'll only upset you more."

My jaw dropped. "Unbelievable. Now I'm not even allowed to listen to the plan? Talk about adding insult to injury. But yeah, sure, whatever. Don't mind me, I'll just be on my way."

I turned to leave, half expecting someone to stop me or at least to say something to try and make me feel better ... but nothing. *They're seriously kicking me out. Assholes.*

Instead of going directly back to my room, I decided to take a slight detour—to Austin's room. I still hadn't seen it, and because of my unceremonious removal from the meeting, I was suddenly in the mood for some snooping. Was I being spiteful? Maybe. But I wasn't the one who caused an unexpected opening in my schedule that I had to fill.

Curiosity rippled through me. What tantalizing information would I garner while rummaging through Austin's possessions? Even though I'd been in his mind, there were tons of small details I still didn't know ... like did he read comic books? Or have a secret anime addiction? Was he neat or a slob? What was his favorite color?

I rubbed my hands together and grinned. *I will leave no corner untouched, and no drawer unopened.* Bursting into his room with excitement, my gaze snagged on a completely naked Jessica. *Not exactly the delicious secret I had in mind.*

"What the hell are you doing? Naked? In Austin's

room?" I averted my gaze, but it was too late. I'd seen *everything*.

And fuck, why the hell would Austin say no to that? Every body insecurity I'd ever had reared its ugly head.

"Get out!" Jessica shrieked, throwing a pillow at my head.

"I'm only going to ask you one more time, what the hell are you doing in Austin's room—naked?" Although from her emotions, I could already guess.

"What do you think I'm doing?" she snarled at me.

"What I think you're doing better not be what you're actually doing."

Jessica notched her chin up, leveling her gaze at me. "I'm going to get him back."

I snorted. "Good luck with that when you never had him to begin with." I was not in the mood to deal with her in any way shape or form. Wasn't she planning on leaving the team? What happened to that plan?

"I did have him ... before you came along. And I'm going to win him back."

"Oh, for fuck's sake, didn't you listen to anything he said to you? In front of Natalie, by the way, so you can't say he was lying. He doesn't want to be with you. Move on and find someone who will love you the way you deserve."

I was pissed and wanted her out, but Austin had treated her like shit, and underneath it all Jessica was a good person. I, of all people, could understand being obsessed with Austin.

I snatched up her discarded clothes and tossed them at

her. "Put your damn clothes on already and get the hell out. Austin is mine. Forget about him."

"Bitch," Jessica spat, scooping her clothes up from where I'd tossed them.

I expelled a long breath through my nose. *You can do this. Be nice but firm. None of this is her fault.* "Look, Jessica. I'm sorry. This whole situation sucks. But you need to understand that Austin was never yours, therefore I didn't steal him. And for the record, I wish you all the happiness in the world, and I hope you can move on and heal from all the pain we've caused you."

I clicked my tongue. "But make no mistake about it—he's mine. And this is your one and only free pass. I won't be responsible for my actions if I find you in here like this again."

Her lips peeled back into a sneer as she let her gaze demonstratively drift around the room, lingering on specific spots. "Yours? You're not the one he'll be thinking about when he looks at any flat surface in this room."

Jealously burned through my veins, and I clenched my fists. Thankfully, since she wasn't an empath, she wouldn't have any idea that her shot hit true.

Feigning indifference, I retorted, "Please, he wasn't even thinking about you when he was inside of you." So much for being nice but firm. But I was only human after all.

Jessica launched herself across the room like some kind of crazed cat. Her fists managed to make contact with my face twice before I was able to take her to the ground. Pinning her arms at her sides, I straddled her, the move exceptionally difficult with her having gone completely feral.

"I will have him again," she snarled as she whipped her head around.

As I stared down at her twisted features, the naked ex-girlfriend and fuck buddy of the man I loved, something inside of me snapped. "Leave us the fuck alone," I hissed.

Without thought, I dove into her mind, throwing every image, every memory, every tiny moment of Austin and me being together. It was a barrage meant to cause her sensory overload, and also to simply make her understand. Austin was mine, and what we were, what we experienced was nothing like what he had with Jessica in any way.

"No!" she screamed. "No! It's a lie!"

"It's not," I grated. "He loves me. Not you. You have no future with him. Let him go." I kept pouring the images into her mind, one after the other, over and over again.

"No!" she screamed again, writhing against me. "Stop!"

"*See* it. See how he loves me. See how it's different with us."

"What the hell?" Nixon's voice echoed as if a million miles away.

"Sam, no!" Austin's voice joined in, bellowing from the same distance.

I was yanked off Jessica a moment later.

"Stop. Sam, you have to stop. Let her go before you hurt her."

"No," I growled. "She has to see. I have to make her see." The control of my mental assault faltered with me no longer touching her.

"Nixon, get her out of here, now."

"Yeah, on it." Nixon scooped Jessica's convulsing body off the floor, wrapping a sheet around her before he made a hasty exit.

"Sam. Snap out of it. It's me. Come back to me." Austin's voice in my mind was like ice water dousing my brain. Shuddering, I blinked up at him.

"What?" I reached a finger up to press at the worry lines between his eyebrows.

"You don't have enough training to do that to someone like her. If we hadn't come along when we did, you could have broken her. Permanently."

I ground my teeth together. "I just wanted her to understand so she'll leave us alone. I tried to handle things calmly, but she attacked me. I don't know, I just snapped."

Austin tried to put his arms around me, but I moved out of reach. "She was waiting for you, naked, in your bed."

His eyebrows lifted before he turned to make quick work of pulling the sheets off his bed. When they lay in a pile on the floor, he reached for me again. "Better?"

"Yes. I mean no." I tugged at my hair. "I didn't mean to, it's just she—"

"It's okay. I picked up what happened from your mind the second we walked in." I opened my mouth to protest, but he continued, "And yes, I know you don't like it when

I pry into your mind uninvited, but under the circumstances, it was a more efficient way to assess the situation so I could know how to handle it."

He tugged me close, pressing his lips gently against my forehead. "I have to say, it was a pretty ... shocking scene." He chuckled. "I think Nixon was a bit turned on by it."

I rolled my eyes. "Of course he was."

"I'm sorry you had to deal with that. If I could have—"

"Please, if I was in her shoes I'd probably be just as much of a mess. It's not exactly surprising." *So why did I let her get to me?*

"Sam, I know it bothers you. Tell me what I can do to make you feel better."

I gnawed on the insides of my cheeks, considering. What could he do to make me feel better about it? Nothing. I mean, it didn't change how I felt about him, or me wanting to be with him, but there was nothing he could do to make what he had done with Jessica go away. The past was unchangeable. "Nothing. It doesn't matter. Time is my ally in this situation."

"I'll move rooms, to the one next to yours." Austin gazed at me tentatively, gauging my reaction to his suggestion. When I didn't say anything, he added, "And then you can be the one to christen every inch of it with me. There won't be memories of my girlfriends' past lurking in any corners for you to think about."

I wasn't sure it would do much good, but it was worth a shot. "Okay. Let's start packing up your stuff."

A FEW HOURS LATER, I was sitting on the floor in Austin's new room, unpacking a box of his things as he lounged on his bed. I scrunched my nose at him. "Aren't you going to help? This is your stuff after all."

Austin gave me a rueful smile. "Well, I figured since you were so keen on snooping through my things, I'd make it easier for you by letting you unpack everything. Then you can put it all where you want it so you'll know exactly where everything is."

I grinned unrepentantly. "You saw that part, too, huh?"

"Yep," he replied with a chuckle. "Too bad I don't have anything interesting for you to snoop through. What you see is what you get."

"Tell me about it. Not even a secret porn stash for me to get mad over."

Austin quirked an eyebrow, his eyes dancing with mirth. "I could start one if you want."

I scrunched up my nose again. "Um ... yeah. That's okay. But why don't you have one? Doesn't every guy have one? I mean, at least a magazine here or a movie there?"

"No need," he said flatly.

"Oh yeah," I mumbled, bitterness riding my tone. "I guess someone like you doesn't need that kind of stuff when he always has access to the real thing."

Sitting up, Austin scowled down at me. "What's bothering you? Really? I've felt your anger and insecurities pushing at me since your little incident with

Jessica, but I figured it was just because you were mad about everything she said to you. I figured you'd be over it by now."

An image of naked Jessica flashed in my mind, and I couldn't keep the words in anymore. They poured from me like verbal diarrhea "Why me? Why do you want to be with me when you could be with someone like Jessica? Or why be with me at all when you could be with almost anyone? Of all the beautiful women I'm sure you've been with, how could you fall in love with someone like me?"

I waved my hands at myself. "I mean look at me. I'm cute, pretty even, but next to someone like Jessica, I'm surprised you even noticed me."

Austin's face softened into something that resembled pity. *Great, exactly what I was going for.*

"Sam, you can't be serious." He crossed to me in two strides, leaning in to cup my face as he pushed into my mind briefly.

His lips twisted into a frown. "But you are, aren't you?" His thumbs caressed my cheeks with tenderness as his blue eyes pulled me into their fathomless depths. "You don't see yourself clearly. You're the most amazing woman I've ever come across—"

"Amazingly stupid to think—"

"To think that I could love you above anyone else?"

"Yeah." My stomach did a little flip-flop as I breathed in his spicy scent. Apparently, despite my doubts, my hormones continued to be on their own schedule.

His lips met mine, gently at first and then with

AVA WIXX

growing intensity, pushing at the doubt that hovered in my chest. *"You own my heart and soul, Chloe. You always have, even before I knew who you were,"* his voice murmured in my mind.

"The name's Sam now," I snapped back mentally.

"You'll always be my Chloe and my Sammy—my good little Sammy girl."

I hated when he called me Sammy girl, the nickname somehow condescending or demeaning ... unless he used it during sex. Because hearing his rough, lust-laden voice murmur that name with approval ... Yeah, it melted things on my insides. "No. I don't—"

His fingers deftly slid under my shirt to caress my breasts before pinching my nipples, which effectively silenced me.

I moaned into his mouth, and his lips turned up slightly at the corners. My clothes found their way to the floor piece by piece, and I didn't come up for air until I lay completely naked under Austin, even though he still had almost all his clothes on.

"No fair," I gasped as he began kissing his way up my inner thigh.

His eyes met mine, burning intensely. "I want to show you how much I love you. I going to worship every inch of your body. And when I'm done, I'm going to start all over again."

"Oh," I grunted as his thumb circled my clit. The man didn't fight fair with his magical fingers.

"Austin, I ..." It was embarrassing, but I had to tell him

before he wasted his time. "I can't come that way, or at least I never have, so you might as well strip now."

He paused with his lips against my thigh to shoot me a disbelieving look. "What are you talking about?"

Squirming away from him, I sat up on my elbows, my face heating as I met his gaze. "I've never been able to come when a guy goes down on me. It feels good enough, and it's great foreplay as you well know, but I can never quite get there from that alone."

"That's about to change," he growled. "If it takes hours, days even, I won't give up until you're coming on my tongue."

Images of us together flooded my mind, causing me to cry out even though he hadn't touched me yet. Against the wall, in the shower, on the floor—image after image spiraled through me, making my body quiver with need.

I screamed, arching my back when Austin placed the first slow lick against my heated center. *My God. It was never anywhere close to this before.*

"Oh yeah," Austin's voice purred in my head. *"I'm really going to enjoy this."*

———

AT SOME POINT, I must have blacked out. Stretching, I groaned and blinked Austin's room into focus. *Nope, I have never felt anything like that before.*

Austin's masculine satisfaction danced along the edges of my mind.

"What happened?" I mumbled.

Goose bumps erupted along my flesh as Austin skimmed his fingertips possessively down my body. "I'll tell you what happened. I discovered exactly how unskilled all your exes were. You should thank God you found me."

"Such an ego," I harrumphed, even though a grin stretched my lips wide.

"I've earned the right to have such an ego." He smirked. "Or are you going to try to deny that?"

I rolled my eyes. "Really? What do you want me to say?"

I rose to my knees in front of him, letting the sheet slide down my body. "Oh, Austin, you are the best lover I've ever had. You are a sex god. I can never so much as look at another man after experiencing what you have to offer."

I dropped down in a mock worshipping stance, peeking up at him from under my lashes. "I humbly beg for you to allow me to be invited back to your bed again." I pulled the sheet slowly down to reveal his naked body. My heart sped up, pushing a spike of lust through my system, all sarcasm draining from me.

"You've ruined me for all other men," I whispered, kneeling to take him fully in my mouth. He grew hard against my tongue, a groan escaping him as his hands slid in to fist my hair.

A few minutes later, unable to resist any longer, I released him from my mouth only to slide onto him.

Clutching at his chest, I rocked back and forth, moaning with each small movement. I was sore, but it didn't matter, I simply couldn't get enough of him. I moaned his name as my thighs trembled.

"Alex. My real name is Alex."

I instantaneously understood what he wanted, and as my orgasm finally shook through my body, I called out a completely different name ... his real name. Alex. A wave of intense emotion slammed into me as he came on a shudder, groaning.

Austin swallowed, his hands kneading my hips. "I haven't told anyone my real name since it was erased."

My heart clenched. Him telling me his name was more than what it seemed on the surface. He was sharing a part of himself that no one else knew and letting me see the vulnerability that lurked under his monumental ego. He wanted me to know him—really know him—the real him.

"I love you," I said in a hushed whisper.

A soft laugh burst from me, suddenly uncomfortable with the serious direction my emotions were headed. "And yeah, you are a sex god. I'll worship you any time."

Austin's knowing gaze snagged mine, but he remained silent. I had no doubt he knew exactly what I was doing. But the truth was, neither one of us was ready to unpack our baggage quite yet. We loved each other, and for now, that was enough.

"I love you, too," he said with a smile, right before he pulled me down to claim my mouth again.

Chapter 23
JUNE, THREE YEARS EARLIER ...

"*This might hurt a bit,*" *Malcolm murmured, his amusement evident.*

His forced presence in my mind was an assault on all my senses, bogging me down and pulling me under into a lake of tar, the thick substance consuming me completely.

Screaming, I tried to eject him, but he was too strong—stronger than I thought—and I couldn't beat him, not like I thought I could. If only I'd listened to—

Jolting awake, I rolled my gaze around the room, spotting Nixon. "Where's Austin?" I croaked, my throat like sandpaper.

"I convinced him to go grab a shower because frankly, he was starting to smell." Nixon frowned. "But he's going to be pissed that you finally decided to wake up after he left."

"So he's coming back?" What if Austin decided to try

and leave me again for my own good? I wouldn't let him of course, but the concern was real.

Nixon's brow furrowed. "Of course he's coming back. Why wouldn't he? You're married now."

"I don't know, it's just with what happened, I thought … I thought—" Tears exploded from my eyes, and sobs racked my chest.

"You thought he'd pull away from you again? Despite the fact you're married—because of how much he loves you? Because he's worried about that stupid premonition again?"

"Yeah," I hiccupped.

"I don't think even he's that dumb."

It was then I took note of the fact that Nixon was sitting beside my bed being nice to me again, with none of the bitterness or anger directed at me like he usually had. "Nixon, I'm sorry."

Confusion rolled across his features and then his lips pressed into a thin line as understanding dawned. "Let's not talk about it. I want to pretend it never happened. It's what I need to move on."

"It's just that—"

"No, Sam. You might need to talk about it to get some closure, but I don't. Just do what I ask, okay? Pretend it never happened. You two are married now. End of story."

I swallowed around the boulder lodged in my throat before responding. "Yeah, okay."

"Thank you." He ran a hand through his hair. "Now, I

better go get Austin or he's never going to forgive me." He gave me a small smile that didn't reach his eyes.

"Okay."

He lumbered out of my room as if stiff from sitting for too long. Of course, that was probably the case.

It felt like I blinked and Austin was taking me into his arms. "My Sammy girl," he murmured into my hair. His emotions were a snarled mess, almost indiscernible, except for the abundance of guilt. That one was hard to miss.

"It's not your fault. Please don't torture yourself."

When he pulled back to look at me, I noticed the patchy scruff on his face. I scratched my nails over it, giggling. "I guess you could never be a mountain man, huh?"

The corners of his lips tipped up ever so slightly. "You almost died and you're going to criticize my lack of beard-growing genetics?"

"Well, when you put it that way it does sound a bit silly."

He quirked one dark eyebrow. "A bit?"

"Fine. A lot." I frowned. "You look a mess."

"Stop worrying about me, Sam. So I've been a little lax with my hygiene the last couple of days. I didn't want to leave you." Fresh guilt darkened his eyes.

"If I stop worrying about you, then you have to stop feeling guilty about what happened to me. I was the idiot that went after Malcolm when everyone told me it was too dangerous. Apparently, everyone was right."

"No. I knew what you were planning, and I didn't do enough to stop you. I—"

"Stop me? Last time I checked, I'm my own person who makes my own decisions. You don't get to tell me what I can or cannot do."

Austin's hands came up to bracket my face. "I won't apologize for wanting to protect you. And I won't stop. I don't care how much that pisses you off. I will keep you safe. Whatever it takes."

"What if your life is whatever it takes?" I balled my fists up, resisting the urge to clutch his shirt. "Do you think I could live with that? Do you think I could go on?"

"You could and would because you promised."

Some promises couldn't be kept and that would be one of them. But I didn't want to think about it anymore. "No. I don't want to talk about this. Hold me. Just hold me."

Austin's warring emotions flitted around the edge of my awareness. But he complied and enfolded me in the warmth of his embrace. I shuddered against him, inhaling his heady scent, made sharper from him not showering.

"I was so afraid." Austin's words were so low I barely heard them. "I saw it. I saw all of it. What happened, what he said ..." His emotions twisted and turned like a brewing storm.

"Don't you see, Austin? This is exactly what he wants. You're doing exactly what he wants. Don't let him win."

Not responding, he tightened his arms around me.

It was clear that pushing Austin any more on the subject now was pointless. I sighed heavily. "I need a shower," I declared. "We need a shower," I amended a second later.

"Is that right?" Austin's voice lacked its normal sarcasm, but at least he was trying.

"Um, yeah. I'm afraid to know how long it's been." Disentangling myself from him, I stood slowly, my wobbly legs threatening to give out.

"You going to help or what?"

"So now you want my help? Let me get this straight … you're your own person who makes all of her own decisions, stupid as some of them may be—"

"Hey!"

Ignoring me he continued, "You don't want me to order you around, you claim I'm overprotective, you hate when I try to help you most of the time, but that all goes out the window whenever you feel it's convenient for you?"

"Stop trying to twist things. Just help me."

He obligingly scooped me up into his arms and started towards the bathroom. "Women," he mumbled under his breath.

"Men," I grumbled back, letting him know I'd heard him.

Once in the bathroom, Austin deposited me on the closed toilet seat and turned on the water in the bathtub. He then began rummaging around underneath the sink, searching for something. Moments later he emerged with a triumphant look on his face, holding a bottle of what appeared to be bubble bath.

"I want a shower," I complained. "With you."

"You're too weak for that. You're getting a bath, instead."

"With you?" I asked hopefully.

"No. You're too weak for the kind of bath that would turn into."

I stuck my lower lip out. "No, I'm not."

"Yeah, you are." Austin gave me a stern look, which only made me push my lower lip out farther.

He crossed his arms over his chest and stared me down for several seconds.

"Fine," I relented. "I'll take a stupid bath. By myself."

I pulled myself to my feet and slowly peeled off my clothes. Lust darkened Austin's gaze, but he didn't so much as twitch in my direction.

"Not going to work, Sam. It doesn't matter how much I want you, it's going to have to wait until you feel better."

I widened my eyes, feigning innocence. "I don't know what you're talking about. I'm just taking my clothes off so I can take a bath, like you want."

"Mmm hmm. Then how about taking it."

"I'm about to." I wiggled out of my underwear, smiling to myself as Austin's gaze tracked my every move. Sighing demonstratively as I sank into the hot water, I glanced at Austin just as he scrubbed a hand over his face and turned away.

"Are you going to take a shower?" I asked.

"Yeah," Austin responded, his voice gruff.

As if to illustrate, he reached in and turned the shower

on. I stared at him from my bath expectantly. He raised his eyebrows. "You just going to stare?"

"Not just." I blatantly dipped my hand below the water to caress myself.

He growled something under his breath and turned to make quick work of stripping before stepping into the shower without another glance my way.

"Spoilsport," I grumbled.

But I was just getting started. I dropped the bar of soap just out of reach on the floor. "Um ... Austin. I need your help." Through the frosted shower glass, I saw his head dip forward as he planted a hand on the wall in front of him. I bit my lower lip to keep from laughing.

He turned the shower off, and stepped out of the door, wrapping a towel around his middle quickly. I dragged my gaze down his exposed flesh, admiring the plains and valleys his muscles cut across his chest and abs. The man was a work of art. One that I wanted to study in great detail with first my hands and then my tongue ...

I caught Austin's gaze as I twirled a loose piece of hair around my finger. "I seem to have dropped the soap." I wiggled my fingers and tried to reach it to illustrate my point.

His amused, yet slightly exasperated emotions swirled around me. "I can see that."

"Well, can you please get it for me?"

He rolled his eyes and walked over to retrieve the soap for me. "Here you go."

As soon as he was close enough, I wrapped my hand

around his wrist and tugged him down. He didn't put up much of a fight, ending up on his knees right beside the tub.

I batted my eyelashes at him. "I need some help washing, too."

"Sam, no."

"No? Really? You don't want me to be dirty, do you? Because I'm so diiirty, Austin."

"You're certainly fighting dirty," he growled.

"But you like it."

"Not right now I don't."

"Oh? Well, I did learn from the best."

Austin quirked an eyebrow. "Flattery will get you—"

"Everywhere," I said with a laugh.

I skimmed my hands across my chest and down underneath the line of water. "Austin, I need your help with something else."

He grunted, staring at the spot where my hand had disappeared under the bubbles. I bit my lip harder and circled my clit while staring up at him. When I let a small moan escape, he gripped the side of the tub. "I just can't seem to do it the way you do."

Grabbing his hand, I yanked it under the water and slid it down to where mine had just been. With our hands interlaced, I guided his fingertips in a circular motion, moaning as I peered up at him. "See, you just do it better."

He let out a curse and then took control. His long fingers delved into my engorged flesh while his thumb circled my clit. A moment later, I threw my head back, moaning my release.

He abruptly pulled me out of the tub, placing me on a towel. "I need you," he growled, sliding all the way into me in one quick motion. He rocked forward so that most of his body weight was on his forearms as he cupped my face, his gaze fierce. I wrapped my legs around his waist, digging my heels in just above his ass to urge him on.

"Austin, please," I moaned as he moved languidly in and out of me.

He dipped his head to deliver me a quick yet thorough kiss before pushing up from his hands and pulling my legs onto his shoulders. Wiggling underneath him, he stole the air from my lungs when he quickened the pace, slamming in and out of me until another orgasm darkened the edges of my vision. It wasn't long before Austin joined me in ecstasy, his body tensing over mine.

Our coupling had been fast and furious, with an underlying desperation on Austin's part that concerned me a bit. I was still trying to catch my breath when Austin pulled me up from the ground to wrap me in a fresh towel.

Since he was still naked, my attention snagged on his perfectly formed, muscular ass when I saw it reflected in the mirror. I leaned forward and grabbed it roughly, digging my fingers in.

Austin flexed his muscles and laughed. "I think I might have created a monster."

"Huh?" I mumbled as I continued to knead him,

mesmerized by what I saw in the mirror. He was just the right balance between firm and pliable, with the perfect—

"Having fun back there?"

"What can I say, apparently I'm an ass girl now. In fact, I kind of want to bite it." Abruptly twisting, I sank my teeth into his left ass cheek.

Austin froze. "Did you just *bite* my ass?"

"I do believe that's exactly what I just did. Why? Do you have a problem with it? I mean you can't go around tempting me with such a bitable ass and not expect me to, well, bite it."

He shook his head. "I can't believe you just bit my ass." A grin tugged at his lips. "I bet I bite harder."

Raising my hands, I inched away from him. "Huh-uh. You're not biting my ass."

"What's fair is fair. You bit me, and now I'm going to bite you. You're the one always prattling on about equality. Now's the time to put up or shut up."

"No!" I squealed, dashing for the door.

I scurried down the hall towards my bedroom, glancing back to see that Austin hadn't emerged from the bathroom yet. He probably didn't want to run naked down the hall, so he had to stop to wrap a towel around himself before pursuing me. After all, he wouldn't want random people trying to bite his ass. I chuckled to myself.

I stopped short the moment I entered my room. *Something's not right.*

"Hello, Chloe, or Sam. Whichever you're going by now. Not that it matters. Glad to see you're feeling better."

Pivoting, I found Malcolm standing in my doorway.

"I would have hated for you to die before I was ready for it. I have plans, after all." He shrugged. "I guess you're oversensitive, but now I know."

"Austin," I managed to squeak out.

Malcolm grinned. "Is being detained."

I screamed as Malcolm's inky black mind slid into mine, sucking me into oblivion.

Chapter 24

JUNE, THREE YEARS EARLIER ...

M y heart thrashed against my ribcage, and a dull roar assaulted my ears as I struggled to keep my breathing deep and even not to alert anyone I was awake. I needed to glean as much information as possible first. The angle of my arms and legs, combined with the tingly feeling in my limbs, let me know I was restrained.

People were talking, and I focused on what they were saying.

"Plans have changed, Malcolm baby. I'm sorry," a feminine voice said smoothly.

"Just like that?" Malcolm growled.

"They want her. And him. It was a mistake bringing her here, letting them get a look into her mind and at her abilities." There was a pause in which I strained to hear what else was being said, but my pounding heart was

AVA WIXX

entirely too loud. "At least you get to break her. That should please you."

"You fucking bet, Renee. I'm pleased I get to break her when my goal was to kill her." Something crashed to the ground. "And him. There's no way I can let him come here."

More crashes sounded nearby, and I struggled not to react.

"Calm down, baby. Wouldn't it almost be better to turn her into something he'll hate? To tear her away from him without killing her? To have him see her every day and regret what was his fault she became?"

Silence descended, only lasting a few moments before Malcolm responded, "Hmm ... I suppose if I can't kill her then that would be the next best thing. Leave. She's awake and listening to us. It's time for me to get started."

My breath caught in my throat, but instead of opening my eyes and admitting I was faking being unconscious, I remained perfectly still. Sweat trickled down my spine, and my nostrils flared. Heels tapped out a steady rhythm across the floor, and then a door opened and shut.

"Time to get up and play." Malcolm's hot breath fanned across my cheek.

I jerked into motion, trying to scramble away from him, but my hands were bound behind my back, something I'd temporarily forgotten. I surveyed the small room I was being held in, realizing I didn't have anywhere to go. My world suddenly tilted.

"Awe … I think you got up too fast," Malcolm said with mock concern. "You might want to take it slow."

"Fuck you," I grated.

"That's not very nice, Chloe. I'm just trying to help." He regarded me with doe-like brown eyes that would have been beautiful if there was anything but darkness behind them.

"My name hasn't been Chloe for a long time, it's—"

"Sam. I know, I know. I do suppose if we're going to be working together I really should start calling you by your new name, huh?"

"I'll never work with you," I spat.

"Now, now, *Sam*. Hasn't anyone ever told you to never say never?"

"I'm not going to work with you—*ever*. And you won't take me from Austin—*ever*. We share a special connection. The only way you can break that is by killing me, and from what I just heard, that isn't going to happen. So sorry."

Ignoring me, he tapped his chin. "Now where to begin?"

"Who the hell are you working for anyways? Who would employ a psycho like you?" I mean really, what kind of place would keep a complete sociopath with so much power on the payroll?

A smile ghosted across Malcolm's lips. "The United States Government, of course."

My eyes widened. "Wh-What?" I stammered. "But I thought—"

"Oh, you thought that's who ran your little operation, didn't you? I'm afraid not. Our ex-employer is privately funded by some do-gooder who has more money on their hands than they know what to do with. Kind of a waste if you ask me. But my employer, and your soon-to-be new employer, focuses on political manipulation. I don't think I need to expound on that any further. At your old place of employment, you might have gotten to save some lives, but here? Here you'll get to shape history."

"I'm not interested in shaping history, unless it entails saving lives."

Malcolm rolled his eyes. "I don't have the patience for your sanctimonious, holier-than-thou drivel right now. I want to get started on tinkering with that mind of yours. Or maybe first we should take a trip down memory lane … again."

My stomach somersaulted, and I was swept into a memory. But instead of playing out slowly, it slammed into me, only pieces of it standing out in my mind.

"Oh, Austin—yes, Austin!"

"I'm sorry, Malcolm. So sorry. More than you'll ever know. But it had to be done. You have to know it had to be done."

"Why? Why would you do this to me?"

"You know why."

"I love her! You know I love her! How could you do this to me?"

"You screwed up. You fell in too deep. You'll get over it and realize what you felt wasn't really love. She had to die. You know she had to die."

"No! I love her! Maggie. Please. I love you. Maggie ... I need her. Please, I need her."

"No! Stop! You're not going to turn me against him!" My chest heaved as I sucked in ragged breaths. "Nothing you can show me will ever turn me against him."

Malcolm was on me in a second, his fingers digging into my throat, his lips pulled back from his teeth in a snarl, spittle flying from his mouth. "You will see. I'll *make* you see."

His inky mind slithered into mine, contaminating everything it touched. "No!" I screamed, thrashing against him.

Images of Austin with a myriad of women swam in front of my mind's eye—him kissing them, him touching them, him fucking them. It was one thing to know he'd been with a lot of women, but it was something entirely different to *see* it. And there was no point in trying to deny the truth of it because I knew that Malcolm had gotten the information I was currently viewing directly from Austin's mind.

Malcolm kept bombarding me with unwanted images of Austin and other women until they choked me, and I gagged on bile. "Stop. Please stop." I curled into a ball, my hands still bound behind my back. "It doesn't matter. I still love him. I still love him," I whispered, trying to comfort myself.

The images cut off just as suddenly as they began. "Then you're a bigger fool than I thought," Malcolm spat. "And the fun is just beginning."

Chapter 25
SEPTEMBER, THREE YEARS EARLIER ...

Y ou can torture someone without ever laying a hand on them, twist them up, and turn them inside out using their mind alone. Some would simply call it emotional abuse, but what Malcolm had been doing to me couldn't be considered anything short of torture. I had become a student, an unwilling participant, of what it truly meant to mind-fuck someone, and I didn't know how much more of it I could withstand.

"Austin," I whispered.

"Is not coming to save you," Malcolm stated. "In fact, he probably already found someone else to occupy his time between the sheets with. You're old news to him by now."

"No." Unwillingly, my thoughts drudged up images of him and Jessica together. *What if he's already replaced me?* No. I wouldn't let Malcolm make me doubt him. I couldn't. Austin married me, that had to mean something.

But then again, what if Austin was grief-stricken and blamed himself for not stopping Malcolm from taking me? What if he wasn't strong enough to fight off advances from someone like Jessica? Hell, even Jessica herself? Was he capable of doing that to me? My heart fisted painfully.

"I was once loyal to him. I believed he thought of me as a brother, as I did him." Malcolm leaned back in his chair, propping his feet by my face in the bed I was splayed in. "But you'll soon find out he doesn't deserve your loyalties."

I pursed my dry lips, glaring at him defiantly. "No. He deserves everything I've given him."

Malcolm rose abruptly, the chair hitting the floor with a loud thud, fresh anger flashing in his eyes. "I guess we're going to have to do this the hard way then."

Despite my best efforts, panic slid down my spine, but Malcolm didn't have to know that. "Do your worst. I'm not afraid."

He clicked his tongue. "Oh, Sam. But you are. I can taste your fear like sweet, sweet wine aged to perfection."

My eyes widened slightly, which brought a small smile to his lips.

"What? You haven't figured out that I'm an empath, too?"

"B-But … how can you kill the way you do? How can you do all those things?"

Malcolm's eyes glinted with amusement. "My dear Sam, I *like* how it feels to walk beside someone in death, to know their last thoughts, to *feel* their last breath. And then, when their heart stops beating, when their eyes have seen their last image ... I walk away more alive than when I started. I walk away having felt death, yet in a way, transcending it. It's even better than sex."

"Then you haven't been doing it right. Sex, that is."

"Enough," he snapped. "You're trying to distract me, stall me. Time to get down to business."

I fought with everything I had left to keep him from sliding into my mind again, to stop the murky sludge of his presence from mingling with my thoughts, moving around in my head, but I didn't have much of my shields left, and even if I did, I wasn't sure I could keep him out. He was too strong.

I screamed until I couldn't scream anymore.

Chapter 26
PART 3: PRESENT DAY - 2013

I'd been given my best and worst memories in one mind-boggling fell swoop. All the missing pieces were now filled in, and the lingering doubts erased. I loved Austin—more than anyone or anything. But our history together was sordid and twisted, with some extremely toxic elements. I didn't care though, and I never would. Austin was the other half of my broken soul, and we fit together perfectly.

Somewhere deep down, I'd known the entire time that I loved him because his name was etched into my heart and soul. But even still, not having the memories of how we met and the complications that initially stood in our way of being together, left me without the most important parts. It was the mundane things just as much as the complicated elements that defined any relationship.

Unfortunately, the bad was also returned with the good, and I now had the memories of Malcolm as well.

With his torture, he'd opened up something dark inside of me, something that had been waiting to be discovered again. And I hated it, hated being faced with a part of myself I didn't know existed and wished didn't.

Uncurling myself from the bed I was in, I surveyed my surroundings, which turned out to be a cheap motel room. Anger surged as my gaze came to rest on Nixon—my fake husband. The man who'd stolen my life and lied to me over, and over, and over again. It didn't matter that he'd done it to protect me from Malcolm because it wasn't his choice to make. None of it was.

Trembling, I came to stand in front of Nixon. I glared at him, my emotions raw and ripped open, my thoughts a tumult of anger and confusion. For several years I'd lived with Nixon like he was my husband, and I'd developed genuine feelings for him, but only because my memories had been altered, my past essentially erased. I couldn't simply unravel those feelings, and yet, I knew they were a lie along with everything else I'd been force-fed by Nixon.

In the end, he'd betrayed me, and that trumped everything else in that moment. "How dare you!" I slapped him across the face. "How dare you steal my life from me! You made me believe what we had was real. That I loved you. But I never loved you at all … it was always Austin."

I slapped him again, and he barely flinched, my hand leaving a red mark. "What you did is unforgivable."

Hurt flashed in his eyes. "I saved you."

"Saved me?" I ground my teeth together. "Maybe you found me and saved me from Malcolm, but then you stole me from Austin—you stole my real life away! You saved someone who isn't really me!"

"When I found you—what Malcolm did to you …" He shook his head as if trying to dislodge the memory. "Fuck, Sam. There was so much darkness in you. And I realized that I couldn't give you back to Austin that way. He wouldn't have been able to handle you."

"What?" I spat incredulously.

"You would have dragged him down with you. I don't have all the abilities you and Austin have. I'm a void—and I'm not an empath—but sometimes I get visions. Which you should remember now."

"What did you see?" Austin's low voice rumbled from behind me.

Nixon's gaze lifted, settling over my shoulder. "I saw what she would become, and what you would become with her. Your vision—of her dying in your arms—it wasn't what you thought it meant. She wasn't really dying, she was just—"

"Feeling death. Feeling someone else's death," Austin finished for him.

Nixon nodded once.

"And I gave that back to her, too."

Nixon just stared at him, his countenance clouding over.

"I don't feel any different … I mean, not really." But how do you know if something inside of you has changed? I was me again, with all of my memories intact in my mind, and therefore I felt like me, but I was also a different me than the one that hadn't had her memories. *Jeez.* If I thought about it much more, I was probably going to give myself an aneurysm.

Unable to resist any longer, not sure how I had to begin with, I whirled around and flung myself at Austin, the reality of being able to touch him again cracking my heart open.

Burying my face in his chest, I didn't know what to say or do, so I just stood there, listening to his heartbeat, wishing I could sink into him and live there forever.

Austin's arms tightened around me, forming a protective cocoon. His hot breath fanned along the top of my head as he rumbled low, "My Sammy girl."

He was attempting to shield me from the full brunt of his emotions, but some were still leaking through the cracks, his control slipping.

He wanted nothing more than to bury himself in me, to forget everything other than the sweet oblivion I could bring him, but he still had to deal with Nixon and the fallout from that. Plus, he was worried about what Malcolm might do, and he was terrified I would be disgusted with him because of what happened with Jessica. Her death was an accident. He didn't mean to kill her, but he'd lost control when he found out that she'd been the one who aided Malcolm in capturing me. It was her actions that had ultimately set everything else into motion. He thought Jessica was the reason I was dead even though I wasn't dead at all.

"I'm sorry," I sobbed into his damp shirt. *When did I*

start crying? How could I have let Malcolm break me like that? How could I have let Nixon steal me away like that? Every time Nixon touched me, slid inside of me, I should have known something was wrong, but I didn't. I should have known *everything* was wrong, but I didn't. *It's all my fault.*

"No. Sam, you have nothing to be sorry for." Austin grabbed my shoulders and pulled me back from him so I was looking up into his piercing blue eyes from inches away. "None of it was your fault."

I cupped his cheek, his eyes sliding closed as he turned his face into my palm. "I thought I'd never see you again."

Austin's lips came crashing down on mine, fueled by a feverish desperation. I opened up to him instantly, letting his tongue slide in to take control of my mouth. *The reality of being in his arms is so much better than any of my memories or fantasies.* I wrapped my legs around his waist, and he supported me with his hands under my ass. As I pivoted my hips, grinding myself against him, Austin let out a low groan.

"What the fuck do you think you're doing?" Nixon growled.

But I couldn't find it inside of myself to care. Maybe once I would have, but not after what he did, not after he tried to deny me the very thing I was trying so desperately to have at the moment: Austin.

There was a loud scuffle, and the door opened and shut with a slam, then silence. I knew Taryn probably had to drag Nixon out of the room, but again I couldn't bring myself to care. We'd deal with everything later. Now the only thing I could think about was getting Austin naked and inside of me.

"I need you," I gasped out as Austin dropped us down on the bed.

We didn't say anything else as we fumbled with each other's clothes. We shared the single-minded intent of getting naked as soon as possible, but neither of our fingers went as fast as we needed them to. Finally, when we were skin to skin with our hands running all over each other, Austin slammed into me. I cried out at the suddenness of the invasion, scoring my nails down his back, but I was ready—more than ready—for him.

"Show me how much you missed me, Sammy. My good little Sammy girl," Austin growled as he pounded into me.

Both of us reveled in the simple bliss of just being in each other's arms again. And as I screamed his name in ecstasy and he released his pleasure into me moments after, reality finally came crashing down on me. I'd been taken from Austin and completely mind-fucked. I had my memories back, but my emotions were still twisted and snarled, fiction and reality intermingling in my brain. Much to my shame, I started to cry.

"Sammy, what's wrong?" Austin's voice was still flavored from sex, but concern was woven into his tone.

I was overwhelmed and uncertain of everything ... except him. "I—" Lifting my gaze to his, I tried again to put my feelings into words but there was just so much, too much. "It's just that I—"

"Let me see." He touched my temple and slipped into my mind. He grunted his displeasure before saying, "Sammy, no. Please. We'll get through this. I promise."

Malcolm's laugh ricocheted inside my head. "He really shouldn't make promises he can't keep."

Stupid garage door was jammed again. Sighing in frustration, I made my way around the side of the house, setting down a bag of groceries so I could fish my keys out of my purse. It wasn't that big of a deal, but I couldn't shake the paranoia that someone had been watching me, and I would rather have unloaded the groceries in the garage with the door down and locked.

"I wouldn't call it paranoia," an unfamiliar voice said as a hand slid over my mouth, hot breath fanning against my ear. "More like being observant."

His hand muffled my screams as I kicked and thrashed, even as my body slowed, and I lost control over my muscles. My attacker laid me gently on the ground, forcing me to stare up at him. I was paralyzed, and yet I was fully aware of everything going on around me.

The man was handsome, young, and not the type of person I would feel uneasy sitting next to on a bus or the subway. But when he smiled, I saw my death in his eyes. My mind abruptly turned to my husband and our children. Who would find my body? Would my family know how much I loved them and thought of them even at the end? I didn't tell them enough, not nearly enough. I should have let Michaela go to that sleepover.

She was so angry that I didn't and now I'd never get a chance to tell her I'm sorry for calling her a spoiled brat. I didn't mean it, not really, and if I could—

The man jammed a gloved hand into my mouth and lifted my tongue. The pinch of a needle bit into the sensitive flesh, followed by a burning sensation as the contents were pushed into my system. My captor leaned back against the wall like he had all the time in the world as I lay immobile and helpless on the ground.

My heart stuttered and fell into an erratic pattern, and I had the urge to clutch at my throat as my breathing became difficult, but I still couldn't move. I realized he must have injected me with some kind of poison. I heard him inhale sharply as my vision began to dim, my thoughts slowing, my resignation that any breath could be my last ...

Gasping, I arched up, knowing an unwanted smile lingered on my lips.

"Sam." Austin's voice filtered past my current state of euphoria—for I had experienced someone else's last breath, and I kept on breathing. The high like nothing else in existence. Before this—this darkness had been reawakened in me, before I remembered it, it wasn't like this at death scenes for me. But now everything was different. Or rather things were back to the way they were before.

"Fuck, Sam. Just—fuck." Austin buried his face in my hair, his emotions skittering through me.

It had finally come to pass ... Austin's vision. And just like Nixon claimed, I wouldn't actually die in Austin's arms, but instead, feel someone else's death while in his arms. So what did it mean? That I was destined to go down this path no matter what any of us did? Was there no hope for me then? Was I already lost?

Gritting my teeth, I fought back the urge to revel in the euphoria the death brought me. "We need to stop him, Austin. Before ..." Before it was too late? It probably already was, for me at least.

"We will." But his grip only tightened around me, his face pushing farther into my hair. I knew he was dealing with his own demons at the moment, but we didn't have the luxury.

I brushed my hand down his back before pulling away from him. "We need to—"

Austin's gaze captured mine and held me in thrall. "We wasted so much time being apart, Sam. If I'd known what my vision really meant ..." He swallowed audibly. "Maybe I caused this. It's like the whole Oedipus thing."

I almost wanted to laugh. Almost. "Well, not exactly. It's not like we're related, but I get what you're saying. Although rehashing things we can't change is pointless right now. We need to track down Malcolm—"

"And kill him," Austin finished for me. Good to know we were still on the same page.

I gnawed on my bottom lip as I studied Austin. "One thing that's bothering me though, is that I can't shake the feeling that all of this is connected. I mean, even from the very beginning, from the first moment I met you. I just

AVA WIXX

can't quite put my finger on it but there's more than we know. I can feel it."

Austin's phone chose that moment to ring. He strode across the room, utterly naked, to answer, and I sat back to enjoy the view. Even though I'd just been in someone's head while she was murdered, I was currently contemplating going down on Austin while I massaged that perfect ass. The fact that I could so easily push the murder aside highlighted the changes in me internally since getting my memories back. But I wasn't going to acknowledge any of it for the time being, or at all.

"Yeah," Austin growled into his phone. His face pinched with concentration as he listened to whoever was on the other end. He grunted, then said, "I understand," before hanging up.

"That was Natalie." He strode back across the room to rejoin me in bed.

"What did she want?" I pressed open-mouthed kisses to his heated skin, making my way down the hard planes of his body.

His hands caressed my shoulders briefly before I slid farther down, my tongue tracing the contours of his abs. They bunched under the attention, and he let out an almost indiscernible hiss. "She wants me to bring you in so she can talk to you." His voice broke low, and I smiled against his hip bone. "But it can wait a little while longer."

"I thought you'd say that." An image of Maggie lying dead in Malcolm's arms flashed across my mind, and I shuddered. Would Austin be the one assigned to kill me if I ever truly became like her?

Austin's hands slid into my hair, and he pulled my head back so I could meet his gaze over the line of his body. "I'll never hurt you." His eyes bore into mine, fierce and protective. "And I'll kill anyone who tries."

"But what if I deserve to die?" I whispered.

"No, you listen to me right now. There's nothing more important to me than you. Fuck everything else. I don't care anymore. If you needed to kill someone every day for the rest of your long life to survive, God fucking help me, I'd bring you your victim every time, if that's what it took. I love you unconditionally and I won't let anyone take you away from me again. Knowing what it feels like to think you were gone forever … it changed everything."

A single tear escaped my eye, sliding down my cheek. "I love you."

I wished I had something better to say in response, something heartfelt and appropriate, something poetic and epic, but I didn't. So I settled for the next best thing. I would *show* him how much I loved him.

I dropped down to take Austin fully into my mouth as I began my worship of his body. I wasn't always good with words, but I was with my mouth.

AUSTIN WAS SPLAYED across the bed, one arm under his head and the other outstretched as if reaching for me. The cheap motel sheet was tangled around his middle, leaving his sculpted torso and muscular legs exposed. His dark hair was rumpled and in repose, his face was softer, gentler, younger even. I traced his profile lovingly with my gaze, wanting nothing more than to press my lips against his, to run my hands through his silky locks, to—

But it wasn't the time for any of that.

I'd come to a decision. One that hopefully wasn't as asinine as it seemed, even to me. But the risk would be worth it if I could protect the ones I loved, mainly Austin. I was going to offer myself up to Malcolm, hoping I was now strong enough to hold my own with him. The only reason Malcolm had targeted me to begin with was to get at Austin, and I simply wasn't going to risk him again. I was already broken—tainted—and I would save Austin from the same fate.

With one last wistful glance in Austin's direction, I slid from the bed and silently got dressed, glancing over at him every so often to make sure he wasn't awake yet. As I tried to close the motel door behind me as silently as possible, the oddity of how soundly he was sleeping finally struck me. Something wasn't right.

"He always was a light sleeper," Malcolm said as he stepped out from the shadow of the ice machine.

I wasn't surprised to find him there. Maybe on some level I'd already sensed him. "What did you do?"

Malcolm's lips curled. "He'll be fine. I simply slipped into his mind while he was … vulnerable."

"Oh." And he'd been vulnerable thanks to me.

"I think you already know he's fine." He sucked on his teeth. "Don't want to deny myself the grand payoff. After all, I've put a lot of effort into getting us here, to this moment."

Dread dragged icy claws down my spine, goosebumps erupting. "And what is your payoff exactly?"

Malcolm's brown eyes glinted as they met mine. "You, of course."

"You may have opened up something inside of me that I never would have found on my own, but I won't be like you. Or her." Of course, I meant Maggie. She didn't just enjoy feeling someone's death. She killed people, just like Malcolm had begun doing.

Malcolm's anger beat at my senses. "Time to go," he grated. "That is if you want to protect Austin."

My pulse thundered in my ears. "You know I would do anything for him."

Malcolm grinned. "Yes, it's something I counted on."

Chapter 27
THREE AND A HALF MONTHS LATER ...

Death, with its frigid, slithering touch, takes many by surprise. For those ripped out of their lives abruptly, there is little time to process the reality of what's happening. They don't have time to ponder the ramifications of what their death would mean for them and those left behind ... not like, say, someone who's been ill for a long time. A person who is prepared for death, especially after much suffering, welcomes its cold embrace with a certain level of relief that the living seldom understand. People meet their deaths in all kinds of ways, and I experienced them all—and walked away with my life still firmly in my possession.

Malcolm took it upon himself to teach me not only what it meant to feel someone's death and revel in the experience of walking away, but how to appreciate the subtle differences between the manners of death. Once I thought all death was the same, in the end at least, but I couldn't have been more wrong.

Much like wine, each death had a flavor, body, aroma, and of course, finish. The finish was the most important part for someone like me. You see, a violent death, in which someone is taken by surprise, would carry more of an adrenaline surge with it, leaving me in a euphoric state. But a long, drawn-out death left me feeling maudlin, and I usually found myself on the verge of depression afterwards.

One I craved, and the other I despised. If only it were the reverse, then all I would have to do was camp out at a hospice to get my fix. But instead, I was learning why Malcolm did what he did, and why he enjoyed killing.

"I won't do this anymore." My voice held a calm belying my inner turmoil. "I won't just stand by and watch you kill any more innocent people."

"Relax," Malcolm snapped. "This one is a sanctioned kill. I got the orders this morning." He slid out of the car and started walking towards what looked like an office building.

Digging my nails into the leather consul, I tried to stay in the car, as if I could burrow in and remain there indefinitely. But the news that Malcolm was about to kill someone under direct orders from the US government assuaged the guilt that usually rode me when he was just murdering someone for kicks.

"Wait." Clambering from the car, I raced to catch up to him.

"I knew you wouldn't be able to resist." Malcolm's mouth twisted into a smug smile. "If only Austin could see you now." He chortled.

I bit my tongue to keep from saying anything in response to Malcolm's comment. At the mere mention of Austin's name, my heart threatened to burst from my chest. I was doing all of this for him—I was risking my life and my sanity, everything for him.

And yet, I was becoming someone that Austin would despise. My endgame was to kill Malcolm, although I was positive he knew my plan. It didn't matter though, I simply had to wait for him to slip up. In the meantime, I was fighting a losing battle with the darkness that seethed within me, and I couldn't help but wonder if Nixon had been right about hiding the true me from even myself.

"Oh, for fuck's sake," Malcolm spat, his nose crinkling with disdain. "You and Austin are a matched set with all the self-flagellating, introspective drivel that's constantly going on in your heads. It's depressing."

I kept my gaze straight ahead as we rounded the corner of the office building, and Malcolm pulled a security key out of his pocket. "Well, no one is forcing you to spend time with me. It was actually the other way around the last time I checked."

"Quiet," Malcolm hissed. "We're on a job now."

I rolled my eyes. "Right," I muttered under my breath.

I was beginning to wonder if Malcolm was enjoying my company in some twisted way, despite his constant protests. He excelled at shielding his emotions from me, but it didn't take empath abilities to figure out that he was exceptionally lonely.

There was a soft beep, followed by a click, and Malcolm swung the door open. I shuffled along behind him as he strode confidently through the lobby, giving a smile to those eager for one, and a head nod of acknowledgement to others. He exuded an aura of authority, and people simply accepted his presence. Me, on the other hand ... well, I averted my eyes and hoped I went unnoticed as I followed in Malcolm's wake.

We rode the elevator in silence to the twelfth floor, the air thick with tension. Once there, Malcolm headed straight to the door marked 'Men's Room'. He lifted a brow before disappearing inside, the door swinging shut in my face.

I dodged into the Ladies' Room, deciding to wait for him there instead of in the hallway. Making my way over to one of the small sinks, I hesitantly peered into one of the water-speckled mirrors. Each time I was met with my own reflection since being with Malcolm, I was almost sure I'd see the darkness that was spreading inside of me visible in some manner.

Sagging with relief, I ran my gaze over my gaunt features and haunted eyes. *Nothing. Well, unless you can see my soul's taint. Bet my aura's black as night now, too.*

"Join me, won't you, Sam?" Malcolm's voice purred in my mind. I knew what he wanted: For me to slide with him into his current victim's mind as they died. And it wasn't a request.

"*No.*"

"*As if you have a choice.*"

And he was right, twofold. If I didn't do exactly what he demanded, I was risking Austin's safety in the long run, but Malcolm also knew how much I craved what he was offering me. My grand plan with him—all of it—I had to wonder if a part of me merely was using Malcolm as an excuse to feel the deaths I didn't want to admit I yearned for. At any rate, resistance was futile, and we both knew it.

Regardless, I tried to resist. Staring myself down in the tiny mirror, I gripped the sink so tightly my knuckles turned white. Sweat gathered along my hairline and upper lip.

Malcolm's mind tugged on mine, and I gritted my teeth. "No," I croaked. "Not this time."

Malcolm's taunting laugh ricocheted inside my skull. "*Every time, Sam, every time.*"

And with that, I was no longer aware of my body's surroundings because I was seeing out of someone else's eyes.

Dirty fucking bastards double-crossed me. I should have known. I should have been more cautious. Shoulda, coulda, woulda—didn't—fuck. My father always said my ambition and lack of scruples would be the end of me one day. Fucking old coot, guess he was right. What the hell is this sick fuck waiting for? Why doesn't he finish the job instead of leaving me here paralyzed? I can't move a damn muscle. We both know he's going to kill me, so why doesn't he just get it the fuck over with?

"*Ready Sam? This one is going to be a fast high.*"

Shit, that's a big gun. I hope this doesn't hurt too much. Fuck, why doesn't he just do it already? Why the fu—

The click of the hammer was the only distinguishable sound before everything exploded in a wash of red. I squeezed my eyes shut as I became aware of my own body again. Goose bumps erupted across my skin, and my breaths were quick and shallow like I had just sprinted up a few flights of stairs. The familiar euphoria pumped through my system, leaving me floating on its bliss. The death that both Malcolm and I had just experienced was a shock to my system. The suddenness of it so powerful, so—

Feverish lips crashed into mine as a large, solid body lifted me and pushed tightly against me. Instinctively, I wrapped my legs around that body, not even bothering to open my eyes, grinding myself against the source of my newfound pleasure. The death's euphoria only served to heighten all of my senses, and my nerve endings danced with anticipation of what would happen next.

Austin's image danced through my mind, his piercing azure gaze filled with love and devotion as he stared down at me.

My eyes flew open, and I registered Malcolm's pale face so close it was a blur. Bile climbed into my throat as I wrenched myself abruptly away, shoving at his chest. "What the hell do you think you're doing?"

Blinking his doe-like eyes, he slid reluctantly away from me. "I-I—" he stammered before regaining his composure. "I needed to share the aftereffects with someone, and you're as good as anyone." He shrugged before donning a signature smirk.

Shuddering with revulsion, I wiped my lips with the back of my hand demonstratively. "You mean like you used to with Maggie?" I bared my teeth at him. "So sorry. Just like her, I'd rather have Austin."

Anguish followed by anger flashed in Malcolm's dark eyes. Before I had time to move, the back of his hand cracked into the side of my face. My head whipped to the left, and I hit the other side of my face against the wall. The sharp metallic tang of my blood bloomed in my mouth.

"Don't ever speak of what Maggie and I had together. You could never begin to understand."

Turning to look at him, I ran my tongue along the inside of my cheek "Oh, I'm more than beginning to understand."

Glaring at him defiantly, I dared him to hit me again because this time I was ready. But he just stood there, staring at me with hatred rolling off of him in palpable waves, despite me having a lock on my shields.

"She probably never really loved you, and I'm guessing you never really loved her. What just happened between us proves it. I hate you, and I'm pretty sure you hate me, and yet—" I shuddered in revulsion again. "We were just …" I couldn't bring myself to say it out loud.

Pain erupted everywhere at once, like millions of tiny

needles being stabbed into me. I sank first to my knees, then crumpled into myself on the floor. It was Malcolm. I'd pushed him too far, and since I was unprepared for his attack there was nothing I could do about it.

Or maybe that's not true anymore?

I was stronger than I used to be, more in control of my abilities than I'd ever been before. Now was my chance to test and push, to see how far I'd come. Focusing, I gathered up all of my anger, fueling it with thoughts of Austin, and how I longed to be with him but couldn't because of Malcolm. Ah, Malcolm. The man that tortured, twisted, and then violated me on countless levels. He was the source of all of my problems, and I couldn't let him win.

Immense pressure built in my gut, bursting from me a moment later. My pain instantly stopped as Malcolm cried out in agony of his own. I pulled myself to my feet, my knees wobbly, and stared down at his prone form writhing on the bathroom floor.

Now's my chance. I groped for the knife I had tucked into my boot, but before I could take the few steps that would put me in striking distance of Malcolm, he rolled into an awkward crouch.

A humorless grin twisted his lips. "Getting better, I see. But you still can't beat me." He unfurled himself and dusted off his clothes nonchalantly. "We need to leave before the body's discovered." He turned and stalked out of the bathroom like nothing unusual had just happened.

I clenched and unclenched my fingers around the handle of the knife, grinding my teeth. *I was so close. So close to ending him once and for all.* I smiled at the closed door. *Next time for sure.*

Chapter 28

"Don't you think it's time I got some real answers?"

Malcolm schooled his expression, locking down all of his emotions nice and tight. None of his usual snide comments or teasing remarks meant to torment were forthcoming either. Somewhere along the line, he'd realized my abilities were strengthening and that I was merely biding my time until the right moment to kill him presented itself. We were like two cobras slithering around each other, each waiting for the perfect time to strike.

"You already have all the answers you need," he said flatly.

"But that's not true, is it? I never got my standard villain breakdown about everything you've been up to. I kind of feel gypped." I raised one eyebrow at him in challenge.

"Maybe you should talk to Austin about that. He's the real villain."

Anger roiled my gut, and I bit the insides of my cheeks. "You at least should tell me what you plan on doing next."

Malcolm sighed heavily. "We're going to keep on doing what we've been doing."

"So work for the government, or should I say keep using the government for sanctioned kills, and keep up the serial killer tendencies on the side? You have to have a bigger plan—grander aspirations."

"If I do, I'm not sharing them with you," Malcolm grunted, pretending to focus on driving.

"It's been over three and a half months since I left Austin in that motel room ..."

Despite my best efforts, my mind swirled around thoughts of him, I could never seem to help myself when it came to Austin. One day, less than 24 hours was all I had with him before I was forced to separate from him again. He was out there, even now, searching for me, and all I would have to do was open my mind and we would connect instantly. But I couldn't, all I'd done couldn't be in vain, I had to protect him.

When Malcolm was dead, then and only then could I return to Austin—if it wasn't too late for me by that point. My plan was flawed from the beginning, a calculated risk with a huge downside if I failed. But I'd do it all again if I even had a slim chance at protecting the man I loved.

"Brace yourself. Now," Austin's voice commanded in my mind.

With no time to contemplate how he'd gotten past my barriers, I braced myself against the dash in Malcolm's car. Glancing in the rearview mirror I spotted a black pickup truck barreling down on us. Knowing what was about to happen, I unsnapped Malcolm's seat belt before bracing myself fully again.

Malcolm's gaze darted between me and the road. "What are you—"

The truck smashed into the back of the car, shoving us forward while Malcolm struggled to keep us on the road. The truck revved, and tires squealed, as we were pushed towards the line of trees off to the right of us. Reflexively I screamed, the sound of grinding metal filling the air.

What the fuck is Austin thinking? Sure this might kill Malcolm, but it could kill me, too.

"*Trust me,*" Austin rumbled low in my mind.

Adrenaline pumped through my system as the car lurched forward in a sudden motion. Malcolm sailed through the windshield as we rammed into one of the trees. With a pop and a hiss, the car came to an abrupt stop, the sudden lack of motion jarring. I watched numbly as Malcolm dragged himself to his feet and staggered towards the trees. A loud shot rang out, and he crumpled to the ground in a heap.

I didn't even hesitate to slip into his mind.

This isn't the way it's supposed to happen. She promised me I would win. She promised me I could make Austin pay by using Sam. This isn't the way it's supposed to happen. Why would she lie? Why would she—

Gasping, I snapped back into my own mind, the now familiar feeling of euphoria surging through my system. It was made that much better with the knowledge that it was Malcolm's death I'd just experienced.

He's dead. He's finally fucking dead.

Although after everything he'd put me and everyone I loved through, it was anticlimactic, too easy.

Thoughts of Malcolm and his death fell by the wayside as Austin pulled me from the wreckage of the car. "I got you. I got you, my Sammy girl." He pressed his face against my neck and inhaled, his arms holding me snugly against him.

Trembling, I choked out, "I'm sorry." The meager apology was not enough but I knew he'd understand.

Dropping the block in my mind fully, I let Austin in— let him see everything being with Malcolm had cracked open inside of me. The darkness, the longing, the pain ... I didn't want to show him, not really, but there was no other way between us. He had to know it all.

"It's okay, Sammy. It's over now. We'll fight it together. I meant what I said before. There is nothing I wouldn't do for you."

He then threw open the doors to his mind, letting his unconditional love for me wash through my system. He didn't care about anything but keeping me safe, and he didn't care what that meant anymore.

In that moment, it all clicked into place, Austin and I shared a perfect understanding of each other. We willingly bound our souls together, and there was no going back. And we would do whatever it took to protect that bond.

But the complications surrounding us were far from over. And although Malcolm's death was satisfying, his untimely demise left a lot of unanswered questions behind. There had been someone helping him or pulling his strings, I wasn't sure which, when it came to the situation with me and Austin. That much I'd garnered from his death emotions. But then why did that someone let Malcolm die so easily after everything else?

There was a seemingly insurmountable number of issues that I didn't grasp and quite possibly never would. Plus, my time with Malcolm changed me. I no longer resembled any past versions of myself, the craving for death emotions a burgeoning addiction I wasn't sure I could fight, even with Austin's help.

And what about my job? What I'd come to think of as my purpose. Could I go back to work for Natalie's team? Would Nixon go back to work for her team as well? If so, could I face Nixon? Would I even be wanted there anymore? I was changed—different, dark. Austin truly loved me, so accepting me wasn't that much of a stretch, but how would it be for everyone else?

"But will it ever really be over?"

"No," Austin said. "Not really, because nothing ever truly ends."

Acknowledgments

As an overthinker, acknowledgments are quite an arduous task for me. I wonder if I'm being lackluster or too intense with the thanks. Or did I forget someone? Possibly I gave too much credit to someone and therefore slighted someone else who actually did a ton. A part of me doesn't want to include these in my books at all because the people I appreciate should know it already ... or do they??? No matter how I look at it these damn acknowledgments make me friggin' sweat.

But here they are anyways since if I don't include them then people will probably think I'm ungrateful and weird. I mean, I am weird, but I don't want people to think that. I am grateful though, so I'll just go-ahead and make this uncomfortable for everyone. Heh.

Okay, here I go. Right now. Actual acknowledgments to follow. Hopefully, they represent an appropriate level of gratitude to all the people in my life that deserve it.

(And yep ... I have totally copy & pasted what comes next from my *Replayed* book acknowledgments, which I originally took from *Virtual Reality Bites* acknowledgments. I thought maybe after *Replayed* that I'd come up with something better. Or at least something new. Obviously not. So this is now copy & paste edition #5. Or 6? 7? Who even knows anymore. Therefore, I'm thinking you should probably get used to it.)

My amazing Hubby! Words can't begin to explain how supportive and truly amazing he is. Hmmm ... I think I already used the word amazing. But unlike in books, when honestly applied to someone, the word amazing means something, well, amazing. And my hubby is all of the things that word implies. Romance heroes are nothing compared to him.

Lindsay Tiry ... what would I do without you? I hope I never have to find out. From cover design to interior graphics to logos, you do it all. Your talent is awe-inspiring, and I hope one day everyone else will be able to appreciate how you shine.

Melissa Ringsted ... my illustrious editor. Without you, this book probably would have gone straight into the trash. Thank you for giving me the confidence to publish when I convinced myself that I was the worst writer in the history of writers, and for fixing all the words.

Ren, Kristin, Shona, Ruty ... my O.G. chicas ... I wouldn't be here without you. I'm beyond lucky to know all of you.

And last, but certainly not least, thank you to everyone who has taken the time to read this book. Hopefully, you enjoyed it, but even if you didn't, I still appreciate the fact that with so many options out there today, you even gave my book a fleeting chance.

About the Author

Ava Wixx escaped into books at a young age and decided to stay there. It was only a matter of time before she was driven to create her own fantasy worlds from fear of running out of places to explore.

Reader, writer, dreamer ... Ava only toils in reality when absolutely necessary. She lives in North Carolina with her husband, and spoiled mini-poodle.